A WILDE]

For Sjt. Cullis
the Wascally Woyalist
and
my dad

"Wish me good speed, for I am going into a wilderness where I shall find no path, nor friendly clew, to be my guide."

John Webster, "The Duchess of Malfi"

ACKNOWLEDGEMENTS

This is the third Babbitt book in the series, though it's actually the fifth, chronologically. (There is a reason I wrote this one out of order but it has nothing to do with the story!) The third book chronologically covers the siege of Lathom House and the battle of Marston Moor (1644), and the fourth ends with the battle of Naseby in June 1645 - immediately before this one begins. Don't worry, you've missed nowt, as the boy Babbitt would say!

In this interim period for some peculiar reason best known to himself Thomas Fairfax has decided to promote Hollie Babbitt up to a full colonel. The somewhat unpredictable Thankful Russell (former secretary to the Earl of Essex) has joined the troop as Babbitt's lieutenant, after a slight and near-terminal case of mistaken identity. Drew Venning has acquired himself a mysterious and extremely bad-tempered little trooper transferred from Oliver Cromwell's own Lovely Company, known only as Gray - and somewhere along the line the troop has been swelled by the acquisition of a young Cornish captain, Kenelm Toogood, his pride somewhat smarting after Essex's humiliating defeat in the West Country. (And his horse Charles. But that's another story.)

That really is as much as the reader of this book needs to know about what happens in those intervening months, I promise....

So. That's where we are, then. Fairfax's campaign of 1645 was really a clean-up operation, pressing the King's troops back into the last loyal Royalist counties of the West Country. Naseby was the last major battle of the Civil Wars. The King lost, and lost badly. Collapse, as Luce would put it, of stout party.

The dates and the campaigns are historically accurate. As ever, I have simply inserted Babbitt and his fictional rebel rabble into places and events where they would have been, had they been serving under Thomas Fairfax. The Governor of Bridgwater's wife is quoted, wholesale, from contemporary sources. I did not invent a word of it. I'm not sure any sane author could!

And the Wilderness of Sin? It's a geographical location rather than a moral statement - it's the desert where the Israelites wandered during their Exodus. Though I cannot guarantee it isn't in part the bitter humour of an ex-pat North Countryman serving in the West Country while his wife is at home in Essex.

Thanks this time to:
Dr Mark Stoyle, who kindly allowed me to read his article on the Naseby Massacre, "The Road to Farndon Field"
The Wardour Garrison, who don't seem to have found me out yet
My big and little boys, who tolerate random acts of stupidity with cavalry backswords in return for authenti-cake
The usual suspects: Tom, Tamsyn, Alan, Geoff, Helen, Wendy-that-is-Jake, Nicky and John… the list is endless. And now Francine, Alison, Jacqui, Andrea, Anna, David….

There will be CAKE.

1 - After the Ball was Over

Naseby, Northamptonshire
June 1645

It was a pale pearl of a midsummer dawn, and Thankful Russell looked like a dead man.

Sitting on his bed, he looked fragile and very, very young. As well he might. He'd turned twenty-one two weeks before the battle at Naseby. He was twenty-one, poor bugger, and as of three days ago, he was blind.

It had been an accident, or a case of mistaken identity, or something of the sort that inevitably happened to Russell. It hadn't even been during the battle. Colonel Hollie Babbitt hadn't got to the bottom of it, didn't want to get to the bottom of it. Thank God, he had spent most of that particular sickening low point in the trajectory of the New Model Army, laid out cold in a churchyard in the nearby village of Marston Trussell, perfectly, and literally, unconscious of the vile massacre being enacted by men he'd fought shoulder to shoulder with. His own troops. *One* of the troops under his command, at least. Hollie had been endeavouring to stand between the ravening ranks of the godly, hellbent on unjustified revenge, and those poor bloody brave, stubborn, doomed Royalist camp-followers. One of the women had had smacked him in the side of the head with a griddle. Collapse, as Lucey would put it, of stout party. It had done no good in the end, either. There'd been over a hundred of those poor women dead or mutilated - hacked apart by good

Parliament men. And there had been nothing Hollie could do to stop it.

Whatever *Russell* had been doing to stop it, he ought not to have, because it had ended with him shot in the head, not to say having been, by the look of him, very badly beaten. Sitting upright on his bed after three days unconscious, Russell was a horrible sight, and he hadn't been *that* lovely before. The scarred lieutenant had a stunning black eye, and a series of clotted, black gouges torn into the cheek that wasn't already marred: his mouth was swollen and torn, and there was old, dry blood on his top lip and his chin. The funny thing was, the pistol ball had only grazed his skull - the troop bonesetter had taken it out from under his skin with no trouble at all. Hollie had always said Russell had a thick head, and now he had actual, slightly-flattened, lead evidence of same. It had been enough to leave him senseless for the better part of three days, though, and it had bled something fierce.

"You can't do this, Hollie." Luce was bumping about like a bee in a bottle, trying every way he knew to deflect Hollie from his stated business of removing Russell to a place of safety. "You can not expect a man with a serious head wound to ride sixty miles. You'll kill him."

Russell turned his head to look in Luce's direction. That was the pitiful thing, that the lad was trying to look as if he was intact. Looking at the blank wall behind Luce's head, his head slightly cocked, looking alert and intelligent and facing in just slightly the wrong direction, his eyes not moving. "I should rather not be left behind," he said, his voice as cool and accentless as ever it was. "*That* would kill me, Cornet Pettitt."

"Hapless!"

"My baggage is packed, sir. I will ride when the colonel wishes to leave. At first light."

Luce looked at Hollie and his mouth quivered. It *was* first light. And proper, impeccable Russell's baggage was shoved anyhow into a saddle-bag, one forgotten stocking still flung across the bed where it had been missed. Hollie reached across and very quietly emptied the bag, smoothing the crumpled shirts and folding them before replacing them. Russell was frowning very faintly, his head jerking almost imperceptibly as he tried to pinpoint the sound. "What are you doing?" he said, and his voice had gone high with anxiety. "Sir? What -"

Hollie put his hand on Russell's shoulder. "Nowt, lad. I'm not doing nowt. I just thought I'd dropped summat a minute ago."

"Colonel Babbitt, sir, I will not allow the lieutenant to leave my care!"

All he needed, bloody Witless. The troop bonesetter, who may have been christened Witcombe but who was definitely Witless, was a fat young man with bad skin who stuttered and blushed and only had any degree of competency at all when he was bloody to the elbows. As a plain trooper he was almost wholly useless. He'd managed to put a pistol ball through the brim of his hat in battle, on one occasion. Clear through, clear enough to see daylight. Give him a lancet or a fleam and he was transfigured. The worst thing was, that lummox had trained Luce in his own image, and now the brat was an eager apprentice in his own right. Frightening.

"Why? You going to give him a better haircut?"

Russell looked uncomprehending. Actually, he looked like a lunatic, with a patch of hair cropped to the skin where Witless had stitched that bloody runnel through his scalp. Witless was never going to make a gentleman's gentleman. He'd hardly flattered Russell's vanity, such as he had had in the first place. What the lieutenant was going to say when he regained his sight - and he bloody well would, Hollie would not have it any other way - and realised that possibly the only beauty he had remaining to him was stuck out at crazy angles to his head and matted with blood. Hollie shook his head, and then remembered that he had a row of stitches of his own, slightly more considerately put in by Luce, who might only be a half-trained butcher but at least he had warm hands. Head-shaking, notwithstanding, made him feel somewhat dizzy.

"I'm not sure you ought to be racketing about the countryside on your own, either, Hollie," Luce said gently, and Hollie scowled at him.

"That'd be it, then, brat." Luce might be his dearest friend in the world, but he was still ten years, and at least one rank, his junior. Brat he was and brat he would remain. "You can come with us. There you go, Witless. Lieutenant Russell's got his own private physician. *There's* posh for you, Russell."

2 - Honey for Tea

Not, of course, that Henrietta Babbitt was anxious, because she had been personally assured by her father-in-law that he would pray for the troop's safety, and, knowing Elijah, he would. A lot. She suspected that God granted more mercies to Elijah Babbitt just to shut him up, than he did to less persistent mortals. Even so. With little Thomazine a bare fifteen months old, and she suspected, a second little stranger expected, she could well do without the Armies of King and Parliament brawling on her doorstep, in this sticky heat.

The battle at Naseby had been a bare sixty miles from here, from her - *their* - home in quiet rural Essex. That was half a day's ride, if that. If Hollie was hurt (and she wasn't going to allow the possibility of worse) she would have known by now. It had been almost a week. Hollie was fine, her husband was about his rightful duties as a colonel in Sir Thomas Fairfax's cavalry, he'd just forgotten he had a wife and a daughter for a while. He had a habit of doing that. Probably Fairfax couldn't spare him. She looked out of the window at the trees by the river meadow, still and shimmering in the heat under a burnished blue sky. Luce, too. He was a junior officer, he was Hollie's cornet, as well as Het's baby nephew and a dear friend of the family - if anything had befallen him she would know, someone would have told her, after this long. It wasn't as if either of them were inconspicuous; both officers, both tall, Luce fair-haired and Hollie russet. There was no reason, other than the absurd fancies of a breeding female, why she should be so uneasy.

Thomazine was burbling contentedly to herself, sitting in the cool shadows by the unlit hearth rolling a ball of rags to and fro between her feet. She was a happy baby, with a comical crest of orange hair and her father's level amber-green eyes. Stripped to her little shift in this heat, with the sweat drying sticky in the creases of her chubby little knees and elbows, but still happy. The child had a nasty speckled scarlet rash on her poor little back, and Het hoped and prayed it was merely the heat, and not some terrible childish ailment. She wasn't sure she could bear to see her baby sicken and fail, though she knew it happened. *To other people*. She was doing it again, borrowing trouble. Thomazine was fine, happy and healthy and thriving. Hollie was fine, just off smiting the heathen hip and thigh and too busy to recall that he was a respectable husband and father as well as a senior officer. Luce was - well, Luce was Luce, and she could never think of him as anything more than a solemn little boy who'd been forever hiding in dark corners with a book, even though he was a man grown now.

And as if she'd dreamed him, as if the force of her will had summoned him out of thin air, she saw her husband's familiar clumsy brown gelding in the distance, between the trees from the Braintree road. With the red mare at his side, and a second dark horse between them that she didn't recognise. The sun glinted on metal. They were in plate. Not a visit in civilian guise, then. But they seemed intact, the horses coming on at a casual pace, not an urgent gallop. She felt almost sick with relief, her hands and head suddenly cold. "Thomazine," she said, and the little girl stopped in her play. "Thomazine, daddy - your daddy's coming home." And then, as those clear green-gold eyes blinked up at her uncomprehendingly, she caught the child under the arms and swooped her up in a wild hug. "Daddy's *home*, Zee!"

He was home. He was whole, though there was a great curving black gash - "My mending, sorry," Luce said wryly - just above his ear, where Luce had cropped his lovely russet hair to the skin to put the stitches in. It gave him an oddly lopsided look.

"Taken out with a griddle, of all things," her husband said, touching his fingertips to the wound gingerly. "See how the mighty are fallen, and the weapons of war perished. Taken out of commission by some bloody Welsh bint with a frying-pan. She was sorry afterwards, mind."

"Yes," Luce said, and his grey eyes darkened as if he was thinking of something he'd rather not recall. Het shifted Thomazine on her hip, and the little girl wrapped her fingers in her mother's kerchief and stared at the soldiers, wide-eyed.

"You are - all well?"

Hollie sighed. "We are all well." She didn't believe him. "Been a bit of a journey, lass, and I got a thumping headache. Any chance of a drink? Got a mouth on me like a gunner's pull-through."

She handed over his daughter, and Thomazine squeaked as her bare skin came into contact with the warm metal of her father's breastplate. Even had she recognised him - even had she seen him since she was more than the size of a kitten, her eyes still baby-blue - the two of them stared at each other in mutual astonishment. "I'll just go down to the kitchens and see, husband. Are you going on to Witham, Luce? I'm sure your mother -"

"No," her nephew muttered, "no, I will be rejoining the troop, as soon as, uh, as soon as may be." And he glanced sideways at the third member of the party. "Russell, can you come here a minute?"

And Russell took a deep breath, audible across the parlour, and lifted his head and stepped forward.

He looked no different. The same impassive, lovely features, marred by that livid purple scar on his cheek. The same look of frigid disdain. The same dark eyes, the only bit of Thankful Russell that ever displayed any human feeling, bleak and burning with rage and pain. Black and bloody with bruising, which looked the worse against his fair skin and thick barley-blonde hair - but he was whole, and alive, at least. Russell turned towards her, that disconcerting black gaze on her face, and as ever, Het felt very small and very awkward under his scrutiny-

Luce gently touched the scarred lieutenant's elbow. "I'm *here*, Russell. That's Auntie Het."

Russell blinked, though his dark eyes never shifted from her face. And then a slow tear made its way down his marred cheek. "He's blind, lass," Hollie said awkwardly. "On and off. Shot in the head at Naseby. I said you'd - he could stop here, while he mended. That you'd look after him."

She'd thought Russell was cold and dispassionate and that he had no feelings. He never had. He never would. It shocked her when he dropped, at Hollie's words, to sit on her parlour floor in a forlorn heap, a forlorn and unrestrained heap, sobbing as if his icy heart was breaking, and Het fell to her knees in a tangle of skirts and put her arms round him quite without thinking and held him as if he was little Thomazine, stroking his back, his tangled, sweaty hair. She'd known Russell for a long time. He'd been at her wedding. (He hadn't *danced* at her wedding. That would have been too much like unrestrained celebration.) In all that time she had never touched him. He wasn't - he hadn't been - a man who invited intimacy.

Over the top of his head, she looked at her husband. Hollie looked awkward, and then quite absently rubbed his cheek in his daughter's red-gold curls, as if the sight of his lieutenant's distress had driven him to seek some comfort of his own. "*P'ickles*," Thomazine said crossly, shoving her father's bristly face away, and he laughed.

"Aye, lass, it probably does. Come on then, baby girl. Let's see what we can scare up in the way of treats between meals. You like cheese, Zee? *I* like cheese -" he hoisted the child over his shoulder, then glanced at Luce with that rare, shy, teasing grin. "You coming too, baby *nephew*?" And then, almost as if it were an afterthought, "Hapless turned twenty-one, two weeks back, lass. Be kind."

She rested her hand on Russell's back. Still little more than a boy, under the plate and the ice, as fragile and bird-boned as a child. Her shoulder was hot and wet with his tears. "Husband - on your way to the kitchens, when you go to get that drink - tell Williams to make up a batch of honey cakes, dear. I hope you like honey cakes, Thankful. My cook makes a very nice honey cake. They are quite excellent when they're hot."

3 - Comforted. And Apples.

Thomazine settled for her afternoon nap, covered only by a cool sheet, in the shadowy leaf-dappled nursery at the back of the house. And Het settled Russell, two doors down the landing, flat under the coverlet with the tears soaking into his pillow, staring open-eyed at a ceiling he couldn't see. No one knew quite what to say to him, and after Luce had very gently and somewhat uncomfortably helped him to unbuckle his plate and dealt with the buttons on his buffcoat, they left him.

Het said nothing until she reached the top of the stairs, and then she turned to Luce and said, quite briskly, "Well, we shall have to see what can be done with him, shan't we?"

And Luce knew that at turned twenty-one, Hapless Russell had just been relegated to the same status as fifteen month-old Thomazine. Because he was now in Auntie Het's very capable freckled hands, and if he could be mended, he would be mended, because Het was possibly the mending-est lady in Essex. And that might comfort him. Or might not. Luce tried to imagine how it might feel, to be suddenly alone in a strange house, surrounded by people you couldn't see, in a room you didn't know. Not knowing where you were, or how you might go on -

He stopped, bowed very politely to Het to indicate that she might go downstairs without waiting for him, and wheeled about and stood on the landing again. Listening to a silence that was all the worse for its emptiness. "Russell?"

"Cornet Pettitt?" Sounding stiff and wary, on the other side of that door.

"I've got your Bible here. D'you want it?"

A long pause. "I can't read it, Lucifer. What do you expect me to do with it?"

"Know it's there," Luce said sadly.

Another long pause. And then - "I might as well. Thank you."

Hollie, downstairs with a cup of medicinal feverfew tea, carefully said nothing about any of it. Mostly because despite the feverfew tea, he had a thumping headache and every time he moved too suddenly the room had a tendency to shift alarmingly. Wouldn't have minded a lie down in the cool upstairs himself, but he'd rather die than admit it. Het put her hand on his shoulder in passing and he leaned his aching head against her arm. "I was trying to avoid touching your poor head," she said lovingly. "*Wretched* man. What hour do you plan to return, tomorrow?"

"I hadn't intended to stay -" he started, and she squeezed his shoulder again.

"I shall put it another way, husband. What hour do you plan to leave. *Tomorrow*?"

"All right, I consider myself told. Black Tom's headed south to relieve Taunton, lass. We'll catch him up. Me and Luce, travel a damn sight lighter than the army mob-handed."

"I'm glad you said you and Luce, dear. I don't think -" she glanced upstairs, where it was very quiet, and where Luce had not yet returned, "not for a while. Let us see what Dr Sleep can do for that poor boy. Rest, and care, and decent feeding." Her hand moved gently on his shoulder, and it was less of a caress than an assessment. "There are times, Hollie, when I could wish I had care of the entire Army of Parliament. I am glad to see you, dear love, but I should rather -" very, very carefully, her fingers touched the stitches above his ear. "I should rather have you returned entire, than piece by piece for repair. Does it hurt?"

"Not as much as it did."

"I have *never* taken to the Welsh," she said primly, and Hollie swallowed feverfew tea the wrong way and choked.

"I believe the lass in question found me somewhat intimidating, gal."

"I imagine. I note that your daughter did not. Prickly, indeed." Her fingers moved down, consideringly, over the angle of his jaw. "Though you are, somewhat. Do you mean to do something about that, before you come to bed?" And then, as he stood up, "Not right this minute, Holofernes, you incorrigible - *creature.* Sir! You return in several pieces, and your first thought is of bed."

"Often is," he agreed, and since he was standing up and the room was staying mostly right way up, bumped his nose gently against hers. "D'you mind kissing me, then?"

"I *never* mind kissing you."

On the whole, Luce decided that it was more tactful at that point to go back up the stairs and keep Russell company. Who could still raise a somewhat sardonic eyebrow, even if it evidently hurt. "I see there are potential advantages to having lost my sight," he said tartly.

"Yes. I hate to say it, but I - yes." Luce still hadn't recovered from the sight of his scruffy, cinnamon-haired commanding officer advancing purposefully on the square and unromantic person of Auntie Het with the explicit intent of anticipating his marriage vows by all of half an hour - and that had been almost three years ago, but it still gave Luce the nightmare. Hollie was that sort of man, and it was that sort of a marriage.

"What's that noise?" Russell said, turning his head sharply. Luce couldn't hear anything. And then, a tiny mew, barely audible through the plaster and lath -

The scarred lieutenant blinked at him, almost in his direction. "Go and get her, Lucifer. Don't leave her. Not on her own."

And it was an odd sight, the three of them in that clean pale room above the kitchen - two fair young officers and the sturdy, red-faced, squalling infant. "She weighs a ton," Luce complained, hefting her under his arm like a parcel. Thomazine quacked like a duck, and for the first time in a week Hapless Russell smiled.

"You have nieces, Russell? Nephews?"

"*My* sister? You are joking."

"Didn't know you had one?"

"Let's say if there's a man laid a hand on Fly, he's a braver soul than I. And I include her husband in that assessment."

"Fy?" Thomazine said warily, her tears forgotten. Still hanging upside down under her young uncle's arm, and apparently happy about it. "Who Fy?"

"Fly is my sister, child." As Russell tucked his feet obligingly out of the way Luce dumped the little girl on the end of the bed, from whence she proceeded to roll herself industriously in the sheets. "What is she doing, Lucifer? - ow! she *bit* me! Ow, you little besom!"

"Ba," she said happily, and dumped a sticky kiss on the back of Russell's injured hand. "Tom'sin."

"Hapless," he said firmly, and gave her his hand back to gnaw upon.

"*Ap*ple?"

"Comfort me with Hapless," Luce said unhelpfully, and knelt down at the side of the bed, for the little girl to burrow in between them both like some kind of benighted grub, cackling maniacally. "Gets that laugh from her father's side of the family, if you ask me."

"I believe she gets the *elbows* from his side of the family. I have had the misfortune to be standing in the colonel's way before now. Ouch. Child. That hurt. Cease." Whatever it was that Thomazine was doing to Russell's knuckles in the folds of sheet, it moved him to more animation than Luce had seen from him in years, never mind weeks. "Tammasin now stop that!" he said sternly.

"Good lord, Russell, you have an accent," Luce said, startled, having never been able to place that cold, impersonal voice till now. Russell coming over all warm country Buckinghamshire was about as startling as the sun rising green. The child reared up between them, narrowly avoided head-butting Luce, and threw her arms round her uncle's neck, a great gummy grin on her face.

"Do you want me to try and settle her?" he said, with his niece standing in his lap with her cheek pressed against his affectionately.

"It doesn't sound hopeful."

"I could take her to her mother -"

"NO!"

"I think she disapproves of that idea."

"Hug," she said firmly, and gave Luce one. "*Nice* hug. Horsey?"

"She is a - talkative - child, is she not? And unafraid."

"What should she be afraid of?" Luce said over the child's head as she made a laudable effort to climb over his shoulder and down the other side. "She is loved - safe - no, all is well in her little world." She dropped onto the bed with a plop, and assaulted Russell instead. He wasn't expecting it, but he braced himself and held her, looking as wary and terrified as if he were holding an unexploded mortar. "Then God grant it remain so," Russell murmured, almost inaudibly.

4 - The Love of Hopeless Causes

Het burrowed drowsily against her husband's warm side. She pretended to complain about his snoring, but secretly she found it rather endearing – and oddly comforting. She always knew he was there, in the dark beside her, even without opening her eyes. And she missed it when he wasn't there, for all her protestations.

She'd never known a man so besotted with a child. There'd been times this afternoon, after they'd retrieved her from her new-found uncles, when she thought Hollie couldn't have been more fascinated by little Thomazine if he'd given birth to her himself. And that little fifteen-month-old scrap was fascinated by her father in return. The babe was currently sleeping face-down on Hollie's shoulder, her hinder parts hoisted into the air like a small flannel-wrapped caterpillar, and one minute hand tangled in his loose hair.

"Must you go?" Het said softly, not sure if he was awake or asleep, but needing to ask anyway.

She felt him laugh, or not quite laugh. "Aye, lass, I must, or poor old Black Tom's going to find himself somewhat light in the cavalry department."

"Now?"

His hand slid under the quilts and stroked her shoulder – comfortingly, like she'd seen him do to his horse when it was fractious. "Not right this minute, owd gal. I've got no clothes on."

"You have a perfectly decent nightshirt in the press, Holofernes," she said tartly, and his comforting hand settled slightly further down with an air of finality.

"And I'm very grateful for it, lass. Lot o' work you put into that. I just happen to prefer –"

"*Hollie*!"

"What? Zee's dead to t'world, I could set her in front of a gun battery and she'd not stir –"

"That is not the point, sir, you are a respectable husband and father –"

"Now that," he said comfortably, "is a great consolation." He sat up, sliding his dribbling firstborn onto the sheets. Het sat up likewise, stern and sensible in her warm bedgown, and then - as she always did – gave a great sigh and put her fingers against his scars: the great curving white arc that ran across his ribs from his days of youthful stupidity in the Low Countries, the dimple in the meat of his shoulder from Reading. He moved his hair obligingly, and she put her arms round him, and that most fierce and implacable military commander made a contented little noise and snuggled himself against her.

"Could stop like this all day, lass, did thee bed me or not," he said against her hair. Zee, presently buried in a nest of pillows behind her parents, smacked her lips in her sleep and stirred.

She lay awake, after he was asleep, watching the moon slowly move across the window, with husband and daughter tangled in mutual contentment - Thomazine's hands clenched tight on Hollie's loose hair in one hand and Het's shift in another.

She should put the child back in her own bed. The little girl had been overexcited, to the point of naughtiness, this afternoon. She'd been downright impertinent with Luce and Russell, who encouraged her naughtiness in the way of indulgent young men the world over - even Russell, in his own stiff way, encouraged the child's waywardness as if it were a thing to be proud of. She was set fair to be spoiled rotten by her adoring father, and her impertinence had been such that Het had felt guilty for not taking the child upstairs and chastising her roundly, as a responsible parent should. But there had been something that wrung her heart about that bright little girl at her supper, perched in state at the table between her father and Russell, prattling forward nonsense and stealing the choicest morsels from her father's plate. And, on occasion, trying to feed them to Russell. She was a loving little thing, fiercely maternal even at not quite two, and much given to lost causes. The scarred lieutenant seemed too dazed to mind having sticky lumps of gnawed apple thrust into his hand.

Her husband was too thin. Again. Nature had never intended his bones to be visible, and in the silver light he looked no different to the first time she'd set eyes on him - too young, and too fragile, to be in charge of *himself*, let alone a senior command in the Army. He didn't even have two score years to his name, yet. He'd be but thirty-eight in February. Too thin, with too many scars that weren't healing quickly enough, and shadowed eyes. Het smiled, and set as brave a table as she could, and let Thomazine stay up late, and there was a deal of brittle merriment. But she wasn't fooled for a minute. She showed willing, because he was her husband and she loved him, but Het wasn't daft. *Something* had happened at Naseby. Luce was guarded, something he'd never been, even as a boy - quiet and solemn as a child, but never secretive. And he was good with Russell. *Too* good with Russell, for a man just turned twenty-one. The Lucifer Pettitt who'd left his mother's house in nearby Witham three years ago would have been as full of bounce and eagerness to please as a puppy. He'd have had neither the gentleness nor the patience to deal sympathetically with the lieutenant. He'd learned. At twenty-one, he shouldn't have had to.

All she could do was feed them, and keep their linen in good order, and give them a place to come home to. Be a tiny place of order and cleanliness in a world turned on its head. She couldn't do it for the whole Army - although her husband seemed to think they had sufficient room for every man who was broken in his service - but she could set a little light in the window to encourage the rest, and hope that the Lord would comfort them in their adversity. She found herself praying, as she often did these days: talking to the Lord, in her head, with perhaps a little more tartness than was seemly in a virtuous woman. Not precisely asking Him what He thought He was playing at, letting this go on, but - close. Definitely close.

5 - Back to the Day Job

Lucey met him out on the Braintree road early next morning, as Hollie was on his way to scare the lad out of bed - which was a happy coincidence. "Not coming in for breakfast, brat? Het *will* be disappointed."

"I should prefer to rejoin the troop as quickly as may be," he said stiffly, and Hollie glanced at his cornet quickly.

"Christ, is your mother that bad?"

Which, at least, got a laugh out of him. "No. But I feel a bit guilty about deserting them. Even for two days."

"If you think that rabble can create havoc in two days, Luce, you have a worse opinion of them than even *I* do. Don't worry. I left Venning in charge, and whatever Drew's other failings he don't take shit from troopers."

"Even Gray," Luce said, and there was something odd about the way he said it.

Why Gray, Hollie wondered. That little troublemaker seemed to pop up in quite a lot of Lucey's talk, of late. "Missing him?" he said malevolently, and Luce raised those clear rain-coloured eyes to Hollie's face and said nothing. The lad hadn't slept well. He looked troubled. "Luce, what the hell is the matter with you these days?"

And the brat shook his head, pushing his hair out of his eyes with one hand, dismissing it. "Nothing. How's Russell this morning?"

"Bored. Already. Bloody won't be if Het has her way, I tried to tell him he'll work for his keep, but... " But what employment even Het could find for a blinded administrator, he didn't know. "He reckoned he could see a bit, this morning. Said a good night's sleep worked a miracle." And Hollie had told his daughter the moon was made of green cheese, though it wasn't.

"And did it?"

"Did it bollocks." Oh aye, Russell could see just fine, that was why he had his shirt on inside out and had jumped about a foot in the air when Hollie had come up behind him, scattering breakfast across half the kitchen, to the kitchen cat's delight. He was getting better at the dissembling part, after only a week, and that was a little tragedy in itself.

"You going to appoint a new lieutenant to replace him?" Luce asked casually, and Hollie turned on him with a fury that came out of nowhere. "*Damned* if I will. That's Hapless's post, for so long as he bloody well wants it. *Jesus*, brat! Dead man's boots, or what!" And shaking his head, he'd kicked Blossom into a shambling canter, which had surprised the brown horse as much as it had surprised Hollie. Come racketing back after a hundred yards feeling very ashamed of himself, and Luce had looked at him like a kicked puppy, and he'd apologised, knowing it wasn't rational. Giving Russell's post to someone else was too much like saying he wasn't coming back. "Unless you want it, brat?"

"Er, thank you, sir, but - no. No, I'm not good with lists."

"See? He's no more replaceable than you are."

"I think that may be the kindest thing you've ever said to me, colonel. Thank you."

"I didn't say it was necessarily a *good* thing..."

They caught up with the rag-tag of the Army in Somerset after a mere three days, trying to look inconspicuous and smirking hopefully at some of the lads they knew in Okey's troop of dragoons at the back. Damned funny way of getting to Taunton, in Hollie's opinion, sidling across the countryside trying to avoid His slippery Majesty's garrison patrols down the south coast. Bristol, Bath, Bridgwater and - "We know a poem about Devizes, don't we?" he prompted Luce, and was on the receiving end of a wholly filthy look.

"Not one that is better shared, colonel. In decent company."

"You reckon Okey's is decent company?"

"He'm getting cheeky again," the dragoon said cheerfully. "Put a bit o' distance between you and Black Tom, you start getting lippy - ent that right, Rosie?"

"Why, has he been looking for me or summat?"

"Couldn't miss 'ee, sir. He had a lad out looking early this morning, and 'nother bout noon. Felt a bit sorry for him, I did. M'lord Fairfax was getting proper teasy about it, he reckoned."

"Ah, bugger." It was a nice day. The birds were singing. The sun was shining. The turf was flat and smooth enough that even the lack-witted Blossom might not fall over his own feet at a gallop. "See you later, brat."

6 - The Substance of Things Not Seen

Fairfax was at prayer and could not be disturbed, so Hollie ambled up and down the landing outside his general's personal quarters indulging in a habit which drove Het mad, a tendency to, literally, kick his heels. If you happened to be wearing spurred boots on a stone-flagged hall it was quite a diverting pursuit. The musical chime was a rather soothing backdrop to Hollie's internal mental writhing. Did he, or did he not, need a lieutenant? And if he had to - if Fairfax insisted, and he might - who the hell would it be, that he could trust, to not only turn a blind eye to Hollie's somewhat independent accounting practises, but to translate the troop's less conventional means of support into something that looked good on paper. And Chedglow. Who the hell was going to replace *Chedglow* in command of his troop of itinerant God-botherers? For a minute, Hollie was inclined to promote his own appalling father, just for the hell of it. They'd had one slavering hellfire preacher in charge already, they'd be used to being spat on at close range by their commanding officer - and they'd miss the Old Testament if they didn't get a healthy dose every day with breakfast. On the other hand, it'd mean he'd have to deal with Elijah being stern and godly at him on a daily basis, and that he could not bear. Luce didn't want it, even if he'd been any bloody good at it, which he wouldn't be. (Too nice by half, that lad.) He'd have said Calthorpe, once, but Calthorpe had copped it at Marston Moor. Eliot or Ward - sweet Jesus Christ almighty, no.

The bottom line was, since the New Model Army had come in, most of the new lads were decent, obedient, dutiful plain troopers, who served their God and their commanding officer with zeal and efficiency, who turned out to drill smart and eager, who observed the Sabbath and said grace at length before their meals - and they were as stolid as bullocks in a field. They did what they were told. They thought what they were told. And if they didn't, they sure as hell didn't trust their thoughts with a commander they didn't know from a hole in the ground. They were good lads and they were as efficient a fighting body as he'd ever clapped eyes on but what they were not, for the most part, was independent. The Army didn't like independent thinkers. No, that wasn't fair. The *Parliament* didn't like independent thinkers. Look at Lilburne - denied a command under the New Model for refusing to take the Covenant, earlier this year.

No, Hollie was short of like minds, and the one thing he liked at his hand was men who not only knew what they were doing, but could do it without it having been written out for them longhand. Efficient drill was well and good but it didn't give you *initiative*. Venning, now, Venning was competent and efficient and knowledgeable but he either could not or would not think for himself. Luce the same - had the ideas, but didn't have the confidence, the brass neck, to go off and do them independently. General Fairfax had been bloody clever: he'd got a hold of anybody who looked like they might have both the fire and the skill, and he'd promoted them already. (Said Colonel Babbitt, who knew whereof he spoke, having been promoted already.) Cullis wouldn't touch an independent command with a shitty stick. Russell, even were he fit for service, couldn't be trusted not to go off half-cocked, left to his own devices.

Split 'em up. It was all he could think of, break Chedglow's lads up and take a score apiece amongst the rest of the company. After Naseby Hollie wasn't sure he could trust himself to deal with them fairly, as a troop. Not sure if you could discipline men for rape, mutilation and massacre in the Lord's name, not in the New Model. When Hollie could have called his command his own - when he didn't have as many regulations to sign to as the lowest of his troopers - he'd have shot the lot of the bastards, personally, one at a time or collectively it didn't bother him.

"I see you're as hot at hand as ever, colonel."

He stopped musing and looked at Fairfax. Greying, pouchy-eyed, sallow. Christ, he looked ill. "Ah," he said warily, and then stalked - trying not to jingle - into Fairfax's quarters. "That'd be it."

"Was expecting you before this, mind." Fairfax said nothing unkind, it wasn't his way, he'd just turn those fierce dark eyes on you and look mournful. "Where *are* you quartered, Colonel Babbitt? I sent a messenger, but he was unable to locate you?"

"Oh, you know me, usually end up round and about with Pettitt. What's up?"

"Sir," Fairfax prompted, and he came up short, because Black Tom Fairfax was not only his commander but his *friend* - he'd carried Fairfax's little daughter on the front of his saddle one black night across Yorkshire, fleeing the Malignants two years back. Fairfax had sent some of that little daughter's outgrown baby-things, at Thomazine's birth. Fairfax was a North Countryman, same as Hollie was, an exile in this lush green landscape. They talked to each other in their own home accents, betimes, not the stiff and formal words of a commander and his subordinate. Fairfax looked at Hollie and cocked an eyebrow but did not smile. "How *is* your wife, Colonel Babbitt?" And then without waiting for an answer, "It won't do, sir. It won't do at all. I won't ask for an explanation -"

"But I'll give you one," Hollie cut in, because he was bloody cross at that last implication. "Supposed to leave Russell in Northampton, was I? In his condition, in a town relieved of siege not a week past? Aye, I did go home to Essex, and I took Hapless with me, and Luce come because he reckoned it'd kill him doing the sixty miles on a horse so soon after Naseby. So that's where I was, and if the Army couldn't do without me holding its hand for three days, all I can say is God help it."

"You went without asking leave, colonel."

"All right, if you want to make a paper exercise of it - *sir* - mark me down as absent without leave and dock me according. Or have me bloody shot or whatever else it is you do wi' soldiers that misbehave, these days."

"Goring has abandoned the siege at Taunton."

"Good for Goring. *What?*"

"You heard. Goring's headed for Yeovil. At speed." And then, finally, Fairfax's lean, dark face creased in a rusty smile. "If you'd been any later, you'd probably have bumped smack into him. I'm not sure which of you would have been more surprised."

"Bloody hell."

"Quite. I *had* hoped that you might be able to send some of your troops out to reconnoitre the Royalist position."

"I'm hardly the least conspicuous spy in the Army. Sir."

"Did I *ask* you to go personally, colonel? Anyway. You weren't there. I asked someone else."

"Sir." Fairfax wouldn't tear you off a strip, mostly. He'd just take whatever it was you liked to do, and give it to someone else.

"I hope your horse is rested, colonel. Lord Goring has deployed his men along the line of the Yeo, from Yeovil to Langport. My father has decided to base his infantry at Crewkerne, and we will be shortly joining them."

"Sir."

"I trust that will not interfere with any of your other engagements, Colonel Babbitt?"

"Sir." He couldn't quite stifle a sigh, and Fairfax shot him a stern look.

"You will be ready within the hour, colonel. "

7 - Gray's Anatomy

It was stupid, and shameful, and sooner or later someone would notice, but Luce didn't care. He greeted Venning absently, agreeing with the freckled captain’s every word. Thinking he’d turned down the offer of a piece of pigeon pie, but not sure, and if he hadn’t he could see the tip of a brown and white tail thumping gently against the floor under Venning’s chair, so it wouldn't go to waste.

He couldn't eat. Not now. It had been three days – three days, not half a lifetime – but he didn’t know what might have happened in those three days. He kept thinking of the battle, of her eyes gone black-enormous, with the blood soaking into her collar from the shallow runnel Chedglow’s pistol ball had grazed through her hair. She hadn't been beautiful in her distress. She’d been shaking and as white as spoiled milk, and her coat, when he took it off her later in his quarters, had been splattered with blood and soiled with worse.

What she had not been, was dead. (And neither, by the Lord’s grace, was Russell, and Luce thanked God every night and every morning for that one bright mercy.) She’d not been killed either at or after Naseby but oh, God, it had been so close, and she was so dear, and so fragile, that all his hopes and all his dreams could suddenly rest on the narrow shoulders of one scruffy, bad-tempered little French girl in breeches, who could be blinked out of existence at the whim of any Malignant sharpshooter, any passing pestilence, any accident –

“’Ee looks knackered, bor,” Venning said sympathetically. “Bad news is, looks like we’re going to come to grips with Goring any day, the botty owd bugger. I dunno *what* he thinks he's playing at. No, thass not fair, *I'd* not care to have Fairfax between me and hiding behind the King's skirts, were I Goring. He don't want to stray too far from home, that lad, and can't say as I blame him. Our Tom means business."

"That's good." He rubbed a hand over his jaw, not particularly caring for the scratchiness, but - "Where's Trooper Gray?"

"Gray? God alone knows. Sulking somewhere, I do reckon. I swear to God, Lucey, I had more cause to discipline that lad while you been gone – thought he was suffen fierce before, but he been brawling and cussing just about every hour of the day. I'm running out of ideas, Luce. I ent had him flogged – *yet* – 'cause he's a mate of yours, but I tell you what, it's getting close."

Venning didn't know. Her secret was still safe. Him. He. Not her, not Gabrielle, but just Gray. He dropped his eyes, snapped his fingers to the dog and fondled the soft domed head, bending his face to be washed by Tinners' enthusiastic tongue. Anything to hide the look of sudden fierce joy on his face that he couldn't contain. "Where does - he - normally go? To sulk?"

"Hell do I know, bor? Got more important things to think about, what with you three gallivanting about the countryside leaving *me*' with this rabble and bloody Goring creeping about in the bushes. *Now* where's 'ee going?"

He was going to look for his girl. Who might be dressed as a plain trooper under Captain Venning's command, and who might be brawling her way across Somerset, which wouldn't surprise him in the least,

Gray's traditional means of soothing her ruffled nerves being to go and beat the crap out of someone. She was still his girl, and if nothing else he needed to see her. Just to reassure himself that she was alive, and in the world, and unharmed.

No one knew where Trooper Gray was. Several troopers suggested that he might be out of his mind for looking. Someone thought they might have seen him riding off about an hour since, headed west. "He in trouble – again?"

There was a chuckle from the trooper's friends, who evidently thought Gray in trouble was a matter of just deserts.

Luce shook his head. It was a silly thing and doubtless the result of too much reading but the level landscape was beginning to unsettle him. Those narrow, deep drainage sluices, they called rhynes hereabouts, all overhung with rippling grey willows – he couldn't see Gray as Ophelia, not for a minute, not a-purpose. *Could* see Gray sulking by the water's edge, all too easily, and her boots slipping on the wet grass. The Levels were flat. Still. Silent. Eerie. The pale wide skies reflected in the empty water. He kept seeing the masses of drowned grass as a drowned girl's hair, floating just below the surface.

"Gray." He sounded irritable with relief, even in his own ears, and that wasn't how it was supposed to go. "Where the hell have you *been*?"

She gave a great gulp and turned to face him – her eyes wet and red, nose streaming, hair sticking to her face in great sweaty hanks, and she looked bloody awful and he'd have walked on coals of fire for her. And he had no idea where they went from here, none. He'd left her a week ago with any number of things unsaid, undone, and he hoped to God it wasn't too late.

"Don't cry," Luce said awkwardly, and she blinked and her chin trembled and she said, "I'm not crying," in that odd, gruff little voice.

"So I see. Definitely not crying."

"No. I'm not. I've – I've got an eyelash in my eye, sir."

"Do you mind if I sit down?"

"Yes," she said crossly, and he sat down anyway. "See, the thing is, Gray. It can't go on. *We* can't go on like this. Sooner or later someone's going to notice, and then –"

"I don't care!"

"*I* care."

"What's it got to do with you, Cornet Pettitt? It's none of your business! What's the worst you can do to me? I'm a plain trooper –"

"Well, no, no you're not." Luce looked at his fingernails studiously. "If you were a plain trooper, I'm sure Hollie wouldn't mind a bit. But you're a rather not plain trooper, and sooner or later someone is going to pay more attention to your particularly fine eyes than you will find comfortable. And then where will we be?"

She glowered up at him stubbornly. "Any man lays a hand on me and I'll cut his balls off."

"That'll help, I'm sure, in the interests of avoiding adverse attention," he said dryly. "Gray – you're not a man. You're a woman. I know that, you know that, Russell knows that. Venning doesn't know *what* you are, for which I think you must be profoundly grateful, but you scare him rigid and that's hardly fair."

"What – that web-footed frog-fucker?" She spat into the river. "That for what he thinks. I could take him." In this light, under the shifting golden shadows of the midsummer trees, Gray was a rather young, and very pretty, if slightly thin, young woman.

"He'd probably let you, too. Would it be so bad – to be a woman, again?"

She turned and looked at him, cool and level. "Oh, yes, Cornet. You have no idea what it is to be a woman."

"Well. True. I do not. But –"

"I have known freedom, sir. Such as there is only to be known, in the Army. I have known friendship, and faith, and honour. I have had the liberty to speak my thoughts freely. I have taken my place as an equal at a man's side – I have talked of politics, and religion, and women, as loosely as any one of you, and none has told me to be silent, or to hold my tongue. And you would have me tamely put on my skirts and be hobbled again, sir?"

"You might have been talking, mistress, but I don't think you did a lot of listening," Luce said mildly. "Which man of *this* troop likes meek and milky wenches?"

"Oh, for bedding, Lucifer, that's different! You're all the same –"

"That is not fair, Gray!"

"Is it not? Go on, then, which of you would take a woman such as me to wife? I'm a French soldier's daughter, Lucifer," she said coolly, and he made to say something, and she cut him off. "My mother was raped by a French soldier at La Rochelle. I know what men are, Luce. I know what men are better than you do."

"Mademoiselle, I have nothing but the deepest admiration and respect for you, but this conversation is going nowhere," he said stiffly.

"Indeed. No doubt you admire me because I'm a better swordsman than you are."

"In your dreams. I like you, Gray. Even when you're determined to pick a fight that isn't there."

"Exactly, Lucey. You like me. You don't have some stupid out of date notions of chivalry and how a woman should behave, you don't pant after me like some, some dog after a bitch – you don't fancy me –"

"Do I not, then?" he said, quite conversationally, and she stopped, mid-sentence, with her mouth open. "Possibly not, when you have that look on your face, mind. The resemblance to a fish is truly remarkable."

"Don't be ridiculous, Lucifer. You're only saying that because you know I'm a girl and you think it'll make me feel better."

"That you look like a fish?"

She scowled at him again. "*No*."

"If you don't mind that I – may happen to consider you passingly attractive," he said casually, "why on earth are you so determined that I should repeat the statement? Surely, if it were of no matter, you should prefer it unsaid –"

"Lucifer," she said menacingly, "do you, or do you not, fancy me?"

"I thought you said it didn't matter?"

"It doesn't matter! I just want to know!"

"Well, I don't choose to tell you, just to flatter your vanity."

"I am not vain!"

"Very true, you are of all the people I know possibly the least vain. Which is," he said musingly, "a great pity. As I said. Remarkably fine eyes."

"I asked you," she snarled, "I asked you to – you know - after the battle. In your quarters. And you said no."

"You were drunk! What am I *supposed* to do, girl? Three quarters of a bottle of wine to the bad – you didn't want *me*, Gray, you just wanted to not be on your own. *I* didn't want to take advantage of you when you didn't know what you were saying. Regardless of how much I may have wanted to at the time. I've got *some* bloody decency left!" It wasn't how it was supposed to go. Not at all. It wasn't how he'd imagined, all the way down the country – none of the passionate declarations he'd so carefully thought out in his head, she hadn't fallen into his arms swearing her eternal love. "I am, I hope, a gentleman, with some honour. If little else," he said furiously.

"So – " She sat up suddenly and yanked her shirt over her head. "*I* am not!"

Luce sat likewise bolt upright with a most unpassionate whoop of astonishment, because the young lady was - was - unbound, then, put it that way, and although not lavishly feminine, distinctly of the fairer gender. "Trooper Gray!" he yelped, and she gave him a shaky, defiant look.

"I thought you said you wanted to," she said, although she didn't sound much like she did. She sounded like she might be about to cry.

"Yes! *No*! Oh, for goodness' sakes, girl - I thought we had this argument already -"

"It wasn't an argument," she muttered, "it was a disagreement."

"Whatever it was. We did agree that you were - that you are - " he turned his back on her, very deliberately. "Put your shirt on, trooper. I have no intention of dishonouring you."

"But I *wanted* you to!"

Luce turned back round and fixed his gaze on the tip of her nose. It was possibly the least exciting part of Gray's anatomy presently displayed. He didn't care if it made him go cross-eyed. "Trooper - oh, hell, *Mademoiselle Boissevin* - you are a very attractive young woman, and I admire and respect you enormously."

"But," she said flatly.

"But, indeed. I like you altogether too well to - to - well. That. Dishonour you."

"I can stay dressed as a boy," she said unhelpfully, "if you preferred my arse?"

"Gray!"

She shrugged. "Just saying - if you don't fancy me as a girl?"

"As I have never seen you in skirts, mademoiselle, I could scarcely comment. It's not me we're talking about, girl. It's you." He folded his arms and glowered at her. It was a convenient position, because he had a dark suspicion that were she to notice his - interest, say - it would render matters considerably more complex. "It is wholly immaterial whether or not I - like - you, Gray. One day you will meet a man and you will want to - you know. And you'll know if it's the right one, because - well, you just will. And I should be very sad and very sorry if you chose to give me that very precious gift simply because you - because you -"

"Lucifer?"

"Trooper Gray - *bugger* - mademoiselle?"

"You can be a pompous little bastard at times, Lucifer," she said sweetly. "I would rather do it with someone I liked, Luce. I think I sort of trust you. I have thought about it quite a lot, and - well, Captain Venning is a bit boisterous, and, um, Rosie's just too big. And I'm very fond of Hapless but I'm not sure he'd know what he was doing any more than I would."

"Oh, he would," Luce said darkly, knowing exactly what Thankful Russell's not exactly blameless life had been where the ladies were concerned, prior to the battle at Edgehill.

"But you have always been very kind. And," she lifted her head and looked into his eyes, and Luce swallowed hard a couple of times. "I do fancy you, Luce. I think. So I *do* want to. Even sober."

"Mademoiselle," he said desperately, "what of the man you will take as a husband? Surely -"

"Oh, the hell with him. No one's going to marry *me*, Lucey. There's no one that daft."

"I am not going to have this conversation," he said. "I'm not, you know. Gray – what are you doing?"

The shirt was off again, with an air of defiance that was rather alarming. She took off her stockings and rolled them up and stuffed them into her boots, put her hands on her hips, glared at him, and then started to unbutton her breeches. "Gray!" he yelped, and she stopped with one slender white leg out of that ragged garment, and cocked an eyebrow at him.

"If you don't, Lucey, I'm going to walk bare-arsed through the camp till I find one of your lot that will. You want me as a bloody woman, Lucifer, *you* make me one."

"This is tantamount to – to –"

"*Mais oui,*" she said pertly."Well. Now you know what it's like."

"Sit down," he said crossly, and she sat. Bare as an egg and elegantly cross-legged and he was tempted to put his coat round her shoulders but he had a suspicion she'd laugh at him so he didn't, he just examined a beetle crawling up a stem of grass instead. It was still hardly the kind of romantic interlude Luce wrote poetry about – couldn't imagine writing sonnets to Gray's left eyebrow, given the flyaway humour of that slanted mouse-brown attachment, and yet –

"What are you thinking?"

"About your eyebrows," he said, honestly, and she laughed, and after a pause, so did he.

"What about 'em?"

"They're – sort of – brown."

"And you a poet," she said, tilting her face obligingly into the sun, eyes closed.

"And your hair's growing back." He put out a hand to touch the loose waves on her shoulders, carefully. "It's – it's pretty."

She looked at his fingers, and then she looked at his face, and a slow blush rose from where her collar would have been if she'd been wearing one.

"Luce," she muttered, directing her words into her lap. "Luce, if you wouldn't mind –" her head came up again, and she was trembling like one of the willow leaves whose shadows dappled her bare white shoulders. "Would you kiss me?"

8 - Smoke and Mirrors

They had a day of rest, after that scrambled arrival in Crewkerne. A day of fasting and prayer and godly reflection for some, and conspicuous absence for others. Any number of people remarked on Luce's sudden attitude of fervent thanksgiving.

"Exalted beyond measure," he breathed, which Venning thought was going some, even for a bloody verse-monger.

Babbitt just wasn't there, which occasioned some criticism from the more vociferous amongst the late Captain Chedglow's men, but then neither were several of Babbitt's own personal troop, which also caused raised eyebrows. What hotbeds of vice you could find in Crewkerne on a hot midsummer afternoon on the Sabbath, were possibly best unexplored, but whatever they were, it was assumed that Babbitt was finding them.

Gray hadn't started a fight with anyone from sun-up to sun-down and was attached to Luce's heels like his second shadow, and every now and again you'd catch them look at each other like they were planning something unhelpful.

All things considered, Drew Venning didn't think they could come to grips with Goring soon enough.

Yeovil was a hell of a disappointment. There *had* been a Malignant detachment guarding the town, Venning had seen 'em, when he'd gone out with his lads spying out the land for Fairfax. All of a sudden, when push came to shove – soon as they saw the Parliament colours unroll in the sultry July heat and heard the deep roll of the drums giving the order to advance – the buggers were gone, with not a shot fired. And it was too damnable hot to be chasing Goring's spaniels halfway across the country.

That was the problem with Lord Goring. (Who wasn't even really a Lord anything, by all accounts, but the son of an earl, and using the Lord bit as a courtesy title. He wasn't even a peer. Babbitt said he was, but when pressed for clarity on that matter, had suggested that Goring was distinctly a pee-er - peeing him right off. Which had not been helpful, and Major Disbrow, a very devout and humourless gentleman, had not been impressed. The lads had laughed, mind.) All show and no substance, Goring was. Fierce as a rat in a trap if you had him pushed to corner, but he'd rather run and fight another day, which was no good at all when you had six troop of horse frothing at the bit to be at him.

Bottom line was that he was playing silly buggers now – smoke and mirrors, sending his lieutenant-general off towards Taunton with three brigade of horse, thundering off in a great cloud of dust with all *their* colours flying. Looked nice, and it must have had Fairfax fooled, because he'd sent four thousand of their lads to keep an eye on the proceedings and tail the Malignants. It might have worked, too, as an exercise in divide and conquer, if Goring's Lieutenant-General Porter hadn't been as cocky as his commander. Venning reckoned that any officer who was stupid, not to say lackadaisical, enough to neglect to post sentries while his lads were fell out, deserved all he got. If *Venning* had been caught with his breeches down like that, he'd be more scared of what'd happen when Hollie Babbitt caught hold of him, never mind the might of the enemy. Well, Porter had been sitting with his feet up on Isle

Moor, a few miles west of here, and their own General Massie had proper took the lot of ‘em by surprise. They reckoned it was the quickest rout since – well, you know what Parliament men were. It was always the quickest and most complete victory God hath granted, at least since the last one. Five hundred prisoners to the good, although you had to wonder what the hell they were supposed to do with the ones that weren’t worth anything in exchange.

Babbitt, unkindly, suggested the Wagg Rhyne ditch, just to scare them. It worked, too, looking at that russet-haired scarecrow. He had a great streak of sunburn down his prominent nose, peeling in a most alarming fashion, and he spent most of his time lolloping round in his shirt sleeves with the cuffs rolled back to his elbows, and most of the visible bits of him were dotted with great bloody weeping insect-bites where he'd scratched himself raw. Venning looked at his own freckled forearm thoughtfully. Evidently the gnats didn’t like the taste of a Norfolk boy.

"Reckon we're going to bring him about today? Goring?"

Kenelm Toogood, the Cornish captain, bit down on the juicy end of a blade of grass and sucked it noisily. Venning shrugged.

"Be hell of a nice, bor. No offence, mind, but I'd rather be back up along. Good bit o' fishing off the Waveney, this time of year."

"Ah? Where you to, then?"

"Diss," Venning said gloomily. "Norfolk. Can’t get much further nor home than here. Only come 'cos our Rosie asked of me. Been all around the country after that one, I have."

Toogood shook his head regretfully. "That's no good, then. I ent never been north of Plymouth before, me, so might as well be Cathay for all I know. What's 'ee got there, boy? Drop it, sir!"

Took a minute to realise the Cornishman was talking to Tinners, who'd fallen into the habit of roaming loose about the horse-lines in this flat open country. The grinning dog had also apparently fallen into the rhyne ditch, judging by the besmottered state of him, and was presently flinging his sodden stern from side to side with ecstatic abandon at this attention. What he had was a drenched leather sack, which he was dragging between his front paws and worrying.

"God help us all, it's Lucey's snapsack. Aw, Tinners, lad'll be spitting when he finds out you've dropped his poems in a bloody slummocky owd ditch."

"Poems?" Toogood's eyes had gone round and awed. "Cornet Pettitt? What - he writes, say, *poems*?"

"Thass right, bor." Venning was beginning to enjoy himself. "You ent never noticed, the inky fingers and that?"

"Poems. Bloody hell. Poems. Land, I dussent know what my dear old mother'd say if she could see me - knocking about with poets, up the line in Somerset, miles away from home. He any good?"

"Dunno. I got better things to do with my time than read his scribbling. 'S all about, you know, girls. Soppy stuff. Not even the good stuff. Nicked a bit to send home to our Alice and *she* rated it, but then, she d'think I wrote it. There's times when I reckon Luce is a bit wet, meself. Nice lad, but - bit drippy."

"Ah," Toogood said, nodding. "I know that sort. Here. Venning. You seem like a sound lad. You busy?"

"Not doing nawthen much."

Toogood took the grass out of the corner of his mouth and grinned a villainous, gap-toothed grin, nodding across to the hills. "Fancy a little look-see, then? Let's have a see what my lord Goring's getting up to. You game?"

Venning slapped at a whining gnat on the back of his neck and grinned back. "Talking my language, bor."

9 - An Uphill Struggle

"Can I just say," Luce said grimly, "can I just say, I feel like *shit*."

Hollie had been staring off into the middle distance, less than entranced by the sight of the rank ditch that was likely to be his battlefield in the coming hours. They were supposed to be at prayer, and he was, he truly was, though he was feeling neither godly zeal nor enthusiasm. He was mostly praying to God that he wasn't going to puke in front of the rest of the lads, and that if he was going to end up dead, that it be quick, and not messy. It was as good a prayer as any, and, as he shot a quick glance at Major Bethel a hundred yards away with his eyes closed and his lips moving silently, he reckoned it was a heap more heartfelt.

It was odd to have Luce Pettitt at your elbow using language like that, though, most out of character, and he stopped looking at Bethel and wondering how long it'd be before the godly bastard had to stop for breath, and looked at his friend instead. "You all right, brat?"

The brat buried his face in his hands and his – sweat-limp, unbrushed, not like him either – hair fell in his eyes and he took a deep breath. "Honestly? No. But if you can try and not get me killed this day, my mother would be grateful."

"Aye. Well." It was Goring, that was what it was. It was the possibility of facing that unprincipled Malignant son-of-a-bitch, and not knowing quite what the hell he might *do* to you if you happened to fall into his hands. Had a reputation, that one. Venning reckoned Goring was like a rat in a trap but it was all right for Venning, he had a bloody dog to sort out the rodent population. Hollie gave his friend an awkward grin. "I'll do my best."

Luce did look ill, mind. All sort of pale and sweaty, with great smeary black rings under his eyes. And he'd been heaving his guts up for the last day and a bit, now Hollie minded it. He'd just thought it was the heat – or the excitement – or a bad pie or something. Some bloody mate he was, then. "Tell you what, Luce – if we have to, you know – today – you stick on me and I'll keep an eye out for you."

"I said try and *not* get me killed, Hollie?" he said with a feeble attempt at a smile, and then his face changed and he put the back of his hand to his mouth in a very genteel manner. "'Scuse me," he whispered, and fled.

Gray, just coming in, almost collided with Luce on his way out. Where Lucey was Trooper Gray would be five yards behind, like a worse-tempered version of Venning's dog. He'd behaved for almost a whole day now, and he was spoiling for a fight, and he raised his eyes to Hollie's with a look that promised something unpleasant held in reserve for later. Fine by Hollie. He had the best part of nine inches height on Gray and he had a niggling headache and the idea of turning that belligerent little whelp upside down when they'd finished with Goring was beginning to appeal. In a purely informal capacity, obviously. He could break the little bastard any time he chose, although Venning was beginning to despair of ever bringing the little trooper to any kind of discipline. Hollie looked back, long and cool and thoughtful, and then flexed his rackety right hand meaningfully. It was a noisy operation, as ever, and he made great play of smoothing his bridle-gauntlet into place. It'd hurt, if someone with an armoured right hand smacked you in the mouth. Might want to think on that, Gray.

Bethel was still rolling his eyes piously and someone else in Hollie's company had fallen out, almost literally. He could hear them coughing. He hoped it was coughing. And that it wasn't Luce. Apart from his great sympathy for the brat, it was just hugely embarrassing in moments set aside for quiet personal communication with the Lord when your cornet was audibly trying to turn himself inside out. Bethel was still at it, and Hollie looked up and caught the eye of the other galloping Major, who was looking as pale and shaky as Hollie felt. Disbrow nodded abruptly in greeting – wouldn't do to interrupt the Lord's Elect mid-flow, they'd never hear the last of it – and then gave himself a resounding slap on the wrist.

Which was somewhat unexpected, and even Disbrow looked startled at the noise, and looked at the smear of blood on the cuff of his shirt where he'd just crushed some flying buzzy thing out of existence, and turned scarlet and hunched his shoulders in embarrassment.

Too many little flighty pestilences in these parts anyway, Hollie thought sourly, observing the general discomfiture of the horses. Stamping and restless and irritable, tails swishing and heads tossing, being bitten into testiness by this god-damned plague of whining gnats. Even Blossom was teasy as a snake, which was rare. He could see the big rawboned brown horse's head jerking up and down, the white blaze on his nose that gave him that odd wall-eyed look making him distinctive in the line. Couldn't *hear* the wet slobber as the horse shifted the bit restlessly in his mouth, or see the patches of sweat darkening his neck, but he knew the horse well enough to know –

There was an indignant squeal, and a brief flurry of violent equine activity, and Hollie took advantage of the lull in godly reflection to shout, "Amen!" and flee to the safety of the horse-lines.

There was a nip on Blossom's shoulder, and Russell's neat bay Thomas was squealing-furious. It reminded him again of Hapless – who should be here, and was not. His horse was still here because Russell had managed about a hundred yards on Thomas before admitting defeat and taking one of the more sluggardly remounts, a beast not so inclined to require governance. And Percey – Percey would've sorted out that little scuffle, no trouble. Lucey's red mare was sweating and frothing and miserable, in her customary state of restless agitation. "Luce, take Thomas out."

The brat didn't even laugh, just dragged himself wearily into the saddle. Russell's horse laid his ears back and looked like he was thinking about playing up, and Luce gave him an even more uncharacteristic wallop down the shoulder with the buckle-end of the reins. "Don't you play silly buggers with me, or I'll have you kennel-meat," he said crossly.

"Gray – Rosa." Just for the joy of seeing the little trooper bouncing about on that lanky overbred mare like a pea on a drumhead.

Sergeant Cullis appeared at Hollie's elbow. "Looks like we're ready to go, Rosie-boy. Orders?"

"Use the brains God gave you and don't let the bastards back to Bridgwater," Hollie said tersely.

It was like the Promised Land, Bridgwater. If that unprincipled Malignant slithered back in there they'd never poke him out. *And* he was going piecemeal, the bugger. The heavy guns and the baggage had stolen away already, rumbling away overnight. Goring had little ordinance left – two, they were saying, two small ones – and Fairfax had the full might of the New Model Army to his hand. It was probably the quickest Council of War Hollie had ever been a party to. Lieutenant-General Cromwell still eating his breakfast, talking to someone through a mouthful of bread and cold bacon, looking as much like he'd slept in his clothes as ever. Henry Ireton – *Colonel* Ireton, now – be nice to say he hadn't changed a bit, poor bugger, but he had. He had a stiffness to his walk after Naseby, and the scars on his face were still pink and shiny.

That said, he was still at Cromwell's shoulder, not even brushing off the crumbs of the Lieutenant-General's breakfast where they'd spattered on Ireton's sleeve, so Hollie had hope that all was still well with Bridget. It was daft, to be in the middle of a war, and to find time to worry that all would still be well with your friend's love-life, but it was somehow a small, bright thing, a little reminder that the world was not all blood and fire, that Bridget Cromwell should still be sweet on Henry Ireton, even if he had a scarred face and a bad leg. Ireton glanced up at Hollie and smiled. Aye, all was still well - he clearly knew what Hollie was thinking, touched his elbow to Cromwell's, and the Lieutenant-General looked up in his turn and gave Hollie a great big grin.

Fairfax, looking tired and somewhat grim, but peaceful. Up all night wrestling with his conscience, probably, like Jacob and the angel, but he'd come out smiling, even if only faintly. He gave Hollie a formal, stiff nod, at which Hollie wondered what he'd done wrong *this* time, but all seemed to be well. He slipped quietly in between Bethel and Disbrow, murmuring something meaningless.

"Colonel *Babbitt*, sir!"

Bloody Toogood. There was no point in trying to be inconspicuous when you had both him and Drew Venning bouncing up and down opposite trying to attract your attention. He ignored them for as long as he could, though it was hard to ignore two fine, sturdy, strapping young gentlemen both possessed of voices that would carry across two counties. Toogood was bouncing, and Venning was squirming, and then to cap it all Venning's bloody *dog* came bounding in, yapping and bouncing up at his master. Bethel was giving him a very odd look, as if he suspected Hollie of engineering the whole insubordinate scene.

"Intelligence," Venning said happily.

"That'd be nice," Hollie muttered.

"Goring's foot are advanced, sir, come all the way down to the pass, you know the brook?"

"Hedges are full of musketeers," Toogood added. "*Full* of 'em. Like birds nesting in spring, dear of 'em. If you like, me and Drew can scat up and catch us a brace of –"

"Well done, captain," Fairfax said. "*Well* done. Both of you. My commendations, Colonel Babbitt."

There was a small murmur of assent from Cromwell and Ireton, and a pained look from Bethel. "We waiting for suffen particularly?" Venning whispered, in what he evidently fondly imagined to be a discreet voice intended for his commander's ears alone. "Or can we crack on and get righteous?"

It was as good an order as any. The Council of War scattered to the four winds, mounting up and galloping away to get their troops in some kind of order. It seemed no time at all before the gunners started up, thumping away at the Malignants' rather pitifully small force. Toogood was quite forlorn about it, and kept muttering that they were within musket shot, so they were, and he could take 'em from here, until Hollie turned him about and sent him off to rouse up his Cornish rascals and do some damage where it was most necessary.

"What d'ee mean, Rosie?" Venning perked up at that, too.

"Bethel's the forlorn hope."

"Bethel bloody *would* be."

"Hoi. That's *Major* bloody Bethel to you, you cheeky arse. *I* can call him names, I'm his bloody superior. I'm not having that bloody preaching idiot taking over. Fairfax wants a bloody forlorn hope, he's getting *me*."

"You *said* you weren't intending to get me killed," Luce said, halting the bay gelding next to him. "Look at the thing. Belly-deep in water, and you can barely get four horses abreast across –"

"Oh, don't be so bloody soft." Even Blossom was starting to dance on tiptoe as Hollie's wild restlessness infected him. He hated it – *hated* it – hearing the bloody ordinance ringing round this little valley, the cries and shot of the musketeers as they advanced to flush the Malignant birds from the hedges. They were getting all the bloody action, while Hollie and his troop lurked in a swampy ditch getting bitten by midges. And then – "What bugger is *that*?"

"Thass Goring," Venning said, squinting at the colours. "Thass Goring, his very own self."

"Commanding his very own troop?" It was. Lord Goring his very own self, and his troop beginning to advance down the hill, while Major Bethel was still calling on the Lord to strengthen his right arm, and his men getting quite excited about it. Bethel was standing up in his stirrups, yelling with rapture, when Hollie came thundering up at a flat gallop, belted Bethel's horse round the backside with the flat of his sword, and roared, "Stop preaching about it and just fucking *do* it!"

And then was gone, with a clattering splash as Blossom skidded on the stones in the deep and dirty ford, with Bethel half a length behind screeching like a badly-tuned fiddle and two troop of horse milling about in flat-out confusion strung out behind them.

Goring hadn't expected it, either. Bethel might be a prosy pain in the arse but before God that man had brass neck, and he kept on going, yelling his head off the while. Trailing out in a straggling line as they went smashing through the ford in a great spray of water, cold and unexpected as a slap in the face. Hollie whooping with sheer stupid joy and tossing the wet hair out of his eyes, forgetting for a minute that the riders of the red mare on his tail and the white-starred bay behind weren't Luce and Russell, weren't those two most dear and trusted of friends. And then the red mare starting to pull ahead with her ears pinned back to her skull – he could hear her breath shrieking in her red-rimmed nostrils as she went crashing past, barging past Blossom, sending the brown horse staggering off-stride.

"Gray, what the *fuck* d'you –"

"Bolting," Luce gasped beside him, and gave Russell's luckless horse a kick in the ribs that had the big bay extend himself into a startled gallop for probably the first time in years.

It was close work, close and bloody. Goring's own troop were sufficiently taken aback by a red mare coming up the hill at apocalyptic speed that several gave ground all unthinking, and then the mare was in amongst them, amongst them and – gone. In the blink of an eye, she was gone. And Luce, that slight and dreamy and poetic young man, was gone in after her, using Russell's stolid horse as a battering-ram. Which explained how come the colours had ended up in *Hollie's* hand, though he had no recollection of taking them, but since he had them he might as well make use of them, and as one of Goring's cavalrymen turned on him in a roaring fury he had every intention of belting the man somewhere tender with the butt-end of the staff. Blossom didn't like having yards of rippling silk swishing past his ear, so he went pirouetting sideways, the Cavalier lunged past Hollie swearing horribly, and then *Hollie* was enveloped in the middle of Goring's own personal troop as well, feeling like a pearl in an oyster and having to fight down a wild unworthy desire to giggle.

It was a brief, if unsettling, sensation. It must have lasted less than a heartbeat before the Malignants realised they were not only under assault but now actively breached. Thank God – and Hollie meant it for once, thank God – for Bethel, who'd come screaming up the hill like the wrath of God and simply split Goring's troop down the middle, like an axe in a rotten log. There seemed to be thousands of the buggers. Toogood, bleeding from a raw and bloody split across the bridge of his nose, turned up briefly out of the fray, grinning. "Like a nest of emmets," he said happily, and then went back to his bloody work whistling.

He could *see* Goring. That was the funny thing. Wasn't sure, quite, what he had expected of that notorious libertine, but wasn't expecting him to be brave or admirable. Not expecting him to be trying to stand his ground in the face of an inexorable tide of godly zeal, beating him back up the hill. It was bloody, but there were barely any casualties. It was, literally, hand to hand, and shoulder to shoulder, the clash and ring of swords. Horses squealing, whinnying, but not the horrible screams of wounded beasts. Shouting, pushing, clashing, and it was vicious, and it was hard work. But it wasn't lethal.

"Fall back!"

That was Venning. He almost sounded local. "Rosie, will 'ee *pull out*!"

All right, he had been wrong before. There were more Malignants than ever. (Where the hell were they all *coming* from?) He was getting quite used to hefting the colours now, smacking them across the muzzles of two startled Royalist horses, one of whom reared, staggered, slipped and went down in a flailing tangle of legs, pale belly flashing in the sunlight. There was something almost comedic about being armed and dangerous with your own colours. He could hear Bethel yelling again – thank God, there was so much noise, what with one thing and another, he couldn't hear the actual words, or he might have been tempted to shoot the bugger himself. Suddenly Blossom was chest to chest with a great raking iron-grey brute with a wicked eye, and Hollie was half out of his saddle, with some ruffianly Malignant trying to grapple with him. Heavy-set brute, rider as well as mount, and both of them had weight and years on Hollie and Blossom. Blossom's big clumsy feet were scrabbling for purchase on the slippery dry grass, the horse slithering and Hollie slithering with him. The big brown horse starting to panic, head tossing in distress – he just about had time to think, his old Tyburn wouldn't have turned like this – and then with one final heave the Malignant had him dismounted, and Blossom was gone, fled into the fray, and Hollie was in an undignified sprawl on the floor. Spitting mad, because if he didn't stay spitting mad he thought he might be that frightened he'd collapse into a sick and shaking heap under this bastard's hooves, and that would not do.

Blossom gone, and desperately looking for a loose horse, and there wasn't one for miles, and so he did the next best thing he could think of. A brave scarlet flash caught his eye - either a Malignant sash, or a slit belly - and he staggered to his feet and threw himself at the horse's flank, buffeted and bruised by hot, sweaty horseflesh. Blinded by sweat and his own loose hair, Hollie grabbed at the rider's boot, ignored the stunning smack in the face from the Malignant's knee, sudden mouthful of his own coppery blood – caught the man's foot and gave a twist and a heave. Half out of the saddle. Only half. Not enough. Wild with desperation, he brought the colours up, under the Malignant's flailing armpit, and tried to haul the bugger out that way. The staff broke off splintering-short. Hollie had his horse, and what felt like half a hundredweight of screaming, agonised Malignant with the troop colours rapidly turning as scarlet as the man's sash under his shredded arm, slid from the saddle.

He was buffeted again by Disbrow's troops, as the major came thundering up the hill to make Goring's rout complete, but by then Hollie didn't care. He had been sufficiently battered for one day and he'd had enough. He felt as limp as his own troop colours, and the taste of blood trickling down his throat was making him gag, and he wasn't going to find a glass and be sure but it felt horribly like he'd broken his nose. *Again.* The Royalist horse was mercifully short, and so it wasn't too undignified to scrabble into the saddle and then sit there with his eyes closed and his hands folded on the horse's neck while Bethel went off again in one of his rapturous howlings in pursuit of the rags of Goring's fleeing troop.

Someone sucked in their breath close by, and he opened his eyes. Captain Toogood was shaking his head. "That *had* to hurt," he said cheerfully – Toogood was almost perpetually cheerful, and there were times Hollie would have willingly strangled him with his own sash, but today it was oddly comforting. Especially considering that Toogood, with the great split across the bridge of *his* nose, looked about as awful as Hollie felt.

"Lost?" he said, spat out another mouthful of blood and possibly part of one of his back teeth, and started again. "What. Have. We lost?"

Toogood rubbed his hand across his face, leaving a great bloody smear in its wake. "Not a lot. 'Bout ten, I reckon? That lad o'yours, the little scrapper? He's gone down –"

"Oh Christ not Gray, Lucey's going to tear me a new arsehole if I lost Gray -"

"You?" Venning and Toogood, both whole and bloody, smirking at him like a pair of self-satisfied bookends. And the dog. That bloody dog – Babbitt's troop's own battle-mongrel. It had started out as a mocking gesture to Rupert, and his own proud heraldic hound. Boye was a great hunting-dog of impeccable birth and breeding. Tinners had been found in a sack under Sonning bridge at the siege of Reading and God knows what had gone into the making of him, apart from the leftovers of just about every meal that Drew Venning ate. Boye was known to be Rupert's familiar. Tinners was just *too* bloody familiar. "How'd you lose Gray?" Venning said curiously.

"Put him on Rosa. Out of badness." If he didn't breathe through his nose, it didn't hurt. Not much, anyway. And if he squinted his right eye almost shut, that didn't hurt either. "Ow."

"I'll say," Toogood said. "How'd you do that? *I* headbutted one of Goring's lifeguard. They bloody lobster-pots don't half leave a dent."

"Jesus," Hollie muttered, not sufficiently under his breath to avoid a look of censure from his troop chaplain.

"Thee is intact, boy?"

He didn't think he had to answer that, being upright with breeches on, so he didn't, he just glowered at his father and sniffed blood back up his abused nose. "There is trouble," Elijah Babbitt said smugly. "If thee may attend?"

10 - Fired With Godly Zeal

There was always trouble. There was trouble because Hollie had got a bit independent, like he had a habit of doing and in the past that had always been appreciated and Fairfax had always thanked him for it. This time, his tendency towards self-determination was all of a sudden rebellious and insubordinate, because he'd done it in front of the shiny new New Model Army and Fairfax didn't want them to think *they* could get away with it. He knew that. He knew he should have stopped where he was put and come in as the reserve at the end like Fairfax had meant for him to do, instead of throwing his weight behind Bethel and breaking the buggers like rotten wood. And Fairfax had said, in plain words, that he, and Cromwell, and all the other officers who saw it, said it was one of the bravest things their eyes beheld. Hollie quite agreed. He was quite on speaking terms with Major Bethel, at the moment.

So there was that trouble. And then there was the trouble of Goring's men having set the town of Langport on fire – some people were saying it was so they could flee by the light of the flames, and some said it was because they were rapacious destructive bastards and that was an end to it. Whichever it was, it somewhat put paid to the possibility of quartering there, even if the good people of this part of Somerset hadn't been so bloody pissed off with the Armies of both King and Parliament, quite impartially, that it hadn't been more than your life was worth to walk abroad in a buffcoat.

And then there was the bad trouble. There was the grimness of Trooper Gray, resurrected, bloody, and absolutely pig-livid with the specific person of Lucey Pettitt, who had come tottering out of the remains of Langport looking like he'd seen a ghost and promptly been punched in the face by Trooper Gray. Fortunately it hadn't been hard and the only witness had been Hollie, who'd laughed so much he had to sit down. Gray was *furious*. The little bugger screeched like a fishwife when he got mad, as well – which set Hollie off again. It reminded him of Mattie Percey, when he'd first joined the troop and his voice was just breaking, and every time he got excited his carefully-gruff voice would go swooping heavenwards. Gray was spitting because apparently Luce wouldn't let him fight his own battles, and Luce kept trying to say yes, but, and every time he said yes, but, Gray would start yelling at him again.

"I don't bloody need you to wipe my bloody arse, you – you – mimsy verse-monger!"

And then Luce had got mad in return. "And who the hell do you think you are, you – rebellious – *thing*? How dare you talk to me like that? I'm your superior!"

"I bloody know you're superior – *sir! And* smug! And conceited!"

At which point Hollie was actually weeping with laughter, which hurt both his nose and his much-bruised ribs, and at which point Luce turned round and gave his superior a wild-eyed stare.

"Colonel Babbitt, sir, would you mind awfully *fucking off?*"

The red mare was dead – probably the only casualty of Babbitt's troop, and that only because after her uncontrolled flight up the hill she'd put her witless overbred foot in a tussock of rough grass and gone down at the gallop. She'd snapped a foreleg,

Gray had gone arse over tip and missed the battle due to being laid out cold underneath her. Venning had eventually come across the mare in some distress after the fight, walking the field to do a head-count like the conscientious soul he was, and put a bullet in her ear. Hauled Gray out from underneath, although, regrettably, had not performed a like service for that vexatious little bugger.

That was something else Luce was holding against Gray. "You killed my horse!"

"Your horse was a congenital menace! Like you!"

All right, it was funny. But when Gray took another swing at Luce, it stopped being funny. "I'm off duty," Hollie said down the little trooper's ear. "And that means I'm not officially hearing this conversation. But you lay a hand on one of my officers again, you little bastard, and I'll hang you. Are we clear?"

His face twitched. He knew Hollie meant it. "Sir," he said stiffly.

"I don't know what it is with you two, but you argue worse than women." Gray bridled, opened his mouth to prove Hollie's point, and shut up with a very poor grace.

Luce, on the other hand, said nothing, which was unlike Luce enough to be worrying. He looked at Hollie, frowning slightly – started to say something, and then collapsed.

Gray swore. Hollie swore better. Between the pair of them they had about as much medical expertise as Hollie's horse. "Turn him over, or he'll choke," Gray yelled, very practically, under the circumstances. Hollie realised that his cornet was, for the first time in a brief and illustrious career, managing to do two things at once. Regrettably those two activities were being violently and noisily sick, and breathing. Once turned over, he concentrated on the being sick. Hollie didn't recall the lad as having eaten anything, this last day. Possibly more. It sounded painful.

And he was hot. Hotter than he had any right to be. Hollie swore some more. Luce's hand lay limp and upturned across Gray's lap, and the little trooper put his grubby fingers round Luce's, and probably Hollie should have said something, but he didn't.

It explained a lot. And the likes of his father, and the late, evangelical rapist Sariel Chedglow, might call it a sin and abomination, but looking at Luce's appallingly still, bony, ink-stained white hand in Gray's - at his dirty fair hair trailing in the dirt, wet and dabbled with vomit - hell, it was anarchy but Hollie didn't care. If enigmatic, bad-tempered little Gray loved Luce Pettitt, even like this, then Hollie wasn't going to say a word, because the brat was going to need all the loving he could get to bring him through.

Hollie had seen the pox before, ripping its way through Nuremberg while he sat outside the city walls, twenty years ago. He could tell the difference between the bloody, crusted gnat-bites on his own wrists, and the watery blisters starting to rise on the inside of Lucey's.

"Gray."

Luce didn't move, his eyelashes didn't even flicker, even when the single tear dripped onto his face from Gray's chin. The little trooper's eyes darted to Hollie's face, wide and black with fear. "Gray, you had the pox already?" he asked, trying to sound casual.

He had nice eyes, for a little shit. Wide and black with fear at the moment, but sort of - down-to-earth. Like a boy who took no crap from anyone. That, and a quivering mouth that reminded Hollie of his stubborn little daughter when she'd just bumped herself, trying to be brave, and not fooling anyone.

"'S all right, lad," he said awkwardly, and put his own hand on Gray's shoulder, feeling the little bones all birdlike and so appallingly fragile. "I have. I'll stop with him."

11 - From the Hills, Whence Cometh My Help

It was not one of Hollie's better days. Limping through the streets of Langport with Gray, Luce drifting in and out of consciousness between them, mostly upright and occasionally coherent. He knew what Bethel and Disbrow were saying, that Colonel Babbitt's loyalty to the Cause was distinctly questionable - that rather than pursue the fleeing Malignants as was his duty, he'd chosen to slink about the town with a notorious troublemaker and what appeared to be a debauched subordinate. Not that Hollie cared what they said, but he also knew they were a pair of *noisy* zealots and that gossip had a habit of sticking.

They'd pulled Lucey's sleeves down to cover the rash, which was dissembling at his worst, but it was that or have the boy turned away. No one in their right mind would take in a soldier with the pox. God knows where he'd picked it up, any one of the half-dozen squalid quarters where they'd been based over the last God knows how long. Hollie had been in no state to remember his own experiences with the pox. He'd been all of twenty-six at the time, and he'd been sick as a dog, and he hadn't died by the Lord's mercy and that was pretty much all he needed to know. Luce knew what was going on, that was the worst of it. Kept apologising, and saying he was fine, let him stand on his own feet. They had, a couple of times, but they got fed up with picking him up after a while. Hollie looking like the fifth Horseman of the Apocalypse, Gray bristling and tearstained and filthy, and Luce staggering like the town drunk between them. Fairfax was going to kill them when he got wind of this.

And that was if the pox didn't kill the brat first, or if he didn't burst something vital with his agonised retching, or if they could find somewhere to shelter him in this half-burned town. It was coming on for dusk. The air smelt of burning - burned wet wood, burning thatch, burning meat - great flakes of ash falling like black snow, and if Hollie had had a hand free, what with holding Luce up and carrying the lad's weapons and his own slung over his shoulder, he might have rubbed his stinging eyes. A charred timber cracked like a pistol shot as it cooled, and Gray yelped, and then jumped and glowered at Hollie as if it was his fault.

He was getting pig-sick of Gray, to be honest, and nothing to do with the boy's unnatural habits. Luce muttered something incoherent, and there was a wet patch on the shoulder of Hollie's buffcoat that he was trying not think about, where the brat had been resting his head, and Gray's contribution to the whole enterprise was to scuttle along beside them *snivelling.* "Shut *up*," Hollie snarled out of the corner of his mouth, "or I'm going to put *him* down, and I'm going to break *your* neck."

Felt a little bit guilty watching the lad's mouth quiver, but then Luce puked down Hollie's shoulder again, so he was too busy with trying to clean things up to pay the whelp any attention. "You have some facility with this," Gray said, and he wasn't in the mood for polite conversation either so he just glared up and carried on wiping his cornet's face with his handkerchief.

"You need a hand there?"

All he bloody needed, company. He couldn't turn round quickly, so he shoved Luce sprawling onto Gray and tried to look defiant. "Do I hell."

"Not what I heard, Rosie? Long time no see, lad."

He couldn't place the speaker. He knew that voice. He knew the face - from somewhere - but he looked different, without -

Without a seaman's bonnet, and he wasn't likely to have that, since the bonnet in question had been claimed as battle honours in Hull, two year back. Hollie had won it from this man in a bet - a somewhat drunken bet, to be fair, in celebration of the news of Hollie's impending fatherhood - that he wouldn't ride his big black horse into the tap room of an inn in the middle of Hull on a busy night. Tyburn had obliged, and both Hollie and Rainsborough had got the bollocking of their lives the next day from Sir Thomas Fairfax for such unofficerly behaviour. The bonnet was still around, somewhere. Rainsborough appeared to have abandoned the sea, though.

As well as common sense and decency. The silly bugger appeared to be in charge of a troop of musketeers, and most of them were sweaty, filthy, and grinning.

"He been on the hoy?" Rainsborough asked. "Thought public drunkenness and debauch was your remit, Rosie?"

"Up yours, you web-footed bugger. You was worse. And you know it. The lad's sick."

"So I see!"

"And like to die," Gray whimpered, and almost sobbed before he remembered he was the roughest little terrier in Captain Venning's troop.

Rainsborough's expression changed, narrow-eyed, almost suspicious. "What ails the lad?"

"Bloody pox," Hollie said quietly. "I've had it. And it didn't kill me, neither, Gray, so straighten your face."

"Oh aye *I've* had that an' all," Rainsborough said, sounding quite relieved. "Can't speak for this lot, but I'll send 'em about their business. Where you quartered?"

"Dunno. Where I can get. Where he -"

"We," Gray said firmly -

"*They* are. I'm not leaving him, Rainsborough." He was tired. He was tired and shaking and just about every bone in his body ached and he was too bloody old for this, which was why he was pitiful enough to look up at the musketeers and snarl, "If I have time for any man living, it's this one, colonel. I will not leave him."

And Rainsborough shook his head indulgently, as if he wasn't surprised. "Well fair enough, Rosie, I wasn't asking to keep him. Couldn't stand his poetry for any length of time, meself, but there you go. What I was going to say, is, if you got a bit o'spare floor, you can put him in my quarters, which is both private and well-appointed, what with - " he leered good-humouredly at his own men, who groaned as if it was a long-standing joke, "me being a senior officer and needing my home comforts and that, and I'll shake down with your lot for the time." He cocked his head. "Got to ask, by the way. What the *hell* happened to your face, lad?"

The joke about Rainsborough's quarters turned out to be that they were distinctly private, being in a building that seemed to have seen previous service as a cow-byre, at the end of a muddy field about a mile and a half outside the town. There was a roof on the building and it had a door and there was a fairly comfortable straw pallet on the dry floor, but other than that, it was a cow byre and it smelt of its previous inhabitants. It had the advantage of being some distance from any civilisation, so whatever contagion ailed the brat, it was going to stay right where it was.

"*I* will take care of him," Gray said stubbornly.

"No you bloody won't. You belong to Captain Venning's troop, boy, you're not my problem. You're a soldier, not a god-damned nurse."

Witless had had a good poke already, and he reckoned if the brat lived, it'd be a good month before he was fit to see service again. And he'd stuttered on the *if* bit, the way he did when he was telling you news you didn't want to hear. (The way he had after Marston Moor, when he'd took Mattie Percey's mangled hand off. Hollie tried not to think about that.) Hollie wasn't going to leave his cornet in Gray's volatile little hands for a month - and he certainly wasn't going to stick around Langport for the next four weeks twiddling his thumbs, dear God, there were already dark mutterings about his dereliction of duty and how he cared more for his men than he did for his God and his Cause, in that order. "There'll be a woman in the town who'll take him."

"I can be a woman."

Hollie stopped dead. "I don't care what you two do in the privacy of your own quarters, Gray." Wished he hadn't put it *quite* like that. Thought it was too late to take it back. "You two want to indulge your - whatever it is you do - fine. Do it. But if you ever,

ever, *ever* lay a hand on me, I swear to God I will cut your balls off. Are we clear?"

And Gray - tearstained, snotty Gray - put a hand on his sleeve and looked up into his face and batted his eyelashes and said, "But Colonel Babbitt, you have *remarkably* fine eyes."

And then when Hollie had picked himself up off the floor and Gray had finished hooting with very unkind laughter, the little bastard took a big breath and said it.

"Sorry, Colonel. But I *am* a bloody woman."

12 - The Body of a Weak and Feeble Woman

He might have bloody known it, of course. Always known there was something odd about that Gray –

Oh, give over, Hollie, no you didn't. *You* didn't notice, even bloody Cromwell hadn't noticed, so far as anyone could tell with Old Noll: like most other people in this benighted Army you work on the assumption that if it walks like a duck, quacks like a duck and it tells you it's a bloody duck – it *is* a duck, and don't ask stupid questions. God knows life was complicated enough without having to check which of his other troopers pissed sitting down.

- He was trying not to think about the mechanics of that, and how come nobody had noticed whether Gray peed sitting down or not. He could probably ask. She – he – it would probably belt him, as well. That was probably the answer. Gray had a tendency to smack anybody who asked him – her – it, stupid questions. After a while, people stopped asking, when they'd finished picking up their teeth.

That was the bugger of it. He had plenty of time to think about things like Gray's lavatorial habits, and whether Henry Ireton had come up to the mark yet or whether he was saving himself for his wedding, and if *Ireton* had got his leg over (and if it was the gammy one or not) with Bridget Cromwell, what the hell was wrong with Hapless Russell, who was considerably better-favoured than the very nice but definitely po-faced Ireton? Which led him, almost inevitably, to thinking about Het. Wondering what she was up to, and as often as not, staring absently out of the window at the midsummer-green Somerset Levels thinking of nothing at all. It wasn't the first time he'd ended up quartered in the house of some devout and distinctly shifty cleric. Before Edgehill, it had been the Bishop of Worcester's residence, and he'd managed not to wreck the place, even with his troop quartered there alongside him. (There'd been a minor incident with the late Captain Rackhay, two ladies of negotiable virtue, and Lucey Pettitt taking exception to the behaviour of all parties and putting a pistol-ball in the Bishop's ceiling - but that had been none of Hollie's doing. Much.) He did have a suspicion that he was acquiring a reputation as Fairfax's red mastiff, mind – which involved him doing nothing more than turning up and looking intimidating, which, at two yards high and scruffy, he managed without trying. It was a position of mutual benefit, apart from when Hollie was feeling bored. Sometimes he was happy to play the backstreet bravo, the rough to Fairfax's smooth. There were plenty other times when it was as dull as –

Dull as Bridgwater. That'd do it. He'd been here three days at Audry, just outside some benighted place with the heathen name of Chedzoy, in the Dean of Wells's own private residence, and he was increasingly less inclined to think favourably of Somerset.

It was the lads he felt sorry for. Mostly lads from the south-east, they were a long way from home, and fed up. Gathering in provisions as best they could, with the Clubmen getting pissy if they took so much as an egg that wasn't paid for, and Fairfax on the other side flapping like a hen if it looked like the natives were getting restless. It was a long way from home with no bloody money for provisioning, or indeed much else, and if it had been up to Hollie, and if he'd been a man of independent means which he wasn't, he'd have slipped the lads a few copper cash to keep them on-side. But then, if wishes were horses, beggars might ride. He thanked God, regularly, and quite sincerely, that it was midsummer, for they could at least see the horses decently fed and watered. It fairly warmed his heart to see that ragged band of equines growing sleek and glossy, hock-deep in the long grass, placidly grazing. Russell's bay Thomas nose to tail with Blossom, life not being so kind to Hollie that Blossom hadn't turned up after the battle, looking embarrassed with his saddle all askew, like a bad penny. Seemed funny not to see either Tyburn or Luce's bright chestnut thoroughbred mare in the meadow, but Tibs was in honourable retirement in White Notley, getting fat and spoilt and making the acquaintance of half the better class of mare in Essex.

And Luce's Rosa was dead. That was another reason to get Gray back in skirts: he – she – it, was damnable hard on her horses. Hollie had come out of the battle at Langport the reluctant new owner of one pig-mannered iron grey brute with an even worse temper than his own. On the whole, Blossom was thick, but meant well. Blossom stayed with Hollie, and the iron-grey brute – known henceforth simply as Pig – could go to Gray. She couldn't make the brute any worse than what it already was. And Luce could take the ever-suspicious Thomas when he came back. Which he would. It had only been a week. It took you longer than a week to recover from the pox. He was only a couple of miles away. He'd be fine. He had Gray to look after him – *in skirts, missy* – he was going to be fine. Him and Russell. All would be well, and all manner of things would be well. It'd all be like it was. Soon.

"Colonel Babbitt, sir, were you *asleep*?"
He came upright with a start. "Wha' – no! Of course I wasn't!"

The sun was comfortably warm on his back, and the birds were quietly burbling in the bushes, and there wasn't a cloud in the burnished sky. "I was lost in personal contemplation," he said primly, and *someone* made an undignified noise behind him.

"Will you come, sir? General Fairfax would review his troops."

"'Bout two miles off," Venning said, because Drew Venning, for all his faults, might let *Colonel Babbitt* look like a damn' fool in company but he'd cover his mate Hollie's backside. "Weston Moor."

They were all bloody this moor or that moor, so far as Hollie was concerned, and he couldn't tell the one from another, but he looked intelligent and pulled Blossom's head up out of the ditch. "Let us delay no further, then."

"We was waiting on *you*, you lollopin' gret mawkin," Venning muttered down his ear, and he very deliberately barged Blossom into Venning's mount till the freckled Fen captain cursed, half out of the saddle, and copped for the rough side of Major Disbrow's godly tongue, after which Hollie trotted off, sniggering.

One set of fortifications looked much the same as another, to Hollie. He'd been put off sieges for life, during his youth; belly-deep mud, starvation, disease, rotting bodies, rats, all blurred into one nightmarish vision of hell for a seventeen-year-old mercenary soldier straight off the Lancashire moors, and he'd hated it. It had all got mixed up in his head, afterwards, with the death of his first wife: he'd had the letter bearing news of her death whilst he was outside the walls of Nuremberg, twelve years ago, and it had nearly killed him. No, he had a bit of a thing about sieges. Just the prospect of one made him cold and sick and shaky. Luce knew that, but Luce wasn't here to keep him straight. Russell probably knew that. Russell knew a hell of a lot about a hell of a lot, but said nothing about any of it. Venning – no. And it was bloody stupid, stupid and superstitious and downright pagan in him to be twitching already at the fortifications going up because *nothing would happen to Het.* She was fine. She was not Margriete. She was Het, she was her own dear self, and nothing would happen to her. *Had* happened to her. There was not a letter following him round the country with news of her death. He would see her again. He would go home, and Russell would be there, he would be fine too, and Lucey would come back safe from Langport, and –

"Colonel *Babbitt*, sir!"

As if Disbrow had never seen anyone puking in a ditch before. Hollie straightened up, and Blossom swung his unbeautiful head and shoved his nose under Hollie's arm, which was comforting. He leaned his head against the brown horse's flank. It was still sunny, and the birds were still singing, though he was suddenly bitter cold. "Got what Lucey's got," he said thickly. "Sorry."

Venning looked at him sideways, frowning slightly. "No you haven't – *oh*. Got you."

"I suggest, then, sir, that you – retire," Disbrow said stiffly, his expression making it clear that he thought Hollie was either drunk or a coward.

"'S all right. Gone." Christ, he wished it was. "Be all right in a minute."

"You want a drink?" Where Venning was, Toogood would be. The sight of those two was ridiculously heartening – Venning mousy and freckled, Toogood fair and sunburned, and wearing almost identical expressions of concern. "Can get you one, Rosie, no bother?"

Disbrow was looking even more horrified. Hollie shook his head, and heaved himself back into the saddle. "Thanks, Kenelm. No. Best crack on."

"Let us know if you change your mind," Toogood said cheerfully.

He'd have preferred the drink to Disbrow's earnest exhortations for the Lord to favour their endeavours, which seemed to go on for hours, and the sun was getting hotter and hotter on the back of his neck. He could smell old, rotten water. Green, rotten, stagnant, stinking water. There was the oddest high-pitched whining in his ears, and he jerked his head, thinking it was one of those bloody vexatious gnats buzzing round again.

"You're game, then, Rosie? Good man!"

Cromwell seemed to think whatever it was he'd just agreed to, was a prime jest. The stocky Lieutenant-General had stopped in his pacing, hands behind his back, and was grinning across at them. "Come on, then, lad."

"What?"

"You've got a bit of past with this line of work, haven't you? Well, come on, then! Give us the benefit of your experience!" Cromwell scratched his sunburnt, peeling nose, squinting horribly. "Come up by here and have a look at this dretful ditch. See what you think."

And because he had no choice, having apparently just volunteered, Hollie dismounted, feeling the eyes of every other member of the Lord's Elect boring into his sinful back as he made his way across the grass. Hoping to God he wasn't going to disgrace himself utterly in front of the generals, because Cromwell was eyeing him narrowly and Fairfax didn't look convinced either. "*I* also have some knowledge of laying siege to a town," Major Bethel's middle-aged lieutenant announced stiffly, and stalked over to join Hollie as though it was a personal affront that General Fairfax and Lieutenant-General Cromwell should be attended by some heathen ruffian who might at any point keel over in the ditch.

Not that Hollie cared, and he was happy to let Bethel's pompous subaltern strut along beside Cromwell, pointing out features of significant architectural significance of Bridgwater. "Speaking from *experience,"* he said, wagging a scrawny forefinger, "I should seek to place the guns about *here* –" And he was wheeling about, an arm outflung, mid-proclamation, when some Malignant sniper on the walls of Bridgwater shot him in the back of the head.

Hollie, who hadn't been expecting *that*, said something unfortunate, forgot to breathe, and did keel over in the ditch. Was rescued by Venning, who called him a very rude name, very quietly, and then propped him up with his head between his knees, shivering. Everyone else was shouting and dashing around and making sure the Lieutenant-General was all right – to which the answer was, fine, and alternately demanding the sniper's head on a plate and roaring praise to the Lord for his deliverance. It was all very fine and exciting and it wasn't *Cromwell* who was sticky with someone else's blood. Nor was it

Cromwell who was sprawled in a ditch with most of the back of his head missing. He'd had dark hair, Bethel's prissy lieutenant. Dark, greasy, collar-length hair. Hollie hoped to God he'd had dandruff, because if not, the pale flecks on the grass and on the back of his coat didn't bear examination. Fairfax glanced over at him and raised an eyebrow, then jerked his head in wordless communication. Amazing, the three sentences that had passed between them without a sound having been exchanged. You all right, Rosie? No. Well cut along, then, while it's quiet. Hell, if he could have, he would, but he thought his legs were shaking too much to stand. If he didn't, though, the little runnel of blood snaking from under the ruin of Bethel's lieutenant's head was going to reach him. Venning got his hand under Hollie's elbow and hauled him upright.

"Colour of spoiled cheese, 'ee is, bor. You all right?"

"Bright boy," Hollie said sardonically. Had to hold onto Venning's shoulder as the sunlight blurred and spun round him again. "I'm sorry, Drew. I'm going to have to get out of here."

"Fuck was all *that* about?" Toogood said, scanning the trees as if there might be a sudden onslaught of Malignant activity. The birds carried on singing. The ditch carried on stinking, overlaid with a certain –

"Rosie, don't 'ee *dare*. Not in front of that missish bastard. Look!" Venning pointed at the cloudless sky, and Hollie looked, quite reflexively. "What?"

"Nawthen, much. Just rather 'ee looked over there than down that-ways. 'Scuse me –" And with an unlikely grace, he swept his grubby coat off and over the lieutenant's face, and then very briefly bowed his head, closed his eyes respectfully. "Poor bastard."

"Heads up," Toogood said, and cocked his pistol.

"Sir?"

"Jesus God almighty it's Gray," Venning said, and there was a ripple of very unkind laughter from his troop. It was not Gray, though Hollie could see why that would be humorous, had he been feeling humorously inclined. It was a very small, skinny Cavalier on a very big horse, each looking as unnerved as the other. He came out from under the shadow of the castle walls at a nervous trot, not looking at anybody or anything, and then halted about fifty yards from Fairfax and stuttered something that was addressed into the sash at his waist and was almost inaudible.

"Speak up, boy," Fairfax said kindly, and the young man's cheeks turned a vivid scarlet.

"I have a m-message for my lords-General," he said, and the big horse shuffled and side-stepped as if the boy's hands had tightened on the reins involuntarily.

"Aye, go on then," Cromwell said irritably, not being so inclined to bandy courtesies as Fairfax. "And get off the horse, boy, I'm not putting a crick in my neck talking to you up there. Don't worry, I'll get one of my officers to fetch a ladder to put you back up."

Which caused more hilarity, as the girlish little ensign scrambled to the ground, and his big horse wandered off to make the acquaintance of some of its Parliamentarian counterparts whilst its master was otherwise engaged.

“Hat. *Off*,” Toogood said cheerfully, cuffing the boy’s feathered excrescence from his head. “While you’re talking to your elders."

“My horse!” he protested, having just noticed its absence, and Hollie grinned at him, settled by the familiar feel of a velvet muzzle exploring his pockets, and busied himself by adjusting the fit of a bridle which had evidently been slung on in some haste. “We’re all Anabaptists and horse thieves,” he explained. “Hadn’t you heard?”

“Aye, but Rosie Babbitt’s *both*,” Toogood said, with a wink.

“This message,” Fairfax prompted, with a resigned look in their direction.

“Is from M-mistress Wyndham, the Governor’s wife,” the boy said, and you had to feel sorry for him now, because he picked his hat up before he continued and his hands were shaking on its brim like a schoolboy called to recite a badly-learned lesson. “She says that bullet was her –“ he couldn’t go on, and he had to stop and catch his breath, his girl’s mouth twitching and quivering, “was her token, my lords, and if you was a courtier you would return the compliment, and do as –“ the hat was taking a right battering, and Hollie didn’t think it was ever going to regain its previous elegant shape – “As much for her.”

“She wants Fairfax to shoot her in the head?” Toogood was confused, but willing. “Well, if the maid says so, do she come out on the walls, and I’ll see what I can do?”

“Kenelm, you tit, shut up! Lad’s still talking!"

“It don’t make no sense!”

“I reckon she’s trying to say Bridgwater will never surrender to rebel scum,” Venning translated. “Thass right, ent it, bor?”

The little ensign was not heartened by this unexpected ally, possibly because the top of his head just about came up to Venning's breastbone, and no matter how amiable that large, freckled gentleman seemed he had shoulders the width of an axe-handle, and he couldn't help but loom. "She did not say in so many words, sir, no."

"Bet she bloody didn't, neither. Bet what she said was oh hell, I just shot one o'they buggers, I never meant to do that, you want to go out there and smooth it over for me?"

"Captain *Venning*, sir!" Fairfax was stiff with righteous indignation.

"Sorry, sir. 'S the company I do keep."

"If you would be so good as to hold your tongue, sir! Now – what *is* the lady's message, boy?"

"Just, uh, that, my lord. I'm sorry, sir. It's – I've forgot it, sir. I said it, like she told me to, and it's gone clean out of my head now. Sir. What with -" he gave Toogood a terrified look, and gulped.

"Fair enough, Bridgwater will never fall into Roundhead hands while there is a stout Royalist heart within. Got it."

"Is there a reply, sir?" the little ensign said, sounding like he hoped to God there wasn't.

"Tell her to kiss my lily-white arse?" Toogood suggested cheerfully, and Venning inhaled something he ought not to have and had to be pounded on the back, and even Hollie struggled to keep a straight face. Even Fairfax looked as if he wanted to laugh but dared not.

"Colonel Babbitt, I *do* expect to see these men disciplined," he said shakily, and Hollie inclined his head in an ambiguous manner. Fairfax turned back to the little ensign, "Sir, you may tell Mistress

Wyndham to k – um, consider her message received in the spirit in which it was delivered."

A great roar of approval and distinctly profane laughter went up from the troops digging trenches within earshot, and Fairfax, not known for his quick sense of humour, grinned with boyish delight.

"She watching, is she?" Hollie said, close to the little ensign's ear. "From the walls?"

He wondered if the little ensign was hers. Some beloved child, perhaps – a son, a nephew. He saw a blur of movement up on the battlements, a tiny glimpse of kingfisher-blue against the blue sky, and without even thinking he had his hand in the boy's sleek lovelocks and his sword up against the young man's throat, bending his head back till the munitions-quality steel bit into flesh. "Looking *now*, d'you think?"

"Colonel *Babbitt*!" Fairfax shouted, and he didn't care. "Babbitt, you will unhand that boy!"

"I'm making him a fucking Roundhead," Hollie said brightly: too brightly, he sounded stark mad even to himself. The little ensign was whimpering, a great smear of drying blood and brain matter down his beardless cheek where his head was bent back against Hollie's stinking coat. He wound his hand tighter in the boy's long hair, and he could hear the lad trying not to sob as the fair ringlets were torn from his scalp, but that didn't matter. *"Babbitt!"* Fairfax screamed, "you will release that boy and that is an order!"

And he did. He released him with a brutal twist of his sword and a knee in the back, sent him staggering and sprawling into the stinking ditch, and then held up eight inches of well-kept Malignant lovelocks.

"That, you fucker, is for my lads, who'll be sat in this benighted fucking sewer starving and dying by inches while your bitch of a mistress decides how many lives her honour's worth. Trust me. Lucey's not here to call me on it. I don't *do* principles, whelp. I do keeping my lads alive. Tell her that."

Disbrow was behind him, trying to get the sword out of his hand, not gently, so Hollie did something he'd been wanting to do for weeks and he rammed his elbow up into Major Disbrow's nose. Something cracked and Hollie didn't think it was his elbow. And life just got better, because it seemed that Major Disbrow knew even more colourful language than Hollie, when prompted by the pain of a broken nose. "Be still, sir, or I will put you down like a fucking *dog*," Disbrow snuffled, and Hollie started to giggle.

13 - The Walls of Jericho

Venning just didn't get it – but then he wouldn't, he was, what, not yet thirty and he'd never set foot off English soil, let alone fought off it. Even though he, and the dog, were spending most of their free hours at Audry where Hollie was confined to quarters and deep in disgrace, he *still* didn't get it.

"I don't get it," he said, for about the thirtieth time, sitting in the Dean's leafy green, well-manicured garden. "What d'ee *do* it for?"

And Hollie had looked at Tinners' head where the dog was snouting for crumbs in his lap, and said nothing, just rumpled the dog's soft ears. He wasn't even especially fond of the dog, but he needed to touch something alive, for the comfort of it. He'd been cold for days. "It's all going wrong," he said, and Venning didn't get *that*, either.

They were dithering, and that wasn't like Fairfax, or Cromwell. The Council of War kept meeting – without Hollie, which was no great disappointment, probably to either party – and deciding precisely nothing. Both Fairfax and Cromwell had nearly drowned, crossing the river at Dunweir in a rackety boat in a high tide. Floyd's and Fortescue's regiments started to make ready for an assault, each man with a faggot of brushwood in his hand in addition to his pike or his musket, and they'd come to the earthworks and found the ditches ten foot deep in water in places. The rumour round the camps was that the Bridgwater garrison knew *exactly* what Fairfax was about, and they were ready for him.

It just felt *wrong*. And this coming from Hollie, who did not believe in fate or predestination or such fancies, but he had taken to haunting his father's preaching, which he knew was unsettling the hell out of the lads, but he reckoned if *anyone* could persuade the Lord to smile on their endeavours it'd be Lije Babbitt, and if that meant the company heathen had to stand at the back with his eyes screwed shut and his hands clenched at his sides in genuinely-ardent zeal, then so be it.

"What d'ee cut his hair off for?" Venning said blankly, for about the thirtieth time, and Tinners backed off with a yelp as Hollie's hand tightened involuntarily on the scruff of his neck. " - Hey! Leave my dog alone!"

He didn't really have an answer, except that he was half-mad in truth, like some of the other officers said behind their hands, which was no answer at all. "I wanted to stop it," he muttered, and Venning looked blank again.

"Because of what's-her-name? Margaret?"

"Aye. Summat like."

"And you reckoned if you cut that lad's hair off and sent him back to his mother half-scalped, she'd give 'ee the front door keys?"

"I could have sent her his head back. On a plate," Hollie said mildly, and the frightening thing was that he saw the look flit across his friend's face that he wasn't *entirely* sure if Hollie was joking or not. "Oh come on, Drew. It's a pissing contest. *She* kicked it off. She had no reason to shoot – who's his face, ah, Jesus, I don't even know his *name*, Drew –" He had to stop there, because he was starting to feel sick again. Took a long breath and blew his ragged hair out of his eyes. "That's a lousy trick."

"We're at war?"

"No. There'd not been a shot fired, then. *She* upped the game, Venning, and I hope she rots for it, but it's more like to be *us*, more's the bloody pity. D'you know, there's times I think women are fiercer on their honour than gentlemen. She had what's-his-name took out in pride and wilful stubbornness. There was no reason for it. Serve her likewise - I should fucking think so, and if I was any hand with a pistol I'd see to it my bloody self."

"Carry on in this wise, Rosie, and you ent going to be seeing to nawthen, 'cos Fairfax will send 'ee home."

"Well, I wish to God he would!" Hollie burst out, and Venning frowned at him and said, thoughtfully, "I don't get it. What d'ee *do* it for?"

There were times when he wanted to bang his head against a wall, there really were.

Fairfax was a good man. He was careful of the lives of those whom God had hitherto so preserved. There were times when Hollie could cheerfully have banged *his* head against a wall, as well. Half the men were hot to storm the town but no, Fairfax would not have it, he considered it more prudent to sit outside and reduce the town by blockade. Hollie had to keep reminding himself that Tom Fairfax was a decent, kind, thoughtful man who only wanted to do what was best, and was not in fact possessed by the vengeful spirit of the Earl of Essex, that other dilatory siege-loving bastard. Because he was a decent, kind, thoughtful man, and a friend, and because at times he possessed all the sensitivity of an artillery barrage, he felt the need to bear Hollie company when he wasn't out stalking the works. (Cromwell didn't. He kept as much distance between himself and Hollie as possible, on grounds that insanity might be catching. Given Cromwell's equally-wobbly temperament, it quite possibly was.)

No, the people wondered how come Fairfax never seemed to tire – how come he could watch, act, take so little rest, and yet hold out against so much fatigue. And if he said "Come, let us trust God," just once more, Hollie was likely to drop him in the Dunweir.

Goring had left two hundred and sixty oxen in the town, not to mention forty pieces of ordnance of various shapes and sizes. The town was well-provisioned, full of soldiers and ammunition, and fortified both by nature and hard work. The Army of Parliament, on the other hand, was sat outside in a stinking ditch, underfed, underpaid, exhausted, and fired only by godly zeal. Hollie was hoping some of the godly zeal might rub off, and that he might feel a bit more optimistic about his prospects, or he wouldn't choose to spend any time at all with the old bastard who'd sired him.

"Thee must trust in the Lord, Holofernes," Elijah said. A lot. It was his stock answer to everything – questions like, any ideas where the next meal's coming from, when do we come to grips with the Malignant buggers, will it rain any time in the next twelvemonth. The Elijah in the Bible might have been fed by ravens, but the one in Babbitt's company was fed by his son's bloody hard work and sleight of hand, though he had a habit of forgetting *that* when he was saying grace. Him and Fairfax were as bad as each other, for commending them all to Christ and urging them to be valiant in His cause. And Hollie was perfectly willing to start on with the being valiant, he just wanted to get *on* with it, because this dithering was driving him mental. The longer it went on, the more things went wrong, or seemed to go wrong, and it was hard enough keeping half a regiment of horse motivated under siege conditions at best, without them thinking that they were cursed and their commander was a lunatic.

The moon was almost full. When the tide was right, on the ebb, the Dunweir was something like passable. Because Hollie was in disgrace, and camp gossip had him marked as dangerously erratic, he pointedly said nothing to anyone that could be taken as an encouragement to direct action. He said, in fact, absolutely nothing to anyone, but tried to look as meek and biddable as possible and only spoke at council to quote Biblical texts. "Whosoever he be that doth rebel against thy commandment, and will not hearken unto thy words in all that thou commandest him, he shall be put to death: only be strong and of a good courage," he said quietly, looking heavenwards, and that was precisely all he said, for the whole meeting. He happened to personally think that Joshua was a self-promoting murderous bastard, but it clearly flattered Fairfax's vanity to be likened to the Biblical commander, heir to Moses and slayer of the heathen Canaanites. There was much nodding at that, and not a few startled looks that the backsliding Babbitt had been brought to see the light. The Lord evidently *was* with them, after all.

The Lord, and the ebb tide, and the moon. It was a warm, still night, with the moon riding full and high in the sky and the river lapping still and silvery between its banks. If you were quiet, you could hear the Malignant sentries exchange greeting on the walls.

"All's well," one cheerful voice called from the castle ramparts, very clear in the soft summer air, and, “That’s what *you* know, son,” Toogood muttered, and someone in his troop snorted with the giggles.

One of Fairfax’s senior officers turned out to have some facility for designing. He *said*. He’d caused eight bridges to be made, thirty feet long, to span the moat, or to float, if required, and the wagons were bringing them up now. The rumbling of the wagons, and the stifled swearing of the poor sods who were trying to put the bridges in their intended positions, was beginning to attract the attention of the garrison. There was a great echoing thump that split the summer air, and half the birds in Bridgwater rose shrieking from their roosts. “They buggers!” Toogood said fiercely, and Hollie shook his head, holding up a hand for silence –

Two. Three guns. The signal for the attack.

“I ent going over them rackety bridges,” Venning said, and Hollie was inclined to agree, so they went through the water, belly deep and at a flat gallop, through a hail of bullets. Toogood was hit – suddenly there was a flurry of Cornish swearing and a splashing, though judging by the fact that the cursing didn’t stop, it was a glancing wound only. And then they were under the castle walls, and out of the range of the big guns, hooves sparking and slithering on the cobbles – Venning’s big grey horse skidding and going almost to his knees as they came round the corner into the market place, and half his troop in skating disorder as they piled up almost on top of a band of Malignant defenders. The horrible scream of a mortally-wounded horse. Shouting.

“’S just like Wakefield, ain’t it?” Cullis said cheerfully at Hollie’s elbow, and without breaking stride rammed the guard of his sword into the face of one particularly vociferous defender. “Shut up, you noisy bastard. Can’t hear meself think.”

The brief blinding jar of pain as Hollie blocked someone’s downward hack with his own blade, and the vibration went right up his badly-healed wrist and left his arm tingling. He wanted – *needed* - to fight left-handed till he could feel his fingers again but he couldn’t change hands mid-skirmish, been caught that way before, and so he kicked Blossom harder than might have been prudent and the big brown horse squealed, surging forward, confused by what his master was asking him to do. Not enough room for Blossom to go forward, but Hollie’s heels were in his ribs, and so he went upwards instead, rearing and kicking out with steel-shod forefeet in some distress. Not as much distress as the Malignant who’d just been kicked in the face by a plough-horse, mind. *He* wasn’t going to be causing any further discomfort to Hollie. Blossom was scared witless. He’d never done close-quarter work in a town before and the echoes of his own hooves were frightening him, the noise, the shouts, the gunfire, the smell of blood and hot metal. He wanted to be willing, because at bottom Blossom was a kind horse and he wanted to do what Hollie asked him to do, but presently he was so confused he didn’t know what to do but whirl in circles, shying and whinnying piteously. There was a great roar from within the church, and that really was too much for Blossom. He took the bit between his teeth and gathered his hindquarters under him to bolt, and Hollie, hard-pressed by some pokey pikeman intent on winkling him out of his saddle like a snail from its shell, took the opportunity to flee the market square.

Precipitately, as Russell would say.

The attackers of the church were delighted to have their advance swelled by a large, anxious brown horse, as it gave them sufficient surprise to bar the doors closed on a good hundred or so very astonished Malignants within. "They weren't expecting *that*," Hollie said cheerfully, to the great astonishment of the Parliamentarian troop commander. "Keep 'em penned, there's a good lad. Better kept out of trouble, I say." He wheeled Blossom about. "Oh – if it looks like they're thinking about breaking out the windows, just fire the church. And tell 'em Colonel Babbitt said so."

The man looked blank. "You're – horse?"

"What about my – *oh*. Aye. We're cavalry. Clearing the market square. Doing a good job, by the sound of it. Hang on." Clearing the market square. *Cleared* the market square. Malignants penned in the church, and the guns in the fort royal trained on any of the buggers that were daft enough to stand and fight. "What're we waiting for?" Hollie demanded. "You lot wi't' pokey sticks – come on. There's a gate wants clearing. *Now!*"

They had a turn of speed, for a clanky lot of lobsterbacks on foot, though he was not in favour of pikemen running, on the whole. Sixteen-foot pikes being ported at a sprint never looked quite safe to Hollie, and Blossom seemed inclined to agree, so he made sure he was a respectable distance to the rear, harrying the back-markers like a sheepdog and trying to keep up a conversation with the pike commander, Colonel Hewson, at the same time. His right wrist was aching like fire, and he looked at the drawbridge on the east side of the town with the biggest grin in the world spreading over his face. "You going to let me do it, Hewson?"

"Sir?" Hewson thought he was mad. Eyeing him warily –

"You never fancied?"

"Sir?"

Dismounted with a thump. Pikemen at a sprint looked peculiar, but the Lord had never intended a fully-armed cavalry officer on foot to look exactly elegant, either. (Except, possibly, Lucey. Oh, hell, brat, you should be here.) "Sir, what are you – oh. My. God."

"Be up there, then, will it?" His wrist wasn't *that* sore. "Excuse me, gentlemen –" they were only Malignants, and if they were stupid enough to get in the way of a man who wanted to get up a flight of stairs and do something he'd wanted to do ever since he was a boy, one of them deserved to get his feet kicked out from under him and dumped on his backside down that flight of stairs. Which were damp, stone, and by the sound of it, exceedingly hard. The other one protested, drew his sword, looked at Hewson coming up the narrow stairs on Hollie's tail, and handed over his blade with a polite murmur. Not stupid, that one. The little room over the gatehouse where the drawbridge windlass resided was barely big enough to swing a good-sized cat, let alone one full-sized two-yard high colonel and half a troop of pike. It still managed to fit a further three Malignants in it, one of whom was armed with a brace of pistols and feeling belligerent, right until the point where Hewson shot him in the hand and then he wasn't feeling so argumentative any more. "D'you do that on purpose?" Hollie wanted to know, and Hewson shrugged rather uncomfortably.

"Might have. Don't like killing good men. Not 'less they fire on me first."

"Bloody hell," Hollie said mildly – so it *wasn't* just him that seemed to have gone squeamish, of late – and then gave a great sigh of contentment, beholding the windlass. "I *always* fancied doing this."

"Oh. God," Hewson said again.

"What?" He stopped, one foot on the great wooden drum. "All right, I might be a lolloping great object, but I can't drop this by myself. Aw, come on. I reckon if we get a good run at it, it'll go with a hell of a bang. Come on, give us a hand here –"

Heavier than it looked, and the great wooden drawbridge came down with agonising slowness, the chains creaking and squealing under the weight, and Hewson said if Hollie didn't stop giving him a commentary on progress he was going to punch him in the head, so Hollie just worked in silence giggling to himself. He *had* always wanted to drop a drawbridge, though to be fair, he'd expected it to be more exciting. Quicker, too. Well, you learned something every day. "*Will* you mind what you're doing," one of the pikemen grunted, "you get a finger caught in that chain and you *will* know about it." There was a murmur of assent about the general uselessness of donkey-wallopers, especially those large and over-keen ones who stuck their big noses in where they didn't know what they was doing and got in the way of them as did.

It hit the ground on the far side of the moat with a crash that made the chains shake. "'Bout time, too!" a voice called, and then there was a clattering rumble as someone's troop of horse came over, and a cheer from Hewson's lads as they saw the familiar insect-scuttle of pike reinforcements coming across behind. Hollie leaned out of one of the arrow-slits so far as he could, ready to shout good-humoured abuse at the cavalry commander, then realised it was one of Noll Cromwell's own pet God-botherers and that any kind of humour at all was lost on Captain Reynolds.

With a little wriggle of satisfaction at having achieved a boyhood dream, he eased his stiff shoulders inside his buffcoat – bloody hard labour, winding that thing up and down – and headed for the stairs again, meaning to rejoin his lads.

"Where d'you think *you're* off to, then?" Hewson grumbled. "You dropped the thing, *you* can fetch it back up. Not having them so-and-so's sneaking back in!"

14 - Which Burneth With Fire and Brimstone

It was a funny thing, but when he was active, and doing, and occupied, he was fine. (His back and his shoulders and his wrist hurt like hell after cranking that damnable windlass, but he was fine.) He found his way back to the market square, and found Toogood sitting happily on a barrel – an broached one, at that – deep in conversation with a shaggy-haired Welsh musketeer.

"Pembroke," Toogood said. "Just over there, see –" and he pointed vaguely in the direction of Bristol.

"That's good." The contents of the barrel were better, mind, and he joined Toogood perched on top of it with a sigh of relief.

"Five hundred foot, Rosie. Think of that."

"Five hundred foot of what?"

The Cornish captain gave him a look of affectionate contempt. "Keep up at the back, big lad. That's five hundred foot out of Pembroke what have just surrendered theirselves prisoners. With –" and he gave a knowing wink, "benefits."

"And what are we supposed to do with five hundred extra mouths to feed, Kenelm?" Hollie said patiently. "Even the Welsh have to eat."

Toogood and the Pembroke musketeer exchanged a sly glance. "'S funny you say that, see," the Welshman said, "but you know there was two hundred and sixty oxen in the town?"

"Ye-es..."

"Well, there's more like two hundred and forty, now. How d'you feel about roast beef, then, colonel?"

"Your name's not Davies, is it?" Hollie said suspiciously. His own Moggy Davies had been supplying the company with inedible rations since the beginning of the war, and no matter what it started out as, Moggy could reduce it to a watery mass with a floating garnish of charcoal. The musketeer grinned. He had small, sharp teeth, like a rodent.

"It is not, sir. It's Evans. Now, about this roast beef."

"Lead me to it," Hollie said firmly, "and stand well back."

Three hundred of the Welsh prisoners took the Covenant on the spot, saying they were proud to have been defeated by such an enemy as Fairfax. They were well-disposed to Parliament, and Hollie was well-disposed to anyone who was inclined to feed him, so as soon as he'd finished his meat, he introduced Evans to Colonel Hewson, thinking it was better to keep a piratical troop of Welsh musketeers within sight where he could at least benefit from their villainy, than turn them over to Cromwell's elect and have them muzzled and useless. The last he heard was Hewson lecturing Evans on the evils of theft, whilst full to the gills with ill-gotten roast meat. It was half-raw, after no more than an hour's broiling, but by God it was a welcome breakfast.

The sun rose on a town that was almost miraculously intact. They said there were twenty men only killed, and a hundred wounded. And it hadn't been Toogood himself hit in the attack, it had been his horse. Hollie had spoken to Fairfax about that, himself, thinking after the incident of the drawbridge he might be edging his way back into favour, and given that there were sixty Royalist horses taken in the storming of the town that were not otherwise engaged. He was right about the favour, as long as he kept his mouth shut and his eyes modestly downcast, and he spent a happy half-hour ambling along the equine booty with Black Tom, replenishing his own troop. Toogood said he wouldn't part with his Charles, no, not if it was out of the King's own stable, so they agreed that he should borrow Hollie's Rabbit till the glancing bullet-gash in Charles's shoulder was healed.

And then there was Blossom, miserable and frightened and nervous and burying his head in Hollie's breast like a new-weaned foal seeking his mother. The lanky brown horse was stiff, bruised, and wretched, and Hollie felt as bad as the horse. Blossom wasn't a cavalry mount. He didn't have fire and wit and dash, like Tyburn. He was a slow, well-meaning, kind-hearted beast who should be at home, trotting from home to market twice a week, some little girl's beloved pet when he wasn't being a workhorse. He looked like an escapee from the knacker's yard, he fell over his own feet at the gallop, and he had all the subtlety and understanding of a tree falling. "Ah, Christ, horse, we're stuck with each other," he said ruefully, seeing hopes of the gorgeous long-legged roan stallion he'd picked out of the Royalist booty for himself, fading into obscurity. "Thomazine'll bloody kill me if I don't fetch you home safe."

"Thomazine being how old, now?" Fairfax said politely, recognising an excuse when he heard one.

"Rising two. And chipper as a little popinjay."

"Ah, they're dear at that age." Fairfax patted the brown horse's bony nose. "I hate to say it, Holofernes, but you and this beast have a look of each other. No matter how much you feed the brute and how hard you groom him, he will *still* look neglected."

"My wife would be disappointed to hear you say that, sir."

"Really? My wife says much the same of me." Fairfax gave his rare, shy laugh. "I am Nan's despair, at times. But dear, I think – she would not have me else. We will come about, Holofernes. I think even you will acknowledge that we have enjoyed the Lord's favour, this – " There was a sudden screaming whistle overhead, and Blossom threw his head up in some distress and gave the General of the Army of Parliament a resounding thump in the nose that made Hollie wince in sympathy, and Fairfax said through a suddenly-bloodstained handkerchief, "What in the hell was *that*?"

That, it turned out after a messenger was sent to enquire, was the Governor of Bridgwater firing hot shot into the Eastover side of the town, determined to use any means at his disposal to shift the occupying force. "He's burning his own *town* down?" Toogood said blankly. "He off his head or what?"

"Remember who he's married to," Hollie said. "*I'd* be off my head if I had to live with that maniac bitch."

"Language," Elijah muttered, and Hollie just snorted. Because Wyndham would not stop, though Eastover was burning like the flames of hellfire, with barely two houses left untouched together. And there were times when Hollie was just plain bloody proud of the New Model Army, because in the middle of it, in the middle of the flames and the ruin and the screaming shot, there was Major Cowell, with his troop, keeping guard as cool as you please, not moving, not crying about it, just settled quite peaceably and not going anywhere. That took some balls. It took some discipline, too, and he wasn't *wholly* sure his own lads would have done it.

The destruction distressed Fairfax enormously, though. The General was almost in tears over it – especially when the Royalists started ringing their bells for joy. ("And I hope the god-damned bellringers burn their fingers to the bone," Hollie had muttered, and for once Fairfax had not checked his intemperate language.) It distressed Hollie, too, though he wasn't walking up and down wringing his hands over it. It was the destruction that distressed Fairfax, but what did it for Hollie was looking over into Eastover and thinking that was people's bloody *lives* that arrogant aristocratic gobshite and his stiff-rumped Jezebel of a wife were levelling, in their determination not to bow the knee to a pack of rebels. He didn't reckon honour was worth not having a roof over your head, and if the Governor thought it was, then Hollie would respectfully suggest they started with the levelling of the Governor's residence, and see how long he held to that principle. Eastover kept burning through the night. Fairfax kept pacing, and Hollie, grimly sticking it out alongside him when just about everybody else had gone to bed and collapsed, was just getting angrier and angrier.

"What am I *supposed* to do, Holofernes? Tell me that! All very well telling me I have to stop it, but -!"

Blood and fire, and he could not bear it. "That's *people* out there, sir. That's women like your Nan and my Het, sat up through the night trying to work out what they can fetch away safe, and little girls like my Thomazine crying because her bloody doll's got burned up –"

"Do you think I don't *know* that!"

"No!" Hollie shouted, poked beyond endurance by fear and exhaustion. "No, I don't think you bloody do, and I'm damn sure *he* don't!"

And Fairfax sat down, suddenly. "Don't shout at me, Holofernes. Do not, ever, take that tone of voice with me. I'll not brook it, not even from you, dear friend though you are. I am sorry for those people. I am sorrier than you can ever know for those poor people. If it is within my gift, I will give them back what they have lost. The Lord will comfort them. But I can not – I *will* not – treat with that man. He *will* agree to my conditions, or I let him burn. I'm sorry."

It was a warm night, but even so, a cold sweat ran down Hollie's back. "But they – the people – they haven't done anything, sir."

"I know. And *he* has brought it on them. Not me."

"But –"

"No, not "but". I will send a messenger to order the town's surrender, but if he refuses – what more can I do?"

At dawn, they sent an ensign, very brave and very young in his clean uniform coat with his breastplate polished. He was back half an hour later, his eyes red-rimmed with smoke. "Be a no, then," Venning said awkwardly, and Hollie shot him a look of disgust.

"Aye. Look to your weapons."

Eastover continued to smoulder. A second storm failed to move the defenders, and didn't do much for the attackers. A second ensign was sent.

This time it was Mistress Wyndham who received him, apparently sending him away after laying her hand on her bosom with the proud retort that. “These breasts gave suck to Prince Charles, they shall never be at your mercy. We will hold it to the last.”

“She wants fucking shooting,” was Hollie’s considered opinion. Toogood agreed, for slightly different reasons.

“Owd gal don’t make no sense. What’s she on about her saggy old tits for? Wouldn’t touch her nohow, not with somebody else’s.”

“Fucking stirring Malignant *bitch*,” Hollie said, lifting his head and looking up at the castle. “I’ll have her, see if I don’t.”

Toogood and Venning exchanged a significant look behind his back. Colonel’s slipping a bit again. “Fancy a drink, Rosie?” Venning said. “Can’t see nawthen happening this side o’ suppertime?”

“Hm? No, can’t say as I do. I’m going to have a bit of a walk. Anybody wants me,” he untied his sash and folded it neatly, and then glanced at the two young captains, “either o’ you two want to help me out of my plate? If anybody asks, the colonel’s got a bit of urgent business. If Cromwell asks, it’s with Fairfax. Fairfax asks, it’s – you got the idea. If they *both* ask, I’m in trouble. The colonel’s off on Army business.” He shrugged his buffcoat off and tucked his hair behind his ears. “*Hollie* is off down Eastover, see if he can do any good.”

“As a plain civilian?” Venning said slowly, and Hollie nodded.

"That’s right. None of the Army’s bloody business.”

"Give us two minutes," he said. "I'll come with 'ee."

They could do little. There was a wind starting to get up –"That'll do a bit o' no good," Venning said gloomily, watching the ashes stirring and sparkling – and the townsmen, sympathetic though many were to Parliament, were disheartened. They returned filthy and frustrated, weary from the hard labour of what little they had been able to do. Venning's wrist was blistered, and bruised, with a raw weal where a charred spar had collapsed as he tried to clear some wreckage between two houses. Hollie was red-eyed and dirty and limping slightly, but "*That*," he said grimly, "is what you get for being stupid enough to wear riding boots for field-work."

"Rosie," Toogood said, "Rosie, I don't hardly like to say, but, your, er – your shirt's all a-wriggle?"

"Huh?" He'd forgotten. "Want a kitten, Kenelm?"

Not the world's biggest kitten, and not the most elegant, sooty-pawed and squeaking indignantly at being hauled unceremoniously out of the breast of Hollie's sweaty shirt, but it clawed its way up his chest and sat on his shoulder in some affront. Oddly-marked, with a lopsided white eyepatch on its black face and a stumpy black tail with a white tip, and a most unhandsome, cross, singed little creature it was. "Looks like bloody Russell," Venning said consideringly, "with that great splodge on its head. 'Ee going to call it Hapless, then?"

"Not going to call it nothing," Hollie said flatly. "Belongs to someone, this –" he lifted it by the scruff and checked, "little lass does, and I'm going to give it back."

"I swear to God, Babbitt, you are as mard as clarts, betimes," Toogood muttered. "Middle of a bloody war and you're bothering about a kitten."

"You ain't never been in a war before, have you?" Hollie said, favouring the young Cornishman with a level stare. "I have. There's times when it's about all that keeps you going, having a bit of your old life back. A kitten – clean linen – sleeping in a bed again, not a poxy billet in back of a stable. Someone'll be missing her."

The kitten purred as he rubbed under her minute chin with a filthy forefinger. "I should not forget that, Captain Toogood, were I you. Them lot out there – they might be bloody Malignants, but they're people like me and you."

He dropped the kitten back inside his shirt, and gave a curt nod of farewell before stalking out into the blazing noon sun.

"God help us all if there's any more at home like *him*," Venning said, shaking his head, and Toogood could only agree.

Fairfax never gave in, you had to give him that. And Hollie was grateful for it, because it meant that at two of the clock, in his full stinking, sweaty, ruffianly, unshaven, charred glory, he got to go before the Governor of Bridgwater and offer terms that all the women and children might leave before four.

Mistress Wyndham, faced with the unmistakable reality of a very big and battle-scarred officer with an indignant black and white kitten squeaking inside his shirt, took one look at him and her face turned a chalky pale green. Hollie had not looked in a glass of late, but he certainly *felt* like what was left over after the Apocalypse. The Governor assumed Hollie had said something discourteous and he spluttered and snarled and threatened, until Hollie just turned his head, very slightly, and looked at him too, until he shut up. He said nothing. And the Governor got very uncomfortable, and Mistress Wyndham turned whiter, and *still* Hollie said nothing.

And then, after a very long silence which every bird in Bridgwater seemed determined to make as festive as possible, he gave them Fairfax's terms. Exactly in the words in which they had been given to Hollie, no more, no less. No threats. No implied violence. No courtesy, either. The Lady Governess looked him up and down as if he'd just crawled out of a ditch which, in a manner of speaking, he had. "And what is your authority to offer these terms?" she said, in a voice that tried to wither with contempt and just shook. Trying to imply that he was some rebel gallows-bait with no birth and no breeding, and not fit to kiss her morocco-leather slippers. He closed one eye and looked her up and down in his turn – wondered if the bruises had faded on his face yet, or if he still looked the worse for Langport – and did not smile.

"By the authority vested in me by God's grace, and by my lord Fairfax," he said coldly. "Who has a care for the lives of the men in his care, and which he would not endanger in a drawn-out and pointless engagement." He did not say, unlike some he could name, nor did he call her a vicious cold-blooded Malignant bitch who set her name and her honour above the lives of the people her spineless husband was elected to govern. He knew why Fairfax had sent him, though. Fairfax's red mastiff, who stalked at his heel and had only to raise his hackles for a message to be delivered. She knew. Her mouth quivered, and she dropped her eyes.

Wyndham blubbered his thanks for the unlooked-for gallantry. Mistress Wyndham met his eyes again. "My thanks to your general, for his courtesy," she said icily. "Ask him to accept the humble appreciation of one too guilty of the misery of this place."

Toogood was right. She *didn't* make any sense. He kicked around for an hour or so, seeing them off the premises, Lady This and Lady That, looking at him as if he smelt bad – which he did, to be fair – and he looking back at them with a kind of vicious insolence because not one of these high-bred witches was fit to brush the hem of Het's skirt. Not *one*. They looked at him as if he was some sort of dangerous wild animal who might, if they were lucky, spring on them in all his rough soldiering dirt and do something truly shocking. They should be so lucky. Wondering whether Hollie Babbitt was house-trained or not was the most fun they'd had in years.

And then Fairfax started the attack again in earnest – using the King's ordnance taken at Naseby, no less, which struck Hollie as rather humorous. Fireballs, and hot iron, and the red-hot missiles the musketeers called hoggets, and a stiff wind, all served to set the town burning again. He couldn't bear it. Still holding the kitten inside his shirt, because somehow that plump little furry body was become more than just a rather vexatious baby cat, but was a little life to be preserved, a brand to be plucked from the burning if he could do no more, Hollie turned his back on the terror of the inhabitants and rejoined his men. It also struck him as vaguely comical that Major Bethel thought he was clutching his breast in an excess of godly zeal, rather than trying to keep Not-

Hapless the kitten from escape as the guns thumped and screamed. He was, though, praying.

"Rosie."

He looked up. He recognised the big black horse. The rider was almost, but not quite, unrecognisable, having finished the neat Roundhead crop that Hollie had started two weeks previous. "Good lord above," he said mildly, and the boy gave a faint smile.

"I am n-not afraid of you, sir."

"I should hope not. If I'd meant you to be damaged, I'd have done more than cut your hair. Looks better, mind. Now you've neatened it up a bit."

"I should not take up a career as a barber, were I you. Sir."

The little ensign on the big horse turned out to be one of the King's own personal pages, not to mention the darling of the Wyndham nursery. Presumably Wyndham sent him to ask for quarter because of his baby face and charming ways. Fairfax told him, most uncharacteristically, to bugger off, and that the Governor had no one to blame but himself. At which point Hollie gave a sarcastic cheer from the back, and Bethel kicked him, hard, in the ankle – which had more the effect of startling Blossom than it did of reprimanding Hollie, but relieved Bethel's feelings.

Of course, Fairfax being Fairfax, he then gave the lad fifteen minutes to get a sensible answer out of Wyndham, and if he wanted mercy he should have it but it was going to be on Fairfax's terms. "Give him half an hour, and he can probably have the family silver as well," Venning muttered. "That little lad's either going to be a horse-coper, or a courtier."

It was touch and go, that Hollie might actually laugh out loud at the Governor's terms, when they came. That the Governor and his officers might march away with their horses and their pistols, and the common soldiers and their arms, and have a safe convoy to Exeter. That the inhabitants of the two might either stay or have liberty to go with them. And that the like liberty should be given to the clergy.

"Certainly," Venning said, "and would you like jam on it?"

Fairfax heard that, and glared at the officers of Babbitt's company. Hollie glared back. Don't you bloody *dare*, Thomas.

"Do I look like a murderer?" the General said coldly, and it was debatable to whom he was addressing that remark. "*All* shall have quarter for their lives. The soldiers may march out as they see fit without being stripped of their clothes, and the townsmen may enjoy their habitations without plunder. *But.* The gentlemen will be left to the disposal of Parliament, sir. And I will have six hostages sent out to me in token of your good faith."

"That poor lil' bugger's bumping about like a bee in a bottle," Toogood said, watching the little ensign on his big horse return to the Governor for the third time. "Give him ten minutes – ah, here he comes again."

The Governor and his gentlemen could not agree to the terms. "Figures," Hollie said bitterly. "Well, bollocks to you then." And he started to draw his troop off, ordering them to stand to their duty. The little ensign was almost weeping, begging to be given a little more time, a little more leeway, a little more – "He'll do," Fairfax said. "Leave him. He can stand hostage. He's a gentleman. Off you go, boy, and tell

Governor Wyndham it's make your mind up time. And this is his last chance."

As the little ensign passed Hollie's company, Venning urged his horse forward till it blocked the ensign's path. "Understand this," he said, soft and low and all the more menacing for being delivered in a comfortable Norfolk burr. "You tell 'en, bor. Tell 'en if any within do take off so much as a slate, or raise a hand in the least to stop that fire, before that man agrees to terms, and we will fall on like the wolf on the fold. D'ee understand me, bor? He signs –"

"Or we sow Bridgwater with salt." Toogood smiled his engaging gap-toothed grin. "Give you good-day, sir. See you d'rectly, I reckon."

15 - Thorns and Thistles

Essex
August 1645

It was raining, for the first time in almost two months, and Het could hear the water trickling silvery and blessed in the gutters, and down the hall, she could hear Russell sobbing.

It wasn't unusual, poor boy. She thought he might have cried every day since he'd been left with her, and she couldn't wholly blame him. Usually she heard him in the night, and could say nothing, because she suspected that as with many of the things he held to so fiercely, he didn't know his private weakness was so public. Stiff, formal, impeccable Hapless didn't know that he often spilled his supper from its spoon, that his shirt front was often gravy-spotted. That his collar was askew, or inside out, or that his fingernails were dirty. They would have mattered, to the old Russell. Het suspected the loss of them, the loss of that little bit of dignity, would matter even now.

Sometimes he didn't know she was there, and he cried, silently, in the light, thinking himself alone. He had his places where he liked to sit, that he could get to unassisted, without having to put a hand on the wall to guide himself. He liked the big windowseat in the parlour especially, liked to sit with the sunlight on his face, knowing the warmth was there even while the light was denied him. If she was too quiet, she might find the kind sun gilding his wet cheeks, and that made her hot with shame. She'd taken to singing about the house, though the Lord knew she felt little enough like merriment these days. Little Thomazine miserable with a new tooth coming through, wanting to be held and nursed the whole day long. The new babe rising like dough under her waistband, making her queasy and sore. Russell brooding and restless, brittle-bright and black by turns. Mattie Percey tagging her heels like a good dog, just like Hollie had set him on to do, to take care of her in Hollie's absence, but oh, how Het longed for a moment's uncomplicated solitude. She could have sat down and wept, but for the thought of Percey's incomprehension and Russell's anxiety if she did anything so uncharacteristic. Percey, bless the boy, would look at her helplessly and not know what to do, but feel obliged to do *something*. Cushions awkwardly pushed at her back were his especial favourite, or a shawl, and she felt so terribly ungracious refusing him. And Russell wouldn't know what was happening, and would be afraid, and he hated that, for which she couldn't blame him.

And so the two of them wept silently and separately in the darkness.

And Hollie, who was the sturdy bright link between them all, was the Lord alone knew where, and so long as the Lord *did* know and was taking care of him, Het could manage. He didn't know about the child. She kept thinking that - borrowing trouble, she knew - he was somewhere else, and if aught were to become of her, if she or the child were to - no, she wasn't going to finish that thought. But if it happened. He might never know. It had been two months since she'd set eyes on him. She'd had no word, in all that time, and nor should she expect it, with him about Parliament's work and too busy for the silly little cares of home. She blotted her eyes with her apron, and started to sing.

Russell turned his face towards her, and she thought he was still heartbreakingly lovely, in a cold and distant way - like the moon, or a star, frigid and perfect and distant and somehow not real. Even with the livid purple scar that marred his cheek, he was beautiful. Not quite human, even now, even with his eyes red with weeping and a bad attempt at shaving that had left him as furred as a peach in patches and raw in others.

"Mistress Babbitt," he said coolly, and even that was a mask, even that icy and unplaceable accent. She knew he was from Buckinghamshire. Hollie had told her he was. It slipped, betimes, but only ever with Thomazine. Only when he was alone with the child, or thought he was, the dialect gave him away: when he called her Tammasin, and his tibber, and told her long and involved and self-mocking stories. Only ever safe with Thomazine, who would neither laugh at him nor pity him, but simply accepted him as what he was.

"Can I get you anything, Thankful?"
And she would not call him Hapless. *Would* not. He blinked, then winced, and frowned, and shook his head slightly, touching his fingers to the scar above his ear as if it hurt. It often did, and she felt sorry for that, too, but having had a pistol ball all but scramble your brains must take its own sweet time to heal, and all the feverfew tea and lavender posies in the world couldn't speed it up.

"No, mistress," he said softly, "though I thank you." And then looked straight at her, or so it felt. "Would you - mistress, would you mind - would you sit with me a while?"

He hated to be alone in the dark. And she had half a hundred things that should have taken her elsewhere, but still, after all these weeks, she could not bear to have him turn his head towards her in that bright, attentive way, and to know that he couldn't see her, and then to leave him so.

"Of course, dear. I have some mending. Would you mind if we keep company with Thomazine, and give Doraty some peace for an hour or so?"

"She is still fretful, then?"

It was polite conversation, meaningless. He knew well enough the child was fretful. He slept little enough himself to hear her, every hour through the night. Het murmured something courteous and heaved herself out of her chair. Doraty was delighted to give the little girl over, and red-faced, whiny, drooling Thomazine was equally delighted to be free of the nurse, piled in a heap of drapery on the cool parlour floor with a string of corals hanging from her mouth like a dog with a bone.

Het took out her mending. She had precious little, without Hollie and his destructive habits where the elbows of his shirts were concerned. She was embroidering a little biggin for the new baby, but all Thomazine's old gowns were still good, and the tiny cap was an exercise in idle vanity. Thomazine herself had managed to lose her cap again. Het suspected the child of gnawing on the strings, most likely. Certainly despite her ill-temper and fractiousness, the little girl was a bunchy, appealing sight, in her grey-green linsey-woolsey skirts, with her hair in a wild dandelion aureole about her bent head.

Russell was staring in the child's direction, with an expression of such utter terror on his face that Het was on her feet automatically, looking for the poker, or the ancient fowling-piece that Catterall kept loaded behind the door in case of intruders.

"What is it?" she hissed, her voice shaking with fear, though her hands were steady on the heavy iron poker. "Russell, what -"

And he turned his head to look at her. He was afraid. He was afraid like a man beholding angels, lest what he saw should turn out to be fantasy. His dark eyes were wide and wondering. "Mistress Babbitt, she is wearing a - green - dress, is she not?"

Het gulped, sat down, her head swimming. "She is, indeed."

"And her hair is - brighter- than her father's? Yet I should call it rather, red, than fair?"

"Red gold. Yes. Oh, Russell! You can see! Can you see what colour - my embroidery - this silk? Here?" She held one up randomly, and he blinked unwillingly, and a little of the joy faded from his face.

"No. No, mistress, I can only see - shapes. And colours. Not so clear as your figures. I'm sorry."

"Don't be sorry, dear. It is no less than a miracle," she said firmly, and he looked at her and blinked hard again, stretching his eyes wide and shaking his head determinedly. "Russell, do *not* strain your eyes! In the Lord's own time, young man!"

"Rushle?" Thomazine queried. "*Apple* Rushle?"

"No, dear, do not say Hapless. That is what *daddy* calls Thankful. He considers it comical. That is Thankful. Say Thankful, Thomazine."

She sat back on her plump little haunches and considered him seriously, then shook her head. "Apple."

He was blinking again, but this time blotting the tears away with a distinctly reproachable cuff. "She may call me Hapless if she chooses, mistress. Or, er, Apple. She may call me *Bathsheba* if it pleases her. She said no, didn’t she? I saw her, mistress. I *saw* her shake her head. Tammasin? Child?"

The little girl shuffled over on her bottom, pressed her head against Russell's knee, and heaved a very doglike sigh. He put his hand down and rested it on her curls, gingerly. "She - she feels so *hot*, mistress. And little. She's so *little*. Is she - is that *right*?" He looked almost comically astonished by the child, bending so that he could see her more clearly, peering into her sticky, sweaty, dribbly little face, almost nose to nose with her. He would have touched her in awe, put his hand on the fat curve of her cheek.

Thomazine being the child she was, and very much her father's daughter, sank her three extant teeth into his knuckle, and sat there smiling up at him in some satisfaction.

Russell, being now Thomazine's willing slave for eternity, let her do it.

15 - Eating Beetles in the Garden of Eden

His sight came and went, after that, but oddly, he didn’t mind so much.

If he knew it would come back, sometimes better, sometimes worse, but always enough to be something like independent, it wasn't so bad. Het Babbitt fussed over him and he was beginning to like that. His mother had smelt of roses, not rosemary, and her sober skirts had been dark silk, not serviceable grey wool, but - he found, increasingly, that Het's touch was all the comfort he needed. That if he could lean his bursting head in her lap, and have her smooth his hair, sometimes the pain went away.

She was kind. She made him laugh, at which practice he had little facility, but he learned apace, even though she told him he resembled a baby owl at times, blinking at her so solemnly. (He had laughed at that, a little shyly, not knowing if it was compliment or ridicule.) He and little Thomazine made dough-babies in the kitchen with Williams, and stole raisins when they fondly believed no one was looking, and ate scraps of uncooked pastry which Het assured them both was very bad for their stomachs but it was -.

He had to stop there, because Russell didn't have the words for what it was. He'd never done this. Even when his mother was alive, Four Ashes had never been a house like this, warm and shabby and comfortable as an old coat. Even as a little boy, even when he was still lisping his first prayers at her knee, he'd never been allowed so much - liberty, he supposed. Or responsibility. Which sounded odd, but though he was - he couldn’t even think the word. Russell, in this place, you are of worth. No. *Loved.*

Because Thomazine did, very much she did, she would shuffle over to him out of choice when he came into a room and brace her back against his shins when he sat down as if she was his little dog, leaning against him with intent until he'd bend down and hoist her into his lap. Russell had never considered himself in connection with children, in any real or practical sense, but then Thomazine wasn't like any other children, she wasn't a little angel in a spotless apron. Thomazine liked to be hefted like a bundle and given pick-a-backs, it not occurring to her that her willing mount's sense of direction was not always reliable, and many was the time Het had heard stunning thumps and howls from the parlour or the garden and come running to find both parties prostrate and shrieking with laughter. Thomazine laughed at his stories, and told him hers. Hers did not always make sense, and he suspected were not always true, even where coherent, but he liked to listen to her babble. Even when she yanked his hair out in handfuls he didn't mind. Het said sternly that he had no dignity where the child was concerned and he thought she might be right, he did not.

He was still unfit for much, save to sit in the sun and bake like a custard and grow freckles on his nose, and occasionally if directed properly to grub out growing things from Het's garden. That gave him an odd feeling, too; the crumbly Essex soil, dry between his fingers, and he wondered what the soil was like at Four Ashes because he didn't *know*. He'd never been allowed to dabble in it. Weeding by scent, mostly, and the scent of the rosemary hedge when he brushed it with his fingers gave him an odd tight feeling about his heart. Sprawling in the gravel with the sun warm on his back and tingling on his bare forearms where he'd rolled his sleeves up, wearing one of Het's old straw hats after she'd said the back of his neck was turning pink, Thomazine happily rolling in the dirt beside him burbling some nonsense-song and the pair of them likely wreaking a swathe of destruction through Het's herb-garden but they were perfectly content. She had *four* teeth now and he was as proud of those four teeth as if he'd birthed her himself, even when they were buried in his knuckles, as she was still prone to doing. She did it in affection, like a puppy. He actually had scarred knuckles where she'd worried at him. It was marvellous. (It hurt, but he would overlook that.)

Het called him indulgent. He was. But the child was a wonder to him: the fact of her *aliveness*, the idea that this little bright-haired dumpling had been given of God's blessing, made sudden and absolute sense to Russell. The garden, all green and wonderful and alive, was a wonder. His own filthy hands were a wonder. He could sit and look at his earth-stained fingers for hours, seeing heaven in every grimy crease, and the child would sit right alongside him, happy and companionable. Perhaps he was mad. Perhaps he was just reborn. Whichever he was, he was beginning to unfurl, like the petals of a crumpled rosebud in the sun.

What he was getting, was appallingly fanciful. "*Apple*," Thomazine said crossly, and he had the feeling she may have been trying to attract his attention for some while whilst he was peering at his dreadful fingernails in a state of rapture. He rolled over and looked at her, squinting against the sun. Her hat was over one eye, wisps of bright ruddy gold framing her face. She grabbed his hand, bent his fingers flat, and dumped a disenchanted beetle of some nature on his palm. It scrabbled. It tickled. He found himself grinning at it helplessly, its shiny black carapace, its little legs, fine as thread. "'Zat a *good* bug?" she demanded.

"Yes, my tibber, I do believe it is." They were *all* good bugs. Het might disagree, but Russell was finding the world a fairly marvellous place, right now. Thomazine nodded with satisfaction, took it off his hand, and ate it with every sign of relish.

"Was that, ah, pleasant?" He did, actually, want to know. The child trundled into the hedge and grubbed industriously for some minutes, before returning with a slightly different beetle, which she offered to him. He could not in all politeness refuse, but slipped it inside his shirt with what he considered an admirable sleight of hand and pretended to eat it. She was looking at him quizzically.

"Delicious," he said, and she gave another satisfied nod.

"More?"

"Ah - no. Truly, I couldn't possibly eat another thing. Thomazine -!"

"What on earth are you two doing?"
Het's shadow fell across them, and Russell looked up. "Thankful, what are you grinning at?" she said suspiciously, and then reached down and set his -her - hat straight on his head. "And why have you got earth round your mouth? *Thomazine*?"

"Eating bugs," the child said virtuously. "But Zee *shared*, mama. Zee had bug, an' Apple had bug."

"Is this true, Russell?"

"Absolutely," he said, feeling the wretched thing scuttling down his flank and fighting a desire to either wriggle or giggle. Thomazine nodded enthusiastically. "Thass right, mama. *Good* bugs. Apple said."

Dear God, the child was beginning to acquire the accent he fought so hard to hide in company, too. That very faint slur that his voice took on when he was tired, and a hint of a homely country burr. He wondered, for one awful, marvellous moment, if people might think - she was fair - she was going to be tall, the long bones of her - people might believe *she* was his sister, not gaunt, horsy, vengeful Fly.

"Thass right, my tibber." More tired than he'd thought, and he saw Het's eyebrows twitch at their identical inflection.

"Come on, you two. Come in out of the sun."

16 - The Guilty Counterfeited Coin

Nobody claimed the bloody cat, and Hollie kept waking up with the infernal bloody animal under the blankets behind his knees, or padding its needle-sharp claws into his armpit just before dawn and purring like an artillery battery. It took to sitting on his shoulder when he was trying to keep on top of his correspondence, and thus most of his letters were even blotchier than was customary, with a few inky pawprints hither and yon for variety's sake.

The weather turned. He knew it would. At least the rain stopped the fires in Eastover. He was sick of having that conversation with Fairfax. Fairfax thought he'd gone soft in his old age and maybe that was it, maybe he had, but he kept thinking - this is England, such things do not happen here. Them - those miserable, draggled folk trying to rebuild their lives and their houses in the stinking black ash, in the rain - they were plain probably-mostly-honest people, trying to get by as best they could. They didn't know anything about politics, and probably not that much about bloody religion, other than what the Bible said, what they got told at church on a Sunday by men who'd thought about it more than they had the time to do. Most of them were ordinary people, trying to make ends meet. People like his Het, trying to get two ends of a farm to meet in the middle with not much in the way of help and not quite enough money. (And a husband who wasn't there, but doing his best. He knew.)

People like Luce's father and his apprentices, working their backsides off while His soft-handed Majesty had grabbed the cream off the top to pay for his vanity wars. Or like Hollie's own father, fined to within an inch of his life for his Puritan beliefs, though knowing that stiff-necked bugger, and Hollie having been at his old childhood home not so many years back - before the Malignants had took it over as a garrison - not laying out any money on the Babbitt family estates wasn't causing Elijah any lost sleep.

People. That was at the heart of it, and it bothered Hollie's conscience. He had come into this war as a mercenary, bought in out of Europe because he had more practice at this kind of work than most of the English gentlemen in polite society. He'd been a professional cavalry officer since he was twenty - on and off, give or take an erratic patch after Griete died - that was almost twenty years commanding men. He'd not thought much about the moral side of it, then. Left that to Lucey, actually, who spent a lot of time thinking about principles, and putting them into slightly flowerier language. No, when the King raised his standard at Nottingham - *he started it* - so long as Hollie got paid, he hadn't cared much who did the paying. And then after the first great battle of the war at Edgehill, it got personal. Things had started to blur, at Edgehill. Not so much King and Parliament, right against wrong, black against white, but fragment against fragment, rubbing together like the sharp ends of a broken bone. In-fighting. And now the Parliament, having got what they wanted, were turning on their Army, who'd got it for them. And that, actually, pissed Hollie *right off.* If he'd treated any of the lads on the farm at White Notley like Parliament treated its soldiers, he'd find himself rapidly short on labour. Sorry, gentlemen, can't pay you this week, but you don't mind carrying on getting your damn-fool heads shot off for the love of it, do you? Still no money, so you're on half-rations again till the treasure convoy comes through, but you go off and help yourself to a couple of eggs in a barn and one of the locals complains it's not paid for, and you're on a charge.

Making do and bloody mend, and he was sick of it. And *he* was a bloody colonel, on a pound a day, which'd be lovely if it wasn't a purely administrative pound a day written down in a ledger somewhere that he hadn't seen in the better part of a month.

Not-Hapless the kitten licked his ear, and he hunched his shoulder and growled at the little bugger, who just cuddled down and purred. It was a bloody ugly little cat, even now its singed fur was growing back. He turned his head slightly and glowered at its mismatched little face, and it touched its wet nose to his. "I am not being sweethearted by a god-damned cat," he warned it, and he could have sworn that the kitten was smiling. "I am *not* taking you home to Essex. I'm not. I'm telling you, cat. Not happening."

It was getting fat. When he'd first picked it up, a week ago, it had weighed about as much as a soldier's Bible, and taken up about as much room in his pocket. He suspected Not-Hapless was being provisioned in the same place as Venning's dog, with whom the little beast had struck up a wary friendship. Cheese-rinds, pie-crusts, and rodents. The animals thrived on it, clearly. Though if the little cat brought fleas home from Venning's mutt Het was going to - Het was going to do nothing, because he was not being sweethearted by a kitten, and he was not going to take the cat home at winter quarters. Even so he lifted the beast by the scruff of the neck and checked the white fur on its bulging little belly, to his satisfaction and its minute irritation.

"There," he said sternly, "thee is bugless, and long may it continue."

He was simply checking the kitten for fleas, that was all. An upright colonel of Sir Thomas Fairfax's regiment of horse would not be discovered rough-housing a small, homely kitten to the detriment and neglect of his official papers. Hollie straightened up abruptly, banged his head on the underneath of the desk, swore, and Not-Hapless the kitten bolted under the bed.

"*Ow*," he said, realising it was only his father, who couldn't be expected to do anything civilised like knock before entering his commanding officer's quarters. "What d'*you* want?"

"Mail's come in," Elijah said grimly. "Thought thee would want to know. What is thee doing with that cat, boy?"

"Disciplining it for not being godly enough. Now bugger off."

"Got a matter of some dispatch to talk to thee of, Holofernes."

"Does it involve preaching?" Hollie said warily. He was not at his best on his hands and knees on the floor looking up at his sire, who was about as tall as Hollie was himself, and being on all fours put him at something of a disadvantage. He had no desire to have to tell the old man to stop preaching - again. There was some as liked it, in his company. He was quite well aware of Fairfax's feelings on the matter, but when Tom was speaking with Parliament's voice, after the way Parliament had dealt with their soldiers of late, so far as Hollie was concerned what the eye didn't see the heart didn't grieve for.

"Sort of does," Elijah said awkwardly, and that was uncharacteristic enough to have Hollie backing out from under the desk and parking his backside on his dispatches. "Sit. Want a drink?"

"You got summat?"

"I got what I normally got, same as what you lot get. Warm water that tastes like it's been through a horse. I tell you what, my Het'd show this lot o' buggers how to go on. And this the Dean's own residence." Quite tickled him, plain, ruffianly Hollie Babbitt, ringing for a servant to bring him and his equally plain and ruffianly father some ale. You had it to do, though, or they didn't believe you were either an officer or a gentleman, especially not when they'd set eyes on Hollie's linen. Not a stitch of lace to his name. "Spit it out, then."

"If I were to talk to you of unnatural lusts, boy, what would you say?"

"I'd say I wasn't your type. Give over."

"Boy." Elijah fixed him with a fierce glare over the rim of his mug. "This is not a matter for levity."

It never was, with Elijah. Hollie had only ever heard him make one humorous remark, in thirty-eight years of society - and *that* hadn't been that funny. "If you mean Luce and Gray," he said wearily, and Elijah shook his head contemptuously.

"Old news, boy. Did thee not know *that*? Miss Bussyvin has been good plain Mistress Pettitt since this morning. No, I'd talk to you of -"

"You *what*?" Hollie yelped, and the kitten shot back under the bed, growling. "Since when? Who -? What bloody fool did they co-erce into carrying out *that* particular deed of darkness?"

"Don't thee come quoting thy Bible at me in flippancy, Holofernes, or I will turn thee over and tan thy arse, big as thee is," his father said stiffly. "*I* married them, as thy troop chaplain, as I had a right so to do. Would thee rather they was living together in sin, than as man and wife?"

"I should rather they'd asked me first!"

"Why, did thee want to marry her? I believed thee married already, and I reckon your Het'd have summat to say about it -"

All right, that was the second smart remark Elijah had made in thirty-eight years of acquaintance. And that meant the old bastard was in high good humour about having done it. "How long did you know?"

"Me? Thee may believe me or not as thee sees fit, but I never had any doubts on the lass's gender. Especially not when she had half your staff drooping after her like a pair o' dying ducks in a thunderstorm."

"She - *what*?"

"Aye. Thankful Russell made her an offer of marriage after Naseby, though I'd not have married *them* two. He's a decent lad, and I'd not see him shackled to that little virago. Even if she hadn't knocked him back. They'd not have suited."

Hollie took a swig of his ale, feeling like he needed it. Looked at his father, who was flat-serious, and shook his head, drained the mug and poured himself another one. "How. The. *Hell.* Did you know that?"

"She told me."

The kitten leapt onto the desk and he automatically steadied the ink pot from the depredations of that swishing little tail. "She told you."

"Will thee repeat everything I tell you, Holofernes, like some sort of prating popinjay? Aye, she told me. She would talk to someone with a bit o' common sense. Which let *you* out - and the Lord knows that man she's set her heart on is as lacking as thee is, for sense. Aye, Miss Bussyvin - as she was - she would speak with a man of mature years before she made so final a decision."

The old bastard was preening. Trooper Gray - that short, scrawny, belligerent termagant in breeches - had flattered and sweethearted her way into Elijah Babbitt's good graces, something his son hadn't been able to manage in the better part of forty years. "Son of a fucking *bitch,*" Hollie muttered, not quite inaudibly, and big as he was, earned a clip round the ear.

He neither belted his sire back, nor put him on a charge. He just looked at Elijah, probably still with his mouth open. "Did Lucey know any of this?" he said, after a pause, and Elijah looked shifty.

"Aye. Well. He might have known a little of it. This morning."

"So you - and Gray -"

"Miss Bussyvin," Elijah corrected him, "she is not one o' your ragged moss-troopers, boy, she is a respectable married lady."

"What the bloody hell is her name, anyway?"

"Gabrielle. Bussyvin, till this morning. She's Froggy."

"Oh, well, that explains! They do it different over there! The hell - no matter. *Gray* -" it was deliberate, "presumably decided Luce looked like the better bet before she backed that horse, then?"

"Oh, don't be so daft, boy. Gray's been backing that horse, as you so crudely put it, this last six weeks and more, and they've been looking April and May at each other for a sight longer than that. Does thee actually *have* eyes in thy head?"

Hollie ran both hands through his hair, a habit he had when he was wrong-footed, lost the bit of cord that was holding it out of his eyes, and snarled through a russet curtain, "Did *everybody* in my bloody company know except me?"

"Thee would have known if thee had troubled to look."

A horrible thought struck him. "Ah, Christ, tell me Noll Cromwell didn't know. *Please* tell me he didn't pass that hoyden my way because he knew what she was."

"Couldn't say," Elijah said primly.

"You," he said grimly, "can just bloody send Pettitt in on your way out. *Both* Pettitts. With the mail. She still in breeches, or what?"

"Till it starts showing," Elijah said, and Hollie stared at him in horrified silence.

And then there was a horrible rusty creaking noise, like someone cranking a rusted water-pump, and Hollie realised the old bastard was *laughing*.

17 - A Pair of Star-Cross'd Lovers

He just didn't feel up to discussing any further incidents of unnatural lusts with his father today, and so after the door closed behind the sniggering Elijah, he sat on the edge of the desk for a while with his eyes closed and let the troop's romantic entanglements fend for themselves. He thought there might be some ale left in the jug. He thought he probably deserved it, too. The unseasonable rain spattered the window, and he thought he might put some wood on the fire. In a minute. Not-Hapless's little head butted insistently against his hand, and he ran his fingers absently through the soft fur. Feeling the little cat's bones through her skin, and the brave vibration of her purr, humming like a bee, or Het's spinning-wheel at home.

The door opened, and he turned to face the miscreants.

Luce looked like a scabby bag of bones, and a somewhat mildewed one, given that he was quite ferociously bearded. He was upright with breeches on, mind, though it was the *not* being upright that had caused all the trouble. What he did not look like was a respectable junior officer in the Army of Parliament. "By, lad, you look like summat the cat haled in," Hollie said ruefully, all thoughts of reprimand gone. "D'you want me to call for summat to eat? Tha looks like a picked rib."

"I do not, sir." No, he was not the same absent-minded boy that Hollie had left in Langport almost a month ago. Oh, hell. Luce had gone and grown up. He was looking stiffly at a point slightly to the side of Hollie's left ear, with an expression straight out of Foxe's "Book of Martyrs". "I have let you down, sir. I have let the company down. I have –"

"Luce."

"I have disgraced both myself and the good name of my troop, I have –"

"Luce."

"I have dishonoured this lady, though by the Lord's grace I may yet make amends for that anticipation of my vows –"

"Lucifer shut up!"

It came out a bit louder than he intended, and the silence that followed vibrated. "I'm not having this conversation with you. *Ever*. Again. I could have wished you'd done it different, but you didn't, and we are where we are. Now. Are you sufficient mended to resume your duties?"

"I am, sir."

"He is not," Gray said, sounding like Trooper Gray even though she was dressed like Mistress Pettitt, in a plain, decent grey bodice and skirt that was slightly too big for her. Looking like a little girl in her mother's clothes, barely as high as Luce's shoulder, and she was almost as scrawny as he was. She'd covered her ragged hair with a decent cap and somehow that made it look worse, made all the bones of her little face stand out in unflattering relief, her eyes look even bigger. Her mouth was set in a mutinous straight line and she had to look up about a foot to meet Hollie's eyes, and even then she looked like a little wren taking on a cat. It was pitiable.

"Is he not, mistress? Wasn't aware my lord Fairfax had give my command over to you?"

"Hollie, don't!" Luce said before he had chance to catch himself, and Hollie, faced with two married *children*, swung on his cornet.

"Don't? Don't what? Don't expect your wife to behave like a grown-up? You're married to an officer, girl, *you* chose it, and –"

Her chin wobbled, and he felt a bit guilty, but she might be currently playing dress-up but in that little shell of buckram and wool she was still Trooper Gray and that lad – lass – had a backbone of Birmingham steel.

"Don't you talk to my wife like that, Colonel Babbitt," Luce said, with a sudden flash of temper in those misty grey eyes of his that was also new. Gray gave a great forlorn sniff and buried her head in his shoulder, and he glowered up at Hollie, patting her back soothingly. "It's all right, Gray. There is nothing he can do to you. You are not a soldier any more and he is not your commanding officer, and I will *not* allow him to bully you."

Bully *Gray*? Christ, it'd take him *and* the rest of the New Model to bully that one. If Luce thought putting her in a skirt had made her meek and biddable, he was in for a high old time of it. And pretty, she was not. Possibly if her eyes weren't swollen into slits and as pink as sunset, even if her nose hadn't been pink and shiny and wet, if her mouse-brown hair wasn't hacked brutally to the level of her ears – she might have been passable. She was too thin, her mouth was too wide, and she looked as woeful as a drowned puppy. Well, the one thing she was assuredly not, was putting it on for dramatic effect.

"Would you – *one* of you – care to enlighten me as to how this bloody lash-up- started?"

Luce took hold of her hand and gripped it. She even had hands like a boy – blunt-fingered and bony, with nails gnawed to the quick. They both started to speak at once.

"One," Hollie said icily, "at a time. *Mistress Pettitt*. You."

"I came to England to look for my brother, sir," she said in a tiny voice. "He – he was a good boy, and he fell in with bad company, and – and the last my poor mother heard of him he was taking up arms against His Majesty. He- he is my only brother, and my mother is a widow, and – and we needed Luc to support us, and he came over to fight for Parliament, believing it to be his duty as a good Protestant –"

Hollie tried to look sympathetic, and she lowered tear-drenched eyelashes. "Which troop did he join, then, lass?"

"I – I believe Hampden's infantry, colonel, his Greencoats, though I do not know for sure."

"*Fucking* Hapless."

"Pardon?" she said, the French way, and he couldn't help but laugh. "You three. That's *his* old company. Come up with that story between you, did you?"

"I – what – no –"

"May certennmint, madam. I did not come down wi't' last shower, miss. And you will find I'm a bit harder to charm than this pair of crack-brained romantics. Though I'd thought better of both of 'em, to be fair. What's it to be, Gray? His mother's, or my wife's, house?"

"What?"

"I'm giving you a choice. I don't mind you being married –"

"I do not believe you have an option, colonel," she said primly, "your consent was not required. And I am not a virgin. And I would swear to that in any court in the land. So you're not having it annulled."

Wasn't often that Hollie was glad of his father's nose for gossip, but he shrugged. "If you want to get into a pissing contest, Gray, I'm game. I have it on authority that you had a *second* proposal of marriage from another of my officers. Or rather a first - pre-empting Cornet Pettitt by a good few weeks, I believe. So by all means, we can get into the, are you or are you not intact, game, if you want to play silly buggers with me. But I'd not want to be the one to stand up and guess if it was Luce or Russell that got there first. Your reputation, gal, not mine. Or, rather, *his*."

He was expecting her to hit him, and he was not disappointed. He was expecting a girlish flat-handed slap. He got a nosebleed.

He wasn't expecting Luce to challenge him to a duel, either, which was so ludicrous as to be comical. Hollie with his eyes watering and a handkerchief clasped to his much-abused nose, shaking his head and still seeing stars, while a junior officer who presently resembled one of the balls of shaggy fluff that Not-Hapless the kitten dragged from under the bed yelled abuse at him. "You – out!" Hollie shouted – indistinctly – at Gray, who fled, howling.

And then he sat down and rested his head on his folded arms and muttered something dark, while Luce, a young man not intended by nature to be especially fiery, panted and glared at him.

"What gives you the right to persecute my wife, you – evil-tempered, ill-mannered, foul-mouthed – *bastard*?"

"The right of someone who's had the piss right royally took for the last twelvemonth!" Hollie snarled back. "I suppose you think it's sweet and romantic she's been hiding her sex for as long as she's been in the Army?"

"What are you trying to say?" The lad had gone stiff and cold, and his eyes were black instead of mist-pale. "Are you calling my wife a whore?"

"Eh? What? No! Christ, anything but!" He sat up, blew his hair out of his eyes. "Ah, God, I need a drink. Sit down. I'm not in the mood to take shit off you, Lucifer, sit down or I'll knock you down. That wench of yours has been passing herself off as a man for almost two years. I know that, you know that, stop thinking with your balls. I don't care if she wants to dress up as the Pope of Rome in the privacy of your own bedchamber. I do bloody care that she sees deception as second nature. I'll not have it. Not in my troop."

"She's not *in* your troop, Colonel Babbitt."

"*You* are, though. And she is, till I say she isn't."

"I fail to see what concern –"

"*She* has been one of Captain Venning's troopers since last spring. She's lied to me, she's lied to Drew Venning, I wouldn't bet the family farm that she's put you on more'n once and *God* knows what she's said to Russell. You may note, Lucifer, I will tolerate an amount of crap from my troopers but I will not have liars and I will not have deceivers in my ranks. *She* has been both. And if you hadn't noticed, that causes trouble. So. A liar, and a troublemaker. She's not impressing me so far. Makes me wonder what other bullshit she might have been feeding people, and how much more grief it's going to cause me, further down the line."

"I can see you're angry, colonel –"

"Me? Fucking livid, Lucey. In a personal *and* professional capacity."

"Well, I don't see why –"

"Because you knew, brat. You knew and you didn't tell me."

And there was no answer to that, and a faint flush rose in Luce's thin cheeks. He took a deep breath. "Yes."

"And it turns out Russell knew. And fancied a crack at her himself."

"That I did not know. Until – afterwards."

"No. Well. Dark horse, is our Hapless. Two officers, one girl. In my experience of that situation, often ends in tears, brat. How d'you think Russell is going to feel, when he comes back and finds you leg-shackled to the lass who knocked him back? Might be rubbing his nose in it somewhat, even for Master Frigid-Drawers, wouldn't you think, seeing her every day? Could have been him, if it hadn't been for -" Hollie tapped his cheek meaningfully, and Luce looked everywhere but directly across the desk.

"I hadn't thought of that. I – " his eyes were darting everywhere, and Hollie had a horrible feeling the brat was on the edge of tears. "I didn't think."

"No. I *know* you didn't think. You often don't think." The young officer bit his knuckle, hard enough that the skin whitened under his teeth. "Luce, you're an officer. You can't keep doing this. And I have no idea what happened at Naseby, but I do know it wasn't what you three said it was. I'm not commanding a fucking cabal, brat. Are you going to tell me what happened to Captain Chedglow, so that perhaps I might be the *last* person in the Army of Parliament to know what's happening in my own command? Because if Fairfax asks me, I am going to look a complete tit when I tell him I'm probably the only person who does not know. And I'm funny like that. I don't like my commander thinking I'm a bloody fool. There, that's summat else I've got against your Gray. She's let me cop for it, and you've stood back and let her do it."

"I'm." He gulped. His adam's-apple hadn't always been so prominent, either, poor little bugger. "I'm sorry, sir. I truly did not think. I thought she would put on skirts, and no one would ask questions."

"Luce, she looks like a boy in a dress. In *someone else's* dress, at that. And God knows she's not likely to keep a civil tongue in her head at the best of times, never mind when she's expected to act ladylike."

"*I* trust her," he said forlornly.

"Aye. Well. I'm prepared to give her the benefit of the doubt, brat - on *your* say-so. And if she wills it, I'm prepared to keep her in breeches, and we'll say no more about it. God knows it will be easier on the nerves than answering to Black Tom every time she cuts loose in company. Telling your mother – well, that's up to you, lad, and I wish you joy of it." The brat was staring at him, wide-eyed. "What?"

"Sir, what – what is that?"

"What's – oh. Ah, God, that damn cat." He screwed up a sheet of paper – requisition list, damn it – and shied it at the kitten, squatting malevolently with its backside hanging off the earth-box that the staff at Audry had so reluctantly supplied. "I'm no hand at house-training. Bugger it. Ach, Luce, pass us that shirt, will you? It's not clean anyway –" he sniffed the crumpled linen thoughtfully, "no, definitely not clean. Right, you little sod, come here..."

18 - The Way of a Man with a Maid

It somehow wasn't the stern, disciplinarian environment that he would have wished, with the little cat industriously digging in its earth-box and wads of bloody linen strewn about the room. Gray was tearstained and mutinous, and Luce was miserably apologetic all over the place, and that was before those two started sniping at *each other* because Luce wasn't sticking up for Gray against Hollie as much as she would have liked, and Gray wasn't as grateful for Hollie's forbearance as Luce would have liked.

He let them bicker, sitting with the cat in his lap and looking ostentatiously out at the rain sweeping in across the fields. *You* said this, and *you* did that, and all the time the two of them were sitting absolutely identical, both of them with their legs stuck out and crossed at the ankle and their hands folded in their laps, as mirrorwise as a pair of bookends. He wondered if they knew they did it. And how comical it looked, bless them. Babies, both. He couldn't expect the pair of silly buggers to behave like grown-ups.

Not-Hapless (if the damn thing was stopping, he had to come up with a better name than that) jumped into his lap, paddled comfortably and then curled up. "Finished?" he said, eyeing them sternly. Gray sniffed, and Luce wriggled. Hell, maybe when the war was over and done, Hollie could reconsider his place in life. He might make a decent schoolmaster after all.

"Who else knows?" he said sternly.

"Everyone," Gray said defiantly, and "In the company," Luce finished. "I think Venning has an idea. Nobody else. Not Toogood."

"And Chedglow?" He would not let that go. He knew *something* had happened at Naseby. Luce lifted his head and the corner of his mouth twitched in an awkward smile.

"I shot him, sir. Sorry."

Hollie just sat with his mouth open for a minute, before recovering. Faintly. "*You* shot – "

"Well, *he* had just shot Russell. And he'd been aiming for – " he paused, glanced sideways, and blushed even under the ferocious beard. "My wife," he finished, sounding absurdly proud.

"Chedglow saw me kissing Russell," she said, "after I'd told Hapless that I couldn't marry him because I was in love with –" and it was bloody frightening, but she looked up at that hairy, ruffianly fair-haired object and melted - "*my husband*," she breathed.

It probably was neither the time nor the place to laugh, and he probably ought to make a formal report to Fairfax that his own personal company was slightly more lubricious than Imperial Rome in the days of Caligula, but he bent his head over the cat again so neither of the starry-eyed newlyweds caught him grinning. Besides, if he did make a report to Fairfax of that nature, he imagined he'd be accused of having seen one too many revenge plays. "Can you not do that again?" he said mildly. "As a gesture of kindness to me, if nothing else?"

"Kiss Russell?" she said blankly, and Luce stiffened. "I should think *not*, Gray!"

"That as well. I'm sure the poor sod has enough on his plate at the moment. Go about murdering my officers. I did *think* about promoting you to captaincy, Mistress Pettitt. But then I woke up."

"You are not – not going to discipline me?" Luce said faintly, and Gray blinked hard again, and put her hand out to her new helpmeet and gripped his fingers so hard all the bones showed. "You are not going to turn me over to the Commander-in-Chief?"

"Probably should. Unfortunately, life without Chedglow is considerably more appealing. Which is a deeply unChristian perspective. And honestly, Gray? I can't be arsed. The paperwork would be a god-damned nightmare. So. If you're obliging, you're stopping as a lad, for the time, and I want a drink. Luce."

It wasn't a request. Luce gave his colonel a reproachful look.

"It's in the chest under the window," Hollie said meaningfully.

"It always bloody is, with you," Luce sniffed, and rummaged about under Hollie's shirts till he found the precious bottle of wine. Looked at Hollie's expression, and handed it over without ceremony. Gray bridled, and Hollie stopped with the cork in his teeth. "You're a boy, Gray, remember? *Boys* don't mind necking it out of the bottle. Keep up at the back." Out of courtesy, he did wipe it on his cuff before he handed it over, though. "Now, you were saying earlier. About not joining Hampden's Greencoats."

"- that I have a brother." All right, she had a pretty way about her when she tucked her chin in and looked up through her eyelashes. It wasn't flirtatious, it was downright challenging, but she was so short it was rather endearing. "That is not a lie. I do have a brother, and his name is Luc. He is a bloody awful swordsman."

"You still make a habit of keeping apples in your snapsack?" Hollie didn't wait for an answer, but leaned over, opened Luce's bag and rummaged inside. "Want one? Two..."

"Are you *always* so discourteous? Sir?"

"Mm. Pretty much. Luce?"

"*Stop* it."

"You were saying. Luc. Crap swordsman."

"He *didn't* want to come to England," she said furiously. "He talked about it a lot, and it – I was vexed by it."

"Habit of talking bollocks, your Frenchman," Hollie said indistinctly, and settled himself more comfortably against the wall. Picking at some flaking plaster as Gray spoke, as if he wasn't attending.

"I was always better with a sword than he was!"

And then he looked up, grinning. "Now then, Gray, what have I told you about that? Get you riled and you drop your guard. *Every* time. Get you killed one of these days, that will. If you're a better swordsman than your brother, he must fight like my maiden auntie. As I said. I am not stupid. You might be hot at hand, miss, but you can ride a horse, and you know one end of a blade from another. Hampden's infantry, my arse."

"I told you!" Luce said smugly.

"Should've told bloody *Russell.* He's a rotten liar. So you spent too much time listening to Johnny Crapaud talking about the Papist menace, and you reckoned you'd come over and give us a hand?"

"There was a man," she muttered, scarlet-faced.

"You wanted to marry him?"

"I bloody didn't, no!"

Hollie inhaled apple and choked. "Now that I can believe!"

"He was an *old* man. With a wart. Cartloads of money, mind you," she said reflectively. "I decided we should not suit. Besides, I am having far too much fun. At home – skirts, stays, high-heeled slippers. *Yes*, mama. So." She pulled her face into a mockery of prim obedience. "Here – liberty."

"Want to bet?" Luce muttered darkly.

"I had never thought to meet anyone like Lucifer. He is not like other men."

"Which may be a compliment or an insult, brat."

"Colonel Babbitt, you are very rude."

"And *you* are slightly tipsy, missy." Hollie grinned. "Fancy that. Want to watch that lass, Luce. Tell you owt when she's had a glass too many. And there's me thinking the wench was as close as an oyster. Some hope."

"If I thought that was deliberate, sir," Luce said balefully, and Hollie gave an innocent shrug. "Me? Just being friendly, like. Gray, you're on picket duty in half an hour. In breeches. What you do between now and then is your own affair, as long as you don't do it on my bed."

"May we –" Luce indicated the wine. Hollie cocked an eyebrow.

"You may not. The pair of you make my head hurt. I'm off to get pissed with Venning. At least *he's* not a bloody perpetual intriguer."

19 - If They Cannot Contain, Let them Marry

Having then made it all right and tight, he could then hold his head up in the streets of Bridgwater and ignore the behind-handed comments about his troop's immorality and depravity - waiting for that inevitable summons that was going to come for his carpeting from Fairfax. Which came within the day, and Black Tom positively frothing at the mouth, and Hollie stood there trying to look meek and biddable and apologetic, an impression he found difficult at best. He was a bit torn – should he try and divert his commander before the man had an apoplexy, or should he just try and get him told straight out that the lad with whom Luce Pettitt had been caught in acts of immorality was, in fact, a lass? Possibly with a bun in the oven, but married? Or did that make it worse –

"Sir, you are not attending!" Fairfax roared, and Hollie, who was used to being spat on by Noll Cromwell at a short range, looked up and didn't bat an eyelid.

"Was too, sir."

"What did I just say, Colonel Babbitt?"

"Got a bit lost, sir. I were right with you right up until the bit about bringing the Army into disrepute and my officers being a disgrace to the Cause, but I lost the thread round about the bit where you started quoting Genesis at me. Being consumed in the inn – inky –"

"Don't try and play daft with me, Hollie Babbitt. You know as well as I do what iniquity is. If not better."

"Do I? If you say so, sir-"

"I have *met* your father, Colonel. If you honestly think I'm not perfectly well aware that you can probably start at the Book of Revelations and recite backwards, sir, you take me for a bigger fool than I think you do."

To which there was not an answer that wouldn't give offence, so Hollie simply squirmed uncomfortably and tried hard not to think that although raining fire and brimstone was probably all very well, Luce's bit of well-intended fornication was hardly in the same league as Sodom and Gomorrah. Mademoiselle Boissevin – Mistress Pettitt – might not be the most ladylike of ladies, but Hollie was pretty sure she was all female, having seen her in a frock. Scrubbed up all right, for a boy-girl-thing, although he was bloody sure she still wasn't any great admirer of his. And that thing in the Book of Genesis with Lot and his daughters – that was definitely on dodgy ground, that was. Not that Hollie was prim, but if he thought Luce was related that closely to the lass, she'd be out on her arse – Fairfax was eyeing him narrowly again.

"Sir?" he said warily.

"You're not listening again, are you?"

"All agog, sir. And Magog," he added, then realised it wasn't helpful, and shut up.

"What have you got to say for yourself?"

"It's all right, sir, my father married 'em yesterday morning?"

He still liked to put Fairfax on the back foot. As a man, he was very fond of Black Tom. As a commander – well, Hollie just wasn't made not to like wrong-footing his superiors. "What?" Fairfax said, so Hollie repeated it, slower.

"That is a woman?"

"Aye. *Hic mulier*."

"Babbitt, you appal me."

"Do it to myself at times, sir. And no, I didn't know, not till I came in and found the pair of them in a compromising position. On his sick bed an' all. Disgusting. I was proper shocked, I was."

"Were you. Were you, indeed."

"I was, sir." He thought he might be over-egging the innocence again. "Prefer it if it wasn't common knowledge, mind, sir. Not sure how the lads'd feel if – you know – lass tagging round after the Army, they might get ideas, and with our Luce just being back on his feet – I don't want him fighting duels every hour God sends, if you get me. Or him. Her. *Gray*. He – she – *it*'s a fierce little bugger. I'll send her home when we go to winter quarters, and that'll be the last you see of Trooper Gray, you have my word of honour."

Though Fairfax wasn't done with Hollie, not by a long chalk. It was as if that last little bit of taking liberties had frayed a something between them - as if a friendship had been tested, and found wanting.

And that wasn't fair, and yet, it was fair, because Fairfax was Parliament's man, or honour-bound to give the outward seeming of it, and Hollie was his troop's. Hollie owed no duty to a Parliament that saw neither himself nor his men cared for. He was quite open about it. If Fairfax gave an order, he would carry it out, to the best of his ability. It didn't mean they owned his soul, or dictated his conscience. That was between him and his God, and could not be bought or commanded. Seemed he was still an independent free-thinking Puritan boy after all.

Fairfax was furious about it, this sudden turn towards the Independent. "Colonel Babbitt sir, I will not tolerate this - this - *insubordination*!"

And that was fine, because Hollie was furious in his turn, but not so stupid as to flare up at his commander, not in words. He said nothing, but cocked his head. "No, sir," he said stiffly. "Can't say as I know what you mean." This time.

"You know exactly what I mean, colonel! While godly men were resting on this last Sabbath, sir, *you* were careering about the countryside! Drinking with your men!"

Hollie had been trying to head off one of his troopers from desertion. Actually, Hollie had been thumping hell for leather across open country trying to find Lucas Weston's widow's farm before his brother did. Hollie had been trying to explain to Mistress Weston exactly what it was that had driven her husband to measure his life in six feet of Yorkshire soil, shared with Malignants and Parliamentarians both, without so much as a marker to mind him by. (He hadn't done a very good job, but that was mostly because he didn't know, either.)

He'd felt all of three inches high, in that cold, shabby farmhouse on the banks of the river Parrett. He kept thinking of Het, and his own farm like it was when he'd first come there, with the window catch that rattled and the missing tiles off the roof: all the hundred and one little daft things that a woman couldn't do by herself, too busy trying to keep the fabric of the house together. He knew what it was to be running just to stay still, to be so tired at the end of the day that you were as numb and stupid as a bullock in a field and yet to still know there was work to be done that couldn't wait. A household stripped by war could function. His own did. But by God it was hard, it was bone-aching hard, and it took every penny he could send home on a colonel's pay. Luke Weston had been one of nearly a hundred men in Babbitt's own company. Nice enough lad, stolid, never going to set the world on fire, looked enough like his brother Hollie couldn't always tell them apart. Prone to making unhelpful remarks from the back. Died at Marston Moor, shot in the throat. It had been quick. He had no idea if that was any consolation. Didn't know if weary Mistress Weston, with her chapped hands and her three runny-nosed, muddy-footed children at her skirts and her damp house, had loved her husband.

It didn't make it easier to sit in her kitchen accepting her hospitality and tell her he was dead, though. He'd been Hollie's responsibility and he was dead. And the Malignants might have done for Lucas, but Hollie was buggered if he was going to let his own side have Isaac, too. And so he'd been sat there waiting when the big lolloping trooper arrived, because his own Blossom was faster than Weston's shaggy-footed gelding, sat there quite amiably with a mug of cider, and he never let Weston get a word in edgeways about leaving the Army - with or without official consent. Hollie had said he was there because Lucas had died with pay owing and he wanted to make sure she had it. Which was true enough. He just wished he could have afforded to give her all of it. He'd thought for a minute Isaac was going to take a swing at him. Been sticky, for a bit, there. But. It had ended well. Rough cider always took Hollie bad ways, but he expected that a belly-ache was a small price to pay for not having Isaac Weston taken up and punished. Isaac might have got away with it, at the beginning of the war, but not now, not under the new, tight New Model Army. Hollie knew he was on thin ice himself, at times, and he was an officer on nodding terms with both Fairfax and Cromwell. The wages of sin was death, in the New Model, if the devout thought it was a big enough sin.

So, Fairfax had been took in, had he? Hollie filed that bit of information away, and expected no quarter. It was a long list of the troop's transgressions. Allowing a lay preacher to give voice amongst the ranks, after the same had been so expressly forbidden by Parliament not six months ago. Swearing. Wilful disobedience. Looting. Dereliction of duty. Insubordination. Insolence.

"And what have you got to say for yourself?" Fairfax said, and he didn't even sound like himself any more. He didn't sound like a man who'd take his wife and daughter on campaign, like he had at Hull, two years back. He didn't even sound like a man who'd *have* a wife and daughter. Sounded like a dry, godly, eye-rolling straight down the line Parliament lapdog.

"I object to the accusation of looting. *Sir*."

For a moment, something stirred beneath the conventional surface, and Hollie's friend Black Tom was looking at him again. "But the rest you own to?"

"The preacher is my father. Sir. As you well know. I can honour my father, like it says in the Commandments, *sir*, but I don't recall it ever saying nowt about having to honour thy masters in Parliament. Unless they put that one in as number eleven, in February?"

"Holofernes!" Black Tom would have laughed. He'd have been shocked, but he'd have laughed. "I should by rights fine you for that irreligious remark, colonel."

"You probably should, sir, but since you're not paying me anyway, shall we take it as given that I've paid my fine in the same coin as that in which it was received?"

"Colonel, you are grown rebellious."

"I am grown *cynical*, sir. I was always rebellious. Or I'd not be stood on this side of the river, would I?"

Fairfax's black eyes dropped, his sallow cheeks flushed slightly. Didn't like to be reminded he was a rebel, then. "You deny the looting?"

"You know bloody *well* I deny the looting!"

"That's another fictional twelvepence, colonel."

Hollie put his hands on the edge of the table and leaned forward. "Arse. Holes. To the twelvepence. *Sir*. I have never. *Never*. Took nowt that wasn't paid for. Not even Ward and Eliot have took nowt that wasn't paid for, though it might not have been paid for at that exact moment. And they haven't always paid in coin. What with us not having none."

"Will you *stop* going on about that, Holofernes! I can not magic coin out of thin air, sir! If I had coin enough, I would pay the bloody lot of you off today!"

"Twelvepence," Hollie said sweetly, and Fairfax jerked in his seat as if he'd been pricked.

"*Stop* that! And another thing! You are rabble-rousing, colonel - agitating!"

"Me?"

"You know damn well you are! I have been treating till my throat was dry on the matter of - looting, sir, that thing that you don't do - with the Clubmen, under agreement that this Army would pay for all supplies and not harass the people. You know the Clubmen, I assume, colonel. They protest, most vociferously, about the war. That the Army deprive them of their homes, their livelihoods - that men under my command steal, and cheat the people - you are aware of all this, are you not?"

He hated it when Fairfax was sarcastic. "I might have heard a few things. Here and there, like."

"Yes. I rather thought you might. Perhaps, colonel, you might like to explain your remarks to Major Bethel on the subject of Clubmen?" Fairfax leaned forward, and *now* he was mad. His black eyes were blazing. Hollie tried a faint, conciliatory smile. "We spoke at Middlezoy, the day after Langport, at some length with the leaders of the Clubmen. We agreed that we should accede to their requests, so long as they should not aid the Malignant cause. You were heard - *heard*, colonel, you are hardly the quietest man, sir, I imagine they heard you in Taunton! - to be *agreeing* with the Clubmen's cause!"

"Well, *I* wouldn't like it, if -"

"Babbitt." Hollie stopped mid-sentence. "Shut up, Babbitt. For once, can you *not* answer me back? You said, sir, and I believe I quote you exactly. Upon the presentation of the grievances of the Clubmen leaders, you said, very loudly -"

"Christ," Hollie said feebly. "I said, 'Christ, I'm married to a bloody Clubman.'"

"That's not quite what you said, Babbitt, but it's close. I imagine you thought it was funny?"

"No, sir. No, I, ah, yes. Het - uh, Mistress Babbitt - my wife has little patience with this war. She's got no time at all for looters. She keeps her late husband's old fowling-piece behind the front door in case we get any unsolicited Malignant guests paying a call at White Notley. Last time I turned up unexpected she nearly blew my head off -"

"I don't care, Babbitt. Next time you feel moved to give any more public political commentary, might I suggest that you engage what passes for a brain under that ragged mane of yours - and, incidentally, I might add that I have received adverse remarks about your somewhat slapdash personal presentation - and shut the - *hell* - up!"

"My opinions as a private individual are my own affair, sir."

"You're not a private individual, Holofernes, *will* you get that into your thick head? You are a senior officer in the Army of Parliament and you have a duty to represent that Army in all its public functions."

"Aye, well, if I happened to say I thought maybe there was a bit too much being said for

Parliament and not enough for the Army, I reckon I'd be representing the common run of lads there, wouldn't I? The noble cause of Parliament, that doesn't pay its bills to its troops either, never mind the people it's leeching off -"

"Babbitt."

"Sir?"

"Get out."

Hollie stood up and bowed abruptly. He hadn't started, he hadn't hardly started, on his complaints, but he didn't think Fairfax was in the mood to listen. Not in the business of biting the hand that fed him, was Fairfax. Well, at least the hand bloody well fed *him*. He'd been very apologetic about putting the troops on short rations, but half of not a lot was still not a lot. Ah, Christ, he wanted Russell back - Russell'd find something, scratch a ration off bare rock, Hapless would.

And he really ought not to think about Hapless because of all things Hapless's pitiable state summed it up in one neat package for Hollie. Russell, that ruthlessly efficient engine of godly devastation, slumped sobbing and blinded in a shaft of midsummer sunlight on Hollie's parlour floor, while Het held him like a child. Fairfax had never asked after Russell. Not once. Cromwell had never asked. And why should they? They were at war. Men were hurt. Killed. Collateral damage, apparently. It was expected.

Mattie Percey, at White Notley learning to do everything left-handed. Russell, writing almost indecipherable letters where he claimed his sight was coming back and could he be allowed to rejoin his troop, and not fooling anybody. Venning, exhausted and haunted, all eyes and ragged hair as he slowly starved in a fever-ridden ditch in Somerset. Luce, scared half to death most of the time, who cried himself to sleep most nights and hadn't picked up a pen in weeks.

Most of the troop down with something they were calling "the new disease", which looked remarkably like an old-fashioned bloody flux to Hollie, and there was nothing so demoralising as a company with bad guts. It was funny, for a bit, and then it stopped being funny and it was horrible, going out on patrol and you couldn't go more than a quarter-mile to one of your walking wounded having to dismount and squat groaning in a ditch.

Dead, or broken, or disillusioned, all of them, that brave, scruffy, disrespectful company that had taken the field at Naseby. They'd given too much, and they weren't thanked for it. Their masters in Parliament liked to keep a stern hand on the bridle - he laughed silently, thinking of his old mate Rackhay, dead at the beginning of the war, who'd been prone to using that expression. Oh aye, if this particular colt looked like he might be showing a bit of spirit, the great and the good in Parliament were a bit too handy with whip and spur for Hollie's liking, these days. Curbed and leashed every which way. Thank God for Cullis, that square gargoyle, who just shrugged and said what d'you expect, Rosie, if you want to be a politicker you better learn to stop cursing.

To which Hollie had replied, absently, "That one may smile, and smile, and be a villain," and Luce had looked up with more sparkle in his eyes than had been there in weeks and given him, "At least, I am sure it may be so in Somerset."

Which was quick, if not especially funny, but at least the brat was not so lost as to forget the Prince of Denmark.

No, Hollie had not forgot. Parliament might have forgot, after Naseby, now that the King was on the run and by all accounts his army shattered. But Hollie had not. They were Hollie's lads. They had trusted him. If he would not speak for them, no other bugger would.

"Well, well. If it ain't Rosie."

He straightened up with a start. "Oh God, it's you. What's up with you, then - run out of bloody sea to wash about in?"

Colonel Rainsborough, that notorious purveyor of dried-out ship's biscuit and unhelpful remarks, settled himself companionably next to Hollie. "Just come out for a smoke, lad. So long as you don't mind." He filled his pipe with an air of satisfaction. "'M a landlubber, anyway, now. Though I hear you're in the market for a change of career yourself?"

He gave a sharp laugh, and then was slightly astonished how bitter he sounded. "Ach, I'm too old for owt like that. Don't talk daft - even joking."

"Aye?" Rainsborough scratched his head, tipping his disreputable felt hat sideways. "That's not what I heard, Rosie. I heard you was pig-sick of soldiering, big lad. Or is that not right?"

"Oh aye, it's bloody right." The sun was setting. It was funny. It was flat, here - the tallest thing for miles was the tops of the trees where they lined the river. Flat, and so many different shades of midsummer green, all washed over with a scarlet glow. Even the river was wide, and slow, and smooth. It reminded him oddly of home, of White Notley, of the ford near the Braintree road. Just for a minute, he let himself imagine if she was here, or if he was there - her hand in his, warm and comforting, and the swish of her skirts through the long grass, with the lacy heads of the cow-parsley almost waist high. What they might talk of. (Cheese, possibly. Of the things he liked about the West Country, the cheese was an especial favourite. He wondered if she'd ever try it. If he'd ever get the chance to take her some. If that was the sort of thing a dutiful husband did, take a cheese home to his lady wife, or if she'd take that as a slight on her dairying.) At what point she might turn her face up to his, and step into his arms all confiding, like she did - "Fed up to the back teeth with it, but I know what my duty is," he finished.

"Ah." Rainsborough had his eyes closed, and the ruddy light touched his sunburnt forehead, his salt-bleached eyebrows. "I know what mine is, too, for which I thank God. It's a bugger of a thing, Rosie, having to turn your back on your own lads. God-damned lousy I call it, and that's swearing." His eyes popped open. "Tell you what, big lad. You ever fancy a drink and a moan about it, you call by my lodgings. You're not on your own with your thinking, I can tell you that for free. There's them in this Army as is feeling pretty bloody well stitched up right now, and they ain't *all* in the common run of soldier. Just in the interests of getting it off your chest, you understand."

"Colonel Rainsborough, sir, you are preaching insurrection," he said warily, and Rainsborough gave him a snaggly grin.

"Not doing nothing of the kind, Rosie. Purely social invitation to call in one night for a pot of ale and a right good moan. Just a few mates putting the world to rights over a drink, that's all. Most Thursdays. You know where I'm quartered."

21 - A Dinner of Herbs

Essex
August 1645

She felt restless and slightly ill and uncomfortable, all at once. She couldn't settle, the sticky August heat making the soft, well-washed linen of her shift cling to her back and her legs, and her miserable heavy breasts.

There was only Het and Thomazine and the servants here anyway, the people of the house - and Russell, and he was practically family, after three months. Even assuming he could see the state of her anyway, and that varied from day to day. She settled herself back in her chair, blowing the sweat-limp hair out of her eyes. No cap, Mistress Henrietta? Slattern. What *would* the neighbours say?

Just for a moment she imagined hoofbeats on the sun-baked turf. Looking up, out of the window across the sunlit lawn, seeing the dull russet of Blossom's coat slipping between the trees, the brighter scarlet of her husband's hair against his own plain grey coat. The even brighter peeling scarlet down the bridge of his nose, that he'd inevitably have after this summer - typical fair-skinned redhead, he caught the sun and peeled terribly, and it looked so sore when he did, poor lamb. He must be half-boiled, in a stiff leather buffcoat. When the new baby was here - when she wasn't quite so unwieldy - she'd see to putting up some more chamomile lotion. He could take it away with him, then. They needed some at home anyway, what with Thomazine as fire-haired as her daddy, and

Russell without the sense to put a hat on, most of the time.

The little girl was most industriously working her way through a basket of strawberries, pulling off the green hulls for Williams in the kitchen. The smell of the sun-warmed fruit was so strong it almost sickened Het. "Zee one, Apple one, pull one," she chanted softly to herself, her face and her hair all sticky with ruddy juice, her apron and skirts stained. Russell was on the floor beside her, sprawled in a patch of sunlight with the farm account-books four inches from the end of his nose and a pot of ink at his elbow. He looked no better. Absorbed in his accounts, he was absently eating as many berries as the child could put into his inky fingers, to her infinite delight. Hapless Russell was a sticky mess, and utterly at his ease. It was a joy to see.

He felt her gaze on him and looked up, frowning slightly as he looked into the sun as if his head hurt him, which it probably did, poor boy. Blinking owlishly at her. "Mistress?" he said warily, and as ever, "Het," she corrected him, "we do not stand on ceremony, young man, not in this house."

"You are - all right?"

"I am all right," she agreed. "Hot, dear."

"Shall I open a window? Do you need me to - "

"I need you to not upset the ink pot, Thankful. I'm sure *I* can't get down on my hands and knees to clear it up, with this little - prominence - in front of me," and she spread her hand on her belly, rubbing her thumb over her wriggling burden. Feeling an elbow, or a knee, push against her hand, and not able to restrain a smile of absolute wonder. The Lord was indeed kind, to bless her not once, but twice.

"Zee do," Thomazine said happily, and used Russell's shoulder to lever herself upright, thumping purposefully across the squares of sunlight to her mother's skirts. "Where pot?"

"Indeed, 'ware pot," Russell said, and flipped himself upright with the ink in his hand to set it on the mantelpiece. She could have wished he'd done other, but she could always get the inkstains sanded out afterwards. "May I have the book, my tibber?"

He always did Het the courtesy of explaining the state of the farm's accounts to her. It mostly made sense, since he wrote big and simple, it being all he could do, at the moment. The important thing was that they weren't poor, and that they wouldn't starve, not this winter. Enough money, in coin, in actual coin that you could pick up and spend, under the hearthstone in the kitchen, where the fire was in more or less continually and any Malignants who were wilful enough to try and steal it would receive burnt fingers. It was a source of great comfort and satisfaction to Het that no one ever went to bed hungry, at White Notley.

"Madam -"

"Het." Het whose back hurt, and who was not in the mood for Russell's caprices.

He gave her a hurt look - he did hurt looks better than anyone she knew, with those great dark eyes - and went all stiff and indignant, like a kicked puppy. "Het, then. I thought you might like to know. I believe my sister has just ridden into the yard."

Her first thought was that he was trying to tease her. Her second was that he must have mistaken someone else for his sister. Her third was that dear God above, he was right.

Fly-Fornication Coventry stalked into the parlour, unannounced, brushing past Catterall as if the steward was of no account, and it was more than clear that no one could mistake Thankful Russell's sister for anyone but her gaunt, horse-faced self.

She drew herself up to her full height, and she was almost as tall as he was. He cocked his head inquiringly. "May I be of assistance, good sister?"

And his loving sister hit him, with the full weight of her arm behind it. He wasn't expecting it and it laid him sideways. "You filthy, fornicating, vicious adulterer!" she hissed, and Russell yelped - most unmanly, but what the hell was the woman talking about? - and Het surged upright in her chair, perfectly breathless with indignation.

"How dare you, madam!"

"How dare I, you - scarlet woman? How *dare* I? How dare *you* show your face in godly company, you whore? Flaunting your overripe charms at my brother - oh, I know you for what you are, Babylon! You are the talk of all Buckinghamshire, living in sin with a woman not your wife, Thankful. How dare you bring shame on this family! How *dare* you! Where is your *duty*, you vile lecher?"

He was rubbing his arm, where he'd hit the mantelpiece. "Mind your tongue, before the child, if you please. 'S all right, Zee. Nothing to mind."

"*Everything* to mind, sir!"

Thomazine was big-eyed, staring at this strange shouty woman who looked like a nasty version of her Apple, and who was standing between Thomazine and her mother, looking very cross indeed, her face all screwed up and blotchy-red. "Thomazine, dear, come here," Het said coolly. "And you, madam, will do me the courtesy of leaving this house without another word, before I ask the servants to put you out."

Fly's eyes moved slowly from the tall, straight child with the red-gold curls, to the tall, straight young man with the fair hair, to Het's distinctly-pregnant person, and you could see her thoughts fall into place like pennies into a jar. "You dirty little cur," she said, and all of a sudden her carefully-genteel voice had a soft country burr, just like Russell's did when he was rattled. "I hope the Lord strikes you dead for your iniquity. All *three* of you. You filthy little whelp."

Thomazine did what she always did if her mother was out of range. She went to Russell. "Bad lady," she said sternly. "Go way, *bad* lady." And just like Het did when she was ordering one of the house dogs out for misbehaviour, she flung her hand out imperiously, pointing to the door. "Out!"

"Out of the mouths of babes and sucklings," Russell said, and his voice was shaky. "Get out, Mistress Coventry. Or *I* will put you out. And you won't like it."

"You will not speak to my daughter in that way," Het added. Het didn't often get cross. Wasn't a thing you did, out here in the deep country. No point. Cross with whom - the weather? the harvest? the beasts? But when she did, it wasn't ladylike. She tried not to do it. She was slow to most things, but when she went, it was near-unmanageable.

"I have a duty to bring this sinner back to his rightful place, madam! I am a widow and *that* - poor instrument that it is - is my sole support in this world. I have *every right* to expect that - broken reed - to come back to Four Ashes as is his duty before his God, and take up *some* kind of responsibility. You always were an idle, shiftless, *irresponsible* child, Thankful. I tried and tried to bring you to the light and I see I have failed utterly, yet it is not too late. You may still repent, brother." Her voice had softened, now, though her wheedling tones sat ill with her forbidding appearance. "God will always welcome you back into His bosom, if you repent sincerely. Do you know that, little girl? Do *you* know what happens to little boys and girls who rebel against their Maker?"

"They get their hands held in the kitchen fire till their fingers blister," Russell said. Perfectly calm, and perfectly cold. "Or they get locked in the attic in the dark with their Bible for their sole company. Which is well, for I can give you - Proverbs, book twenty-one, chapter nineteen: it is better to dwell in the wilderness, than with a contentious and an angry woman."

"You are unnatural, brother."

"I am a perfectly natural brother. Regrettably, Fly dear, I am not *your* brother, and you cannot dictate your will to me. Not now, and not ever again. I cast you out, madam, like an unclean spirit. Now go forth and haunt some other bugger, and take your vicious tongue with you, before I am tempted beyond endurance to cut it out."

"You are still my flesh and blood, Thankful, and I thank God that if nothing else *I* do not shirk my duty doing the Lord's work."

Het stood up and brushed past Russell's sister. Fly-Fornication was spotlessly clean, almost scrubbed, and close to her skirts smelled of air and sunlight and harsh soap. No softness about her at all. Even her cap was a brilliant white, plain and starched and stiff as paper. Her skin was so pale as to seem unhealthy, unlike Russell's lightly-freckled, ungentlemanlike, outdoor tan.

Het stood beside Russell and her daughter in front of the cold hearth, and for all he looked so defiant he was trembling, close to, his hand shaking on Thomazine's amber curls. "I think you've said all you needed to say, madam," she said. "You've had your answer, and Thankful is needed here."

Felt him go stiff beside her, and looked up at him. "Thankful is *very much* wanted here," she said, looking at him, not at his sister. "This is his place."

"Hiding behind a woman's skirts."

Thomazine buried her face in Het's skirts, still holding Russell's hand, and he dropped to his knees suddenly beside the little girl. "Ah, tibber, tibber forgive me – forgive what I'm about to do, gal –"

And he planted a kiss square on the top of her head, stood up, took two strides across the room, and grabbed his sister by the elbow, hard enough for the plain fabric of her sleeve to pale and dimple. "You, you filthy-minded bitch, are leaving this place."

Her mouth opened in protest and before she'd said a word he rounded on her with such blazing madness in his dark eyes that she subsided with nary a squeak. "No, Mistress Coventry, I'll not hear another word from you. You call *me* unnatural. You have a foul mind and a worse tongue, you godly bitch. Miscall my commanding officer's wife again and I swear to God I will cut your heart out. Mistress Babbitt is not my light o'love, and nor is this my daughter, though I wish to God she were. You have always thought the worse of me – *always*. I wasn't a bad little boy, Fly, I was not cruel or wicked, but you treated me like the worst of sinners. You *still* treat me like the worst of sinners. I was little, and *your* duty – you're keen on duty, Fly, remember? – your duty was to guide me and to take care of me. And you never did. You hurt me and you frightened me. Whatever I did was never quite good enough, was it? Not dutiful enough. Not zealous enough. Not frightened enough, was I? You had to hold my hands in the fire just to show me what I might expect, when I burned for all eternity. I was *five*, Mistress Coventry. I can't even recall what I'd done that condemned me to such a fate -"

"You stole!" she hissed at him, and he flung his head up like a spurred horse.

"I was a child, sister! What did I steal of such import? An apple? A spoonful of honey? A handful of raisins? It was hardly the unforgivable sin! Do you remember when I was sick, Fly? When I was little, and fevered, and miserable, and crying for my mother? D'you remember what you did, my loving sister? You read the Bible to me. I thought I was possessed of *devils*, Fly. I was terrified. You told me I was sick because I had an unclean spirit inside me. I *begged* you to get me a drink and you prayed at me. For hours. Do you remember that? *I* do. Do you remember when I questioned the parson's doctrine – once, sister, I learned *that* lesson quickly enough – I questioned him on a point of theology because *I wanted to know*. Not because I was a stinking heretic, or a miserable unbeliever. Because I did not understand, and I wanted to. I was almost grown up then, I could think for myself. Do you mind that time? Making me stand in the corner of the hall with my face to the wall, while you ate your supper, and you did your mending, and your good husband preached at inordinate length. You said I was not to look on you whilst my spirit was still haughty. Well I'll tell you what, Fly, there's nothing like pissing your breeches at the age of eleven because you may not leave the room, to teach a boy humility."

"Then I failed, did I not? My arm was not strong enough –"

"You left that to your bloody husband, mistress, and his was plenty!"

"And your women, Thankful? Your whores, and your drinking, and your lies? You are *wicked* – you were a wicked boy, and you are a wicked man, stinking with corruption!"

"*Wicked*? Because I wanted to laugh? Because *someone* had to want me there, even if it was only for a night? Well, sister, I was a rebel then, it seems, and I am yet a rebel and by God's grace I shall remain so. And if the Lord has any mercy whatever then *you*, mistress, will burn in hell for all eternity for what you have done in His name. Not me. You are a bitter, twisted, *sinful* woman. You are more unnatural than ever I was, for *you should have loved me*, and you did not. I would have forgiven you everything, Fly, if you had *once* put your hands out to me, and taken me up and kissed me, and said I was dear to you. Instead, you hurt me, and you frightened me, and you shamed me as often as you could, and I will never forgive you, Fly, never. I would call you evil, but there is not sufficient feeling in you for evil. I want you gone from this house."

And then while she stood blotchy-faced and gobbling with rage at him, which didn't bother him at all, and while Thomazine's little face crumpled like paper because she didn't understand and she was frightened and that was unbearable, Russell took his sister by the arm and escorted her from the parlour, with force. Het looked at him, white-faced. She said his name once, and he heard her, but he couldn't stop. Was sorry, but could not. Fly cursed him, she lay full-length on the cobbles outside where he'd pushed her and cursed him with every plague under heaven and a few he thought she might have made up on the way over, and Mattie Percey brought her horse round from the stable without so much as looking at her, though he wouldn't touch her to put her up into the saddle, and the manservant who'd come with her had to dismount and do the necessary.

She had a great smear of good dry Essex dirt down the front of her bodice and as she shook her skirts over the saddle another cloud of dust puffed loose. "May God curse you – may you burn in hell for all eternity, you nasty, vicious, thankless –"

"I heard," Russell said, without looking up. "Learn some new ones, Mistress Coventry. You're boring me."

His head was beginning to ache. More than anything – more than Fly's approval, which he wouldn't get and didn't want – more than even to slope off into White Notley and get viciously drunk – he wanted someone to be at his back. He wished to God Het *was* his wife. Be *someone* who gave a snap of the fingers what became of him. Fly put her heels to her poor old mare, who threw her head up with a blubbering snort and started across the yard at a brisk trot, her hooves slithering on the cobbles.

She didn't look back, and as soon as she was out of sight Russell slid down to the cool stone flags of the hall, back against the warm, rough wood of the open front door, sat with his head on his knees and took deep, shaky breaths.

"Bloody hell," Percey said, sounding alarmed. "Botty owd bitch. *That's* your sister, Hapless?"

"Not any more," he said, and laughed. "Reckon she's cast me off, Mattie."

"Count your blessings, mate. She married?"

"Widow. That's what she came for. My duty, you see. Four Ashes needs a man of the house. Puppet, more likely. Not me, Mattie, not me. Not now and not ever again."

"Well, what'd she come all this way for to tell you that? Couldn't she have just written?"

"She did. I burned it. She can go to hell, the vile-minded bitch. And the house can burn with her."

Mattie, orphaned Mattie, whose family consisted of Het and Hollie Babbitt and, Russell was beginning to suspect, of the neat and pretty nurse Doraty, looked blank for a minute. And then he said again, "Bloody hell, Russell."

"Well, Mattie. Behold the happy Russell family. I thank God I am the last living. At least that particular blight on the earth will be blotted out, with my demise." He paused. Squinted up at Percey, at his look of wary incomprehension. "*Death*, Mattie. Give us a hand up, will you?"

"Stop being so bloody morbid, Russell. You're not going nowheres till we got that colt of Tyburn's broken in. *And* the sheep sheared."

"And the quarter-day accounts to cast, Matthew," he said primly, and then grinned. "I was not planning to assist with the sheep-shearing, mind. I imagine with my somewhat haphazard sight I should be more hindrance than help."

"You can count 'em, can't you?"

22 - A Wish for Joy

He had in the back of his head the idea that he would, quite calmly and with care and consideration, count what coin he had in his pocket, and if it wasn't sufficient, the hell with it, he'd take the fiddle he hadn't touched since Babbitt's wedding and he'd go into White Notley and he'd drink himself stupid. And he might come home again, or he might bait someone into knifing him in a gutter, or –

Or Het might decide that she was going to birth the second Babbitt infant somewhat precipitately and keep him run ragged for the next eighteen hours, not knowing if he was coming, going or been and scared cold-sweaty.

He knew he was a bloody poor substitute for Hollie, she actually *called* him Hollie, when she wasn't trying to break his wrist. The goodwife who was dealing with operations sent him out. He came back with his sword belt, and he put the sword under the bed, as directed, to cut the pain, and then he handed her the thick leather of the hanger to bite on and he ran like hell.

Sitting on the stairs with Thomazine and he wasn't sure which of them was crying the harder, Zee listening to her mother howl the house down or Russell who was frightened witless. Never seen a woman in travail before. Knew about the preliminaries, he wasn't stupid and nor was he innocent, but – before God, if this was punishment for the sin of Eve, Eve must have been a thoroughgoing villain, and he wasn't sure he cared for any God who meted out that kind of punishment on Het Babbitt, who deserved none of it. She had been kind. Kinder than he deserved, and she had said nothing about that afternoon, just rested her hand on his shoulder briefly and said nothing. Thomazine had been afraid of him, when he'd come back in. That had hurt him.

It hadn't lasted, the child was too fond of him for that, which still astonished him. (So you knew *nothing,* Fly.) And eventually the pair of them settled into the window-seat at the top of the stairs, where the landing took a sharp turn, Russell with his back against the bumpy window-glass and Thomazine buried in the curve of his arm with her hot, wet, snotty little face in his shirt. She snuffled. Like a hedgehog. She weighed a good hundredweight and she was absolutely limp in exhausted sleep. His left arm was tingling under her weight, the glass was cold at his back, and he was too tall to quite fit on the windowseat. It didn't stop him, and he fell asleep anyway.

It was something near dawn, a warm, beautiful late summer dawn, and the sun was coming up over the river. Doraty the nurse was kicking him in the ankle, which seemed a harsh way of rousing a man. "Mistress wants you," she hissed fiercely, and Thomazine stirred and mumbled against him and he held her tighter, not wanting to drop the child. "Give her to me."

She was, the midwife said, a beautiful baby. Russell thought she was beautiful, certainly, with her folded-up little red face, so comically cross, and her milky blue eyes and her wet black hair. "Look at her little hands," he said faintly, and Het laughed at him, but he'd never seen a baby so small before, let alone had one placed carefully in his own clumsy, much-too-big hands. The idea that the child had tiny pink fingers and tiny pink perfect fingernails somehow made him feel all hollow inside. “What shall you call her, mis- Het?”

He thought he probably ought to start calling her Het. He was just about getting the feeling back into his fingers after her grip. He thought that informality might now be permissible. Het was propped up against a mound of pillows, pale, her freckles standing out like spilled gunpowder, but lovely. As lovely as her daughter. *Daughters*. “What do you think, then, dear?”

The tiny new one stretched, her little mouth smacking, and he handed her back to the nurse as if she was a hot coal.

"Joyeux," he said. “Happy. For I would wish her that, if I could wish her nothing else.”

23 - And Justice for All

He was filthy and he had been more fragrant in his time, stinking to high heaven of sweat and acrid burned wood, and he looked pretty much what 'Lije called him, a ragged moss-trooper. It ought to have bothered him but instead he stood in Fairfax's quarters - again - surreptitiously trying to itch at a long raw weal where Not-Hapless had scratched him in play, and thinking what else he could be doing with the time.

"Once again, sir, a messenger was unable to locate you."

Not expected to say anything, so he said nothing. What he *had* been doing was skulking with Rainsborough. He was hardly likely to drop Rainsborough in it and say as much. They were doing nothing wrong. Just talking. Passing the time of day, setting the world to rights, over a pot of ale and in Rainsborough's case, that appalling stinking pipe. There was a few of them met, now. An odd, mismatched lot, senior officers, ranters, independents, firebrands, plain troopers, preachers, administrators. Talking, no more. Just some lads who were fed up with being treated like dogs and wanted to sit down in the warm and have a moan about it. Funny, it said a lot in the Bible about the relationship of masters and servants. Book of Deuteronomy was full of it. Paying your servants' wages to time, because they were poor and counted on it. (He'd seen the state of Drew Venning's boots. By God, they were poor.) By reason of the multitude of oppressions they make the oppressed to cry: they cry out by reason of the arm of the mighty. Seemed a bit off to Hollie, that the masters in Parliament, most of whom had plenty, were sitting on it. The sun had *definitely* gone down on Parliament's servants' hire, despite their setting their heart on it. And there was not a few of the shoutier sort of the lads who did not take to being told how they could and could not worship, they seeing it as more than a bit two-faced to be bringing a King to bay for that very same crime. Lot of that going on at the moment, with the left hand giving and the right hand taking away. Still, they couldn't do you for thinking -

"And you may stop looking at me like that, Colonel Babbitt. You can be broken just as much for *dumb* insolence for it being spoken aloud." No, but they could have a bloody good go. "Well, sir, since you have finally troubled to resume your duties, I have some forlorn hope that making them more onerous may curb your rebellious streak somewhat."

He still said nothing, but his head came up and he gave Fairfax a long, thoughtful look. And then since the Commander-in-Chief of the Army seemed to be deliberately provoking him, he said, "Why are you doing it? Why d'you keep having a go at *me*?"

"Because you are a poor example to the men, sir."

He'd asked for that. And Fairfax wasn't wrong. It still felt like he'd been punched in the belly, though. His mouth had gone rather dry, suddenly, and the old Fairfax, his friend, would have told him to sit down and given him what-for and told him to buck his ideas up. "I - thought - we were," he couldn't help it, he was small again and in the dark with the chamber door closing that he might meditate on his sins, "we were *friends*?"

"Ah, God, Holofernes, when will you understand! *Forget* your previous service. This is not war as you have known it, when you were *playing* at soldiers, in the Low Countries. It's nothing to do with friendship. I'm doing a job. My *duty*. Lieutenant-General Cromwell would make this Army into a swift and terrible instrument of the Lord's justice, and I'm sorry if that doesn't fit with your somewhat independent ideas. As it is I cannot trust you, Hollie. I cannot rely on you to carry out orders, I cannot rely on you to *obey*. You are a law unto yourself, and there is no space in the New Model for an officer who will not obey *without question,* do we understand each other? You *are* my friend. You will, God willing, always stand my friend. Tom Fairfax and Hollie Babbitt have seen too much service together to be any other than dear friends. The Commander-in-Chief of the Army of Parliament and his Colonel of Horse are not, I fear, currently at an understanding."

"But," Hollie began, and Fairfax swung on him with his eyes ablaze.

"Aye! But! It's all I ever *hear* from you! I give you more rein than any other officer in this Army. But you are *ungovernable*, Hollie! Stubborn, and wilful, and intemperate, and you surround yourself with staff as - *subversive* as you are yourself, and then you wonder why you're better-liked by the common soldier than you are by your peers! I am not stupid, Holofernes, I know your father is still preaching, I choose to wink at it because I can't be bothered to fight with *both* of you. And you *will* not make this Army a figure of fun by continuing to appear with that damnable bloody cat on your shoulder, because I have found it a new home."

It was a cat. It wasn't even his cat. It belonged at Eastover. It was a stupid and unmanly thing to have to put your hand on the edge of the table and brace yourself till you felt splinters nip your palm, and try and remember to breathe. "*My* cat?"

"Not any longer, Colonel Babbitt. An Army on campaign is no place for a child's pet. It was cruel in you to even think it might be. I have requested that one of the servants at Audry takes that misbegotten animal to its place of new residence in your absence."

"You have taken *my* cat - away? Without asking me? Without even the courtesy of telling me, first?"

"You are being ridiculous. There is work to be done, sir. You have a new troop to take under your command. I always meant to replace Captain Chedglow, and now would seem an apposite time, since in your case idle hands seem to be the Devil's workshop. We appear to have acquired some new recruits since Bridgwater - some rag-tag band in the previous service of the Earl of Newcastle, who have seen the error of their ways. Well, you can take them. Breaking them in should keep you out of mischief. You are dismissed, colonel. *Try* and stay within hailing range of the camp until your new captain arrives."

24 - Old Soldiers, Sweetheart, are Surest

He felt so miserably lonely, with his unpawprinted paperwork in neat, unmolested piles on the table, and Luce sprawled in a chair by the window with a silly grin on his face, humming under his breath. Getting his belly rubbed regular didn't seem to have took the poeting out of the brat. He was worse than ever. Fortunately Gray preferred action to words and Luce's opportunities to find another rhyme for Gabrielle than what Hollie suggested, were somewhat limited.

(He couldn't see the problem, himself. He hadn't suggested it had to be a *bad* smell.)

Venning and Toogood were as thick as thieves, or as two short planks, depending who you asked. Tinners the dog seemed to miss the kitten, snuffing round Hollie's quarters for about half an hour, and then had given up with a canine shrug and gone off to bother some rats. Gray and Luce seemed to have a bloody funny definition of discreet, though it was rather endearing that she'd taken to lolloping like Lucey did with her hands behind her back, she taking great big bouncing strides and he beside her, best part of a head taller, trying to take fairy-steps so she could keep up.

Like Reading, then, all over again. He remembered feeling this lonely, sitting in a tent laying siege to the King at Reading, in the early spring, what would it be now - three years ago? With Mattie Percey sat outside the tent-flap, most of the time, as fierce on guard then as Tinners was with Venning. Luce at the other end of the tent scribbling, not much change there, except there was considerably less romantic sighing these days. There'd been no Russell, in them days. He'd been running the affairs of the Earl of Essex with a somewhat shaky hand. No Het, either. No Thomazine. That wasn't true, Het had been there, a little bright thing in the back of his mind while he was up to the knees in freezing mud at Reading, but he hadn't thought he'd ever have her as his own. And now he had half a letter written to her and he thought he ought to say more but he felt a bloody fool, with Russell there with her. She wouldn't want to be bothered with romantic. Even if he could write romantic. Could've asked Luce, but he suspected that if his wise, practical wife suddenly started getting epic verse detailing how her loving husband burned with desire for her, she'd start asking questions.

It wasn't to say that he didn't, mind. He'd just prefer half the troop were not aware of it. But he missed her. Not just the wise, practical side, but when you had the misfortune to share a tent with Luce and his whispering and rustling when he thought you were asleep, you did come to miss – the other. Het in her sensible stout flannel nightgown, sat cross-legged on the end of the bed with her bare feet tucked underneath her and her hair loose down her back, trying to feed him bread and honey by moonlight. Messy operation, that had been. Gray and Luce didn't seem to have much fun about it, from what Hollie had been obliged to overhear. All a bit earnest and passionate and aye, well, that was all well and good, but it wasn't so nice as bread and honey in bed. Started with bread and honey, and ended with very sticky and giggly loving, and – Thomazine, he rather suspected.

"Eh, reckon I could live here, man. It's lush."

The unknown speaker was right, and Hollie stopped brooding and sat up, frowning, knowing that voice. Hollie had quite took to Dorset himself. Somerset was a bit *too* flat, *too* green, *too* safe for a lad off the Lancashire moors, who was happiest with a bit of wildness in the landscape. Dorset was all curves and unexpected hollows, with just the veriest hint of rock under the softness. Bit like a certain lass of Hollie's acquaintance. He heard Sergeant Cullis's gravelly laugh outside. "Bloody hell-fires, talk about bad pennies!"

"That be it. How ye doin', then?"

If he hadn't recognised the cannonball-round head, as close-cropped as a bowling-green, and the cheerful pink countenance of his old Royalist counterpart Captain Simon Betterton, he'd have recognised Betterton's raking bay horse by the big white scar on its shoulder. Lije Babbitt had doctored that wound two years back, when Betterton's troop had been quartered out in the inimical surroundings of West Yorkshire surrounded by hostile natives. Back when the war had been *fun* – playing knock-a-door-run against the Royalist garrisons, wild raiding parties, no one hurt, just a lot of daft, giddy boys pulling stunts on each other. Before the New Model Army had made it serious. "All right," Hollie said, and meant it. "'M all right."

"Yon glum laddie back there said as he'd put me up with a right rum bugger of a colonel. That's never you, is it?" Betterton didn't wait for an answer.

His eyes were bright and childlike with honest awe. "Not telling me you're a colonel? *You*?"

"Reckon so."

"Aw, man! Well *done*!"

And Betterton – no, *Simon* – punched him in the arm, hard enough to hurt, and stood grinning at him, all keen and happy. "Eh, I reckon I'm gonna *like* being a Roundhead, man."

"Haway," said Hollie, in his best approximation of a Tyneside accent, "and shite. Thee always *was* a bloody crop-head, tha baldy-headed bugger. Tha's got more hair on thy top lip than on thy head. Here – Cullis – see this bugger fed, will thee? I see *Newcastle* never put no food on thy table –"

"Ah, no, Hollie, never say that, lad, no. He were good to us, when he could. He done right by this troop. *He's* not to be blamed." The way he said it, implied that someone else was to be, though. Another dissenter in the ranks? And then his face brightened again, the ends of his moustache turning up in pleasure. "D'ee know what we're about, then, sir?"

There was precious little for a company of horse to do, sitting outside a castle in pearl-cloudy Dorset twiddling its thumbs while the artillery laid it flat, a stone at a time. Mend tack, groom horses, gossip. Tell tall stories. Luce found a stone snail-shell, the size of an apple, just lay in the grass, and brought it home to Gray. Betterton said there was hundreds like that on the beach at Redcar when he'd been there the once. Lije sniffed and said the pair of them was heathens and didn't they know that was from before the Flood when there was giants in these parts, so obviously it was a giant's bone. Gray had just flung her head up as if they were going to wrest the keepsake from her by main force and held it to her breast and said nothing. She was getting a breast, too, these days. Feeding and not fighting was agreeing with her.

The King was, not to put too fine a point on it, stuffed. Goring was on the run, and the West Country was about all His Majesty had left. Be all over by Christmas. It wasn't precisely raining, and it wasn't precisely dry, the air was full of a fine, soft mizzle that drenched you if you sat out in it all day, but it wasn't cold.

"Rosie."

"Hm?" There were worse ways to spend an afternoon than sat with your back up against a tree and your eyes closed, listening to a castle full of Malignants being demolished brick by brick. It was quite restful. Blossom, tethered fifty yards away, had his head down in the grass and wasn't batting an eyelid as the full weight of Fairfax's artillery, and some of the King's that he didn't have any further use for, came to bear on Sherborne Castle. He yawned hugely.

"Rosie, is 'ee minding me?"

"Mm? Every word, Drew. What?"

He could see Venning's cracked boots just at the edge of his sight. A slight shuffle, and then a little crow-hop as Venning edged closer and gave his commanding officer a swift, surreptitious dig in the hinder parts. "Get up, you lollopin' gret mawkin!" he hissed, "Cromwell's looking for 'ee!"

And so he was on his feet, with bark all down the back of his coat but upright, scowling fiercely into Blossom's mane when the Lieutenant-General arrived. Cromwell was at as much of a loose end as Hollie, but being purposeful of nature and square of build he tended to look like he was busy even when he was just advancing on a mate with a conversational glint in his eye and a half-eaten wedge of bread in his hand. "Got a job for you," he said, and Hollie stepped out of spittle-range quite reflexively and let his horse take the crumby impact.

"Ah - sir?"

"Keen on Clubmen, isn't 'ee?"

"...sir?"

"Want to round a few up for me, lad?"

He waved a hand at the wary troop around them. "Fetch this lot, have a bit of a jaunt over Shaftesbury way. Nice run out for us – have a bit of a leg-stretch. Can't speak for your boys, Rosie, but my lads are champing at the bit to see some action. No place for horse, this." He scowled absently at the castle walls, or what was left of them. "I'll not have it, Rosie," he added, perfectly conversationally. "Not having them running around like – anarchists. They want teaching a lesson. They should be *helping* the Cause, not begrudging us a few cows or half an acre of wheat here or there."

Hambledon Hill was an unchancy place, rising above the thin mist as the rain thickened. A freakish hill, rings of man-made terrace put there for some ungodly purpose and abandoned, desolate in the middle of empty fields, with only that one-horse village standing sentinel at its foot. It didn't bother Tinners, who went off rabbiting in an abandoned ecstasy and would not be recalled, to his master's despair. The dog saw no ghosts, clearly. Even Venning, who happily admitted to no imagination whatsoever, muttered that he found the place eerie, too quiet.

"Won't be quiet when us lot get there," Toogood snickered at his side, and that had raised the company spirits briefly, and Hollie had said as much, and then Luce had unsettled everyone by glancing warily sideways and muttering, "It's not the *troop* spirits I'm worried by."

A happy lot they were not, unwillingly superstitious and trying to pretend not to be: something like a thousand men trying to make as little noise as possible in case they woke the ancients who had lived here a thousand years ago. A blackbird came out of the thicket almost under Blossom's nose with a cackling alarm call and the brown horse reared, and Hollie went down the side of its neck swearing, and he even did that quietly. Hambledon Hill was not a place where you could raise your voice. Gone cold, suddenly, and he felt all the skin shrinking on his bones. A muttering, far off in the mist. An unearthly wailing –

"Ah, Christ, they could've picked a cheerier one," Venning muttered, as he made out the words of the twenty-second Psalm emanating from the Lieutenant-General's own Lovely Company.

"If they don't buck their bloody ideas up, I'll forsake 'em myself," Hollie said tartly. "At the gallop."

As they mounted the hill, and the mist started to clear, it became evident just how many Clubmen were encamped there. "Just one or two," Toogood said sarcastically. "No support for that faction, about here. *Not much*."

One or two thousand, more like, and then twice that. Plain, weathered country faces, turning from the upper terraces of the unchancy hill. Flashes of white cockades in hats, as heads turned towards them. No flash of light on blades or musket barrels, because they carried none – only wooden clubs, or billhooks, or scythe blades. “On my command, gentlemen,” Cromwell roared, abruptly, and Hollie, seeing the zealous light of the Lord’s work in the Lieutenant-General’s eye, caught Luce’s eye and said, “Fuck that. On mine. Go.”

The colours came up with a snap – ah, God, he’d forgotten how much he liked that sound, in Luce’s absence: that crisp ripple as the silk caught the breeze, and it must be something in the brat’s wrist action for Hollie surely couldn’t do it himself. Blossom’s head up and his quarters gathered underneath him, stumbling over his own feet as ever but stolid and steady and going like water flowing downhill, unstoppable. A malevolent grunt from Gray’s iron-grey gelding as she leathered him with her heels and the buckle end of her rein, trying to urge him into speed, and Pig just put his head down and pounded along at a bone-shattering trot and would not charge no matter how much she kicked. Russell’s white-faced bay horse with his nose in the air, a weird flash of white in the dusk as the lieutenant’s distinctive horse bounded forward, unsettled by the tearing sound of unrolling silk. Odd, still, to see big bay Thomas without Hapless, but Luce was managing him well enough, even one-handed.

The staff of the colours brushed Hollie’s knee to his left, and – he glanced sideways – Venning and big black Samson at his right, that was good, that was as it should be. The Lieutenant-General liked his troopers to charge knee to knee. “Close order, you sons of bitches,” he yelled over his shoulder, as Pig came barrelling through in the middle, hell-bent on keeping company with his comrades.

“Draw your swords!” Cromwell screamed, “show them a taste of Birmingham steel –“

"Don't you bloody well dare," Hollie said to his own troop. He sounded confident. He wasn't sure he felt it. His hands were sweating, and he thanked God for an armoured bridle-gauntlet that meant at least his right hand wouldn't slip on the reins. Sudden coldness about the spine because Hollie, if you cock this up, you're not only on a charge, but you're a murderer. Collecting Blossom right up on the bit, gathered like a bent bow, so tense he could feel the horse mouthing the bit, and then suddenly digging his spurs into the gelding's heaving sides. Tyburn would have put him on his arse for that, he thought, in a sudden moment of perfect clarity, and then the brown horse took off like an erratic partridge straight through the Clubmen's encampment, scattering their banners and their campfires. There was a howl of outrage from the portly gentleman in the clerical bands who appeared to be currently holding court on the summit of the hill, so Hollie grabbed a banner as he passed and went after the reverend gentleman with the butt-end.

Luce laughed. Luce bloody would. God bless Lucifer Pettitt. Hollie was harrying the reverend gentleman with one of their own banners, and then Luce wanted to play too, and next thing they were playing kiss-chase with the Clubmen leaders, prodding them not too gently, like smock-wearing footballs, from horse to horse.

Blossom was such a clumsy great raking beast, he simply barrelled through knots of stunned yeomen, bowling them like kayles. Hollie's lads had caught on: push and harry, take out of commission, but don't hurt. The Lovely Company were howling with mocking laughter, loving the humiliation of it as gentlemen farmers went skidding on the wet grass, slithering and bouncing and rolling down the slopes of Hambledon Hill.

It wasn't a fight. It was a comedy.

And nobody was hurt.

And even the Lovely Company were enjoying themselves, even Cromwell was having a high old time barging his horse's chest into fleeing Clubmen and knocking them hither and yon. Isaac Weston was thundering up out of the dusk, his feather-footed plough horse kicking up great divots of sod, cutting across Blossom to knock the reverend gentlemen staggering into several of his acolytes – taking four or five down in a struggling mound. "Cush pin!" he yelled, grinning like a fiend, "'s what they call it in Bristol when that happens, sir, cush pin –" And then he was gone again, cackling like a setting hen.

"Right, my lad, I'm having you," Hollie panted, prodding the reverend gentleman from the heap with the butt-end of the Clubmen's banner, and poking him rudely in the buttocks. "Roll 'em up, lads, bring 'em home!"

He ended up dragging the cleric – one of several, by the look of it, but certainly the chief troublemaker – by his collar-band, all the way down the hill. The man was no lightweight, and he wasn't being helpful. The weight of him was practically dislocating Hollie's shoulder, and Blossom didn't like it at all, and he wanted to lean over and say, "Don't you realise, you stupid bastard, *he* wanted to just put you all to the sword?"

Ah, Christ, death before indignity. He loved people like that. Made his life so much easier. Like a hole in the head.

He got hit, spat on, kicked, belted over the knuckles with a club before he had chance to wrest it off the bull-necked yokel who was glowering at him with intent, and sworn at in colourful expressions he reckoned they only ever used in Dorset. He wasn't alone – Luce had a long, shallow slash across his cheek where some bugger had had at him with a billhook. One of the lads had broken his hand. Just about all of them had taken some kind of a pasting. Toogood was loving it, this kind of impartial brawl being right up the Cornishman's alley. To cap it all, Tinners the dog decided to come back from his mission of rabbit-persecution, saw his master involved in hand-to-hand combat with some great hulking rural Hercules, and sank his teeth into the nearest breeches seat he could set fangs to, which was unfortunately Venning's, in the melee.

The clerical gentleman was quickly identified as the Reverend Bravel of nearby Compton Abbas. "And you're going to fuck off back to Compton Abbas and never darken my patch again, aren't you?" Hollie said down his ear, leaning from the saddle under pretext of holding him still by the collar.

"You dare touch a man of God in that disrespectful manner again, you great judas-haired heathen, and I'll kick that banner up your arse, boy," the Reverend muttered back without moving his lips. "Lackey."

Lackey. That smarted. (His hand smarted, as well, looking at his swelling knuckles, but he wasn't going to give them the pleasure of seeing him wince.) And being spoke to like that by a cleric, of all things. Just showed you what kind of bloody ruffians the Clubmen attracted. Well, Hollie was glad the minority of muddy, grass-stained buggers they'd got penned up in the church were going to be staying put, to meditate on their sins overnight. And he hoped it was cold and he hoped their bruises stiffened up. *And* he hoped the Lieutenant-General was going to give them a right good long-drawn-out ranting spittle-fuelled oration in the morning. In fact, he was going to see to it that Cromwell got wound up even before he went back to the village, and make *sure* he was properly in the mood for a good hour of incomprehensible spiritual enlightenment.

He *could* have just let Cromwell's Lovely Company massacre the Clubmen, in the name of godly order.

Instead, Hollie Babbitt found himself unwillingly sympathising with the buggers.

25 - All is Safely Gathered In

Essex
September 1645

"Chamomile lotion," Het said firmly, and looked up at Russell. "Honestly, young man, you truly have more hair than wit. Out in the full sun all day, and you so new-healed." She put the back of her hand to his cheek, and frowned. "I've half a mind to put you to bed, you know."

He said nothing, but he stood and looked down at her with what he suspected might be a silly grin on his face. Which was probably not pretty, but perfectly involuntary. She cared for him. She must have a care for him, to concern herself with what was, after all, a tiny touch of the sun.

"Thankful, dear, you are as red as a strawberry. Now go inside and fetch me the chamomile lotion from the still-room, and stop standing there blinking at me like a mooncalf!" She patted his sunburnt cheek kindly, and then gave him a little push. "Now?"

It had been a long day, and he had spent almost all of it under her kind eye, and at the end of it he was as sore and muzzy-headed and stiff as if he'd been in battle, and yet he felt strangely at peace. He'd never set to this kind of work at Four Ashes. He was a gentleman, not a farm labourer, Fly would have said, and set him back indoors, into that closed, stifling house, to mind his books and attend to his devotions. Oddly, he felt closer to God standing at a sweating horse's head while they loaded a cart with sheaved corn, than he did at his Bible. He had splinters of wheat-straw embedded in his palms, and blisters to his fingers, where the farmhands had been so desperate for aid that they'd allowed a soft-handed ninny like Russell to help. They'd laughed at him, and teased him raucously, and they'd been furious with his ineptitude on occasion, but by dusk, he thought he was learning quite a proficient flick of the wrist, tossing sheaves up on the wagon bed. By then he'd been as sweaty and bare to the waist as the lowest of them, and his shoulders burned every time the soft linen of his shirt grazed them. By the amber light of the setting sun, his skin looked burned-raw, an unflattering, peeling contrast to his sun-bleached hair, and he didn't much care. Het Babbitt had walked alongside him, cool and neat in her soft sage-green linen gown, her dear freckled face speckled with sunlight through her wide-brimmed straw hat. She had been proud of him. Thomazine had been proud of him, and he'd carried her on his burnt shoulders all the way from the Hundred Acre field, which had hurt like hell, especially when she'd bounced with the sheer delight of it. Even Doraty and the new baby had smiled at him, with real kindness - even though Doraty had claimed that little Joyeux's happy grin was wind. Which of course it was not, the tiny child being the best, brightest, dearest unsister a young man could wish for - save only Thomazine, of course.

Het had passed him the jug of lukewarm barley-water with her own hands, and Thomazine had pottered the length of the field, though the sharp stubble scratched her little bare legs under her skirts, to bring him a crumbled pasty in a napkin. Which she had then shared with him, the little poppet. The rest of the men had enjoyed an hour's rest in the full heat of the blazing sun, drowsing in the shade of the hedge. Russell had not enjoyed such liberty. His hour of rest was spent with Thomazine, admiring the treasures she had collected through a morning's harvesting – a field-mouse's empty nest, a white pebble with a hole through it. A garland of wilting flowers which she had painstakingly knotted for her head, and then expected him to complete when her little fingers grew tired. He had one forlorn corn-cockle tucked behind his ear, where she'd thrust it, and a fistful of broken daisies in his waistband. He had a suspicion he looked a proper figure of fun, but he was too tired and rather too happy to care.

The barn was full. The sheaves were stacked in the fields, and the long trestle tables were piled with fragrant loaves and great wheels of sheep's cheese and roast meat. He hadn't realised he was so hungry but suddenly he was, and the sharp smell of spilled cider and new bread and hot meat made him slightly dizzy. Ben Warriner was laughing at him. "Bit sharp-set, then, Russell?"

"Mm," he agreed indistinctly, through a mouthful of bread. Swallowed. Too big a mouthful – choked. "Starved."

"Not a bad day's work. Make a man of you yet, soldier-boy."

He checked, quickly, to see if either Het or Thomazine was watching him. (If he should be so lucky.) Neither of them were, so he gave Warriner a stern look and a rather self-consciously raised middle finger.

Warriner smacked one callused heavy hand onto the sunburnt back of Russell's neck, and he yelped like a stepped-on dog, and various heads turned around the trestles, and various people laughed. Just for a heartbeat he went cold and stiff – what were they looking at? what was so comic about him? – and then he saw Het glance his way and smile, and that was all right, all was as it should be, and so he laughed himself. And then he picked up his wooden plate, piled with bread and cheese and apple pasty .He ignored the ribald comments about preferring to sit with the girls, and the whistles and the cat-calls. He ignored the giggles of some very silly young women from White Notley as he passed, being very well aware that any attention from that quarter was meant in pity, or humour. He held his head up high and he went and sat between Het and Thomazine, and Thomazine scrambled into his lap as Joyeux was nestled in Het's, so that he had to put his plate down, and then she rifled his supper for the choicest pieces – which he'd taken for her anyway, in fairness.

"You spoil that child, dear."

He had his nose buried in a mug of cider by then, so he made no response except to cock an eyebrow at her over the rim, and then realise he'd just downed a good half of the mug in one draught. Unwise. But thirsty.

He really ought not to have sat down: the muscles in his back and his shoulders were stiffening like wood. Het glanced at him sideways, watching him wincing as he struggled to cut up his pasty, and then quite deftly disarmed him and dismembered it. "I see we shall have to have you on light duties for a while, dear," she said, and he flexed his blistered hand ruefully. Which seemed to make her unaccountably sad, and he couldn't understand why, it wasn't so grievous a hurt – and then he remembered Hollie Babbitt's absent-minded trick of easing his stiff right wrist that same way, opening and closing his fingers till the bones cracked, and that made Russell unaccountably sad, too. Possibly it was the cider. Possibly it was the fact that out there in the warm summer dusk, someone had lit a lantern, and someone else was tuning a fiddle. Badly, as it happened, and even with his fingers skinned near enough to the bone he could have done a better job, but he'd not picked up a bow in more than two years. He'd thought he had no more music left in him, not since he'd lost his beauty at Edgehill, but his blistered fingers suddenly itched to tuck a fiddle under his chin again. Thomazine in his lap settled her head against his shoulder, rubbing her nose with her knuckle because she was a big girl now and did not suck her thumb. He rocked her awkwardly, in time with the squeaking music and very quietly, with his aching cheek – what? surely not too much laughter, Russell? – against her smooth hair, he sang to her. His singing was not the most tuneful, and nor was the song what a good and godly parent might have chosen for an infant daughter, but "Of all the birds I ever did see" was the only song he could recall in its entirety, at this moment. Her skirt was stained with apple-juice, her apron creased and dirty. She was hot, and heavy, and she smelt of fresh air and summer, and her little feet drummed idly – and painfully – against his shin. He held her a little tighter, and smiled, and closed his own eyes.

He wasn't drunk, and he wasn't as sunstruck as she feared he might be. (Which was not to say that he did not have the beginnings of the Devil's own headache, but it would bide.) He was just enjoying being in his own body, which sounded foolish, but was a thing of rare joy. Worked into exhaustion, being a thing of some use, and not a burden, and in the company of a lady he adored, and his bright little tibber in his lap; how could he not be content, even if only till the morning? Aching-tired, with a pleasantly full belly and a pleasantly muzzy head, leaning his back against the rough-plastered wall of the barn. Cool to the touch, on skin that was still sun-hot, and he put a hand up behind his head to savour the coolness of the stones there.

Nearly elbowed Het in the side of the head, and she moved aside just in time, laughing. "Gracious, Thankful! Be careful, you almost had my eye out, dear!" And then she stopped, and looked at him with her head on one side, looking him over as if he needed mending. (He did. He certainly stood in need of laundering, badly, after today.) "Are you all right, dear? You look a little flushed."

She had a particular expression that she only ever wore when she was in the business of ministering. It was a very slight frown of concentration, so that her straight brows drew together in the middle a little, and her lips would tighten, but in a good way, so that she looked fierce and kind and considering all at once, and it made him feel very odd indeed, that look. She put the back of her hand to his forehead again, her head cocked as if she were listening to far-off battle trumpets. "You're very hot. I'll get you something more to drink."

He wanted to stop her, as she hefted the baby and passed her to Doraty, but as he was weighted down by Thomazine, he couldn't, hardly. It was wrong for that dear, lovely, wondrous lady to be burdened with cares for such as himself. She should be made to recline on velvet cushions, wearing silks and pearls, and to only crook her finger to have her adoring servants running to her bidding –
"There we go, dear."

Her hand brushed his and it felt as if he'd plunged his fingers into a cold, sparkling brook. He jerked back with such shock that Thomazine stirred and mumbled sleepily, and even Het looked slightly taken aback. "Did I hurt you?" she said, and he shook his head fiercely.

"You could never hurt me, mistress. *Never*."

She sat down beside him again, shaking her skirts out. She had a scent of her own, though he was sure she'd not do anything so wanton as wear perfume. It was a scent of what he could only call cleanliness – not scrubbed-comfortless like Fly, but a sort of clean homeliness, the smell of a well-ordered household. Thomazine had it, too. Fresh linen and sunlight and soap. He felt her skirts brush his foot and it sent a fizzing tingle all the way through him, and he moved quickly away. "Are you quite *sure* you're all right, Thankful?"

No, he wasn't sure, not at all. He didn't know what he wanted: if he wanted to bed his commanding officer's wife, or if he wanted her to adopt him, or if he just wanted to lie in the dust and put his unworthy lips to the hem of her skirts and worship her. He turned his head and looked her full in the face, seeing the way the lantern light gilded the fine curls that peeped from under her cap just beside her ear, the tender lines about her eyes, the gold tips to her lashes. "Mistress Het," he said with as much dignity as he could muster, "you must know that I love you."

He'd never said that before, not to anyone. That felt odd, too. Frightening, and at the same time it was the rightest thing he'd ever said in his life, and he meant it with every shaking fibre of his being. Her dark eyes met his with a look of infinite tenderness. "Of course I know that, Thankful." And then she leaned forward and he thought for one wild moment that she was going to kiss him, right here, right in front of everyone –

And she did kiss him. Very gently, and very sweetly, on the forehead, the way she kissed Thomazine goodnight. "You know that I have been married before, dear? Before I met Holofernes?" She smiled up into his face. "He was a lovely man, my Stephen. He was dark-haired, and not very tall, and quite old when we married. I'm telling you this, dear, because if Stephen and I had had a little boy he would probably have looked *nothing at all* like you. But you might have been of an age with him."

"I don't *care*," he said.

"*I* care, Thankful. I care very much because I like you, and yes, of course I love you –" she cocked her head thoughtfully again, and then a little smile that was nothing short of wicked curved her lips. "There is, in my opinion, an insufficiency of people loving each other in this world, dear. As if it were something to be ashamed of. You are a very nice young man, and I am enormously fond of you, and Thankful – would you do something for me, if I ask it of you?"

"Anything," he breathed.

"There's a good boy. I know how it is, dear, it was exactly the same with Hollie, when he first stayed here. *He* had no head for cider, either. Although he didn't go about the place declaring his affections." She smiled, reminiscently. "Dear me, no, he did not. I practically had to nail him to the wall to get him to admit to *that*."

"Then he's a fool," Russell said fiercely, and a rather beguiling dimple appeared in her cheek as she smiled.

"I don't believe he would argue that point, dear." Her eyes crinkled at the corners. "We were talking about you, not my husband. I don't believe you would be so obliging as to go and put your head under the yard pump, but I imagine a good long walk in the moonlight would work wonders."

"Madam, I can assure you, you may direct me to walk to the ends of the earth and my heart would be none the cooler –"

"Well, that's a blessing, because I can see Alice Warriner from here and she's been trying to catch your eye for most of the night, dear. Ben's little sister, you know. It was remarkably remiss of him not to walk her back home before he went off with his friends. It's a lovely night for a walk, isn't it? I imagine it's just cool enough to be nice out, now. There's a lovely path down through the fields back to White Notley – now, as I recall, you come out just behind the churchyard. It's ever so quiet, dear. I imagine if you and Alice fell to talking, you could be gone for hours, and no one to overlook you." She leaned forward and patted his knee. "She's ever such a nice girl, Thankful. No silly business, now. No turning her head with piecrust-promises."

"Have I ever?" he said bleakly, and she shook her head.

"No, dear. No, you are much like my Hollie in far too many ways. Faithful unto stupidity, the pair of you. I should not care for you so much, were you not. Now go, and keep that girl company."

He had intended to be hurt, and affronted, and sullen. Sent away like a child, banished, cast off. Instead he found himself talking with Alice Warriner, who was a nice enough girl, in a cheerful, uncomplicated manner. She wasn't silly, or flirtatious, but sensible and plainspoken. Alice was a good, sound, level-headed maid, with a lot of glossy hair that could have been any colour in the moonlight, and a very determined mouth. He rather thought he liked her. She reminded him of a younger Het. He wondered if that was deliberate.

"You know my da won't have me married to a soldier?" she said, almost before they'd crossed the first stile, and he'd paused with his hand in hers, helping her down in all courtesy.

"I did not. But had I been in a position to consider marriage, mistress, then I take your meaning." He gave her a stiff smile, and she'd laughed and squeezed his fingers, quite naturally.

"No, sir, I don't believe you do. I said I wouldn't be *married* to a soldier." No sweethearting. He kept that in mind, as she kept hold of his hand. "I'll not lie with you, Master Russell," she said warningly, and he misheard her and said something wholly meaningless about how much he valued honesty himself, and she looked at him as if he was several kinds of idiot.

In all the best romances, he'd have ended with her in his arms, locked in passionate congress. Russell suspected that neither Alice Warriner nor himself were the stuff of high romance. They ended sitting side by side on a dewy bank behind the church, eating the remains of Russell's forgotten apple pasty that he'd tucked inside his doublet, with her head on his shoulder and his arm round her, talking about hazelnuts and sheep and apple pasties. It was sort of how he felt, with Thomazine in his lap. Not afire with ardour, but – happy. Comfortable. Content. *Ordinary.* As Het had said. She was a nice girl. He brushed his lips across her cool, smooth forehead, and she looked up and smiled at him.

It had been a long time since he'd sat in the moonlight with a girl. With any girl. He wondered what it would be like, to sit in the moonlight with Het Babbitt, and decided it would probably be very much like sitting in the moonlight with Alice Warriner, but without the complication of conscience. Her mouth was soft, and gentle, and tasted of apples and of herself. He kept his eyes open when he kissed her, to see if she might flinch, when her hand touched his scarred cheek.

She didn't.

26 - The Plague is A Fretting Leprosy

Bristol
September 1645

"You all right?" Luce said softly, and Hollie looked up and did not smile.

"Not really, brat."

There was not a lot he could say to that. It was late summer, a beautiful heady late summer, the days were long and the air was soft and from where they were quartered you could see the soft blue haze of the Bristol Channel. On a clear day, of which there were not so many, you could see the sails of the Parliamentarian squadron out at sea, blockading the port at Bristol. (Luce wondered where Colonel Rainsborough was, right this minute - if he was lurking out on some high point with a spy-glass and his musketeers, wishing he was out at sea, or if he had finagled his way back onto the quarterdeck and left the musketeers to their own devices.)

Hollie carried on looking at Luce for a minute, in silence, and then returned to looking out of the window.

From what Luce heard, and from what he could see, Bristol was not a happy place, under Prince Rupert's hand. And, despite what Hollie might have you believe, it was nothing to do with Rupert. He had exactly the same problems as Colonel Fiennes had had for Parliament, when Rupert had taken it from him at the beginning of the war. Not enough troops to man five miles of walls and fortifications. And at least Fiennes had had decent, well-trained men: Rupert had troops of raw, untrained Welsh lads, willing and eager, but as green as grass, poor souls. You could tell the ones who'd been around for a while, because they didn't scatter off the walls every time there was a shot from the Parliament guns.

Most of the prominent citizens were long gone, for which you couldn't blame them. It was just the ordinary people left. The ones who couldn't afford to be somewhere else, or who had no other place outside the walls of Bristol to flee to, or no one to take them there. People who couldn't afford to leave their lives behind and run like hell. It was a sobering thought.

"What's up?" It sounded such a stupid question, and it wasn't. Everyone knew Hollie went a bit odd under siege conditions. How odd, was negotiable. "Usual?" Luce prompted, and Hollie shook his head and carried on looking in the direction of the Bristol Channel. He didn't even blink at the next artillery round, though it rattled the glass in the windows. "Hollie?"

"Hey? No. No, it's all right. Stop bothering me."

"Well, look, if there's anything you -"

"Cornet Pettitt." And when he called Luce by formal rank, Luce knew he was in trouble. *"Leave me alone."*

He went. He did not go scuttling back to Venning's company, to seek out Gray and have a good moan, tempting though it was. She was his wife, and his helpmeet, and all, but he wasn't entirely sure that Gray's response would be helpful, given her somewhat ambivalent feelings towards the colonel.

And Drew would probably suggest either taking Babbitt out on the hoy - *seriously* not helpful, in a small space, with both Fairfax and Cromwell on their necks, and his old drinking-mate Rainsborough just up the road - or offer to lead some kind of larky hit-and-run raid with Toogood, which might or might not be successful but which would certainly bring Fairfax on them down like the wrath of God. (Which also meant he couldn't vent his spleen on Kenelm, who was a lovely chap, but who could no more keep a secret if he thought a mate was in trouble, than he could grow wings and fly.)

Crossed Luce's mind that probably the most useful thing he could do was take himself and his conscience out for a good long walk out towards the village at Clifton and see what he could scare up in the way of extra provisions. It was a nice day. Even the dust on the road was soft and powdery. He thought about saddling Leonidas, but decided to let the horse have a day's rest, too. He'd see fire again soon enough, poor beast. It had been very kind of Hollie to let Luce have that very, very handsome roan stallion in replacement for the red mare. Luce had named him Leonidas after the King of the Spartans, a name he thought suitably military and masculine for that proud steed. He did wish Hollie wouldn't insist on calling the beast Leonid*arse*, though, just because he knew it got a laugh out of the troops. He sometimes had the impression that Hollie used bad language as much as he did, of late, purely for the shock value of it issuing from a senior officer in the Army of Parliament. There was still a deal of the old regimental rebel of the Edgehill days left in Colonel Babbitt, be he never so high in authority. It was a comforting thought.

Rupert might be confident that he had enough arms and provisions but - well, as Hollie was prone to pointing out with a degree of vengeful satisfaction, that was Rupert all over for you, wasn't it, the cocky little bastard. And see how cocky he was when Fairfax had his balls in a vice.

He *could* have took Gray. He knew Gray was supposed to be out on patrol, but he could have joined them. There'd have been the usual groans and catcalls if he'd turned up at the back, but he was getting a thick skin about it. And it wasn't like they went riding round holding hands or anything. So far as anyone knew, she was just a somewhat short trooper who happened to have a bosom friend who was an officer, and it was pure coincidence that Gray had asked to be transferred to Babbitt's company from Cromwell's. The only people who knew for sure that he was a she, were either invalided out in Essex or so busy trying to run an army that they weren't telling. Oh, and Lije Babbitt, but he didn't count. It was *that* sort of a day. If he had been just plain civilian Luce Pettitt, ambling knee deep through the lush green grass and brushing his fingertips through the lacy cow-parsley as he walked, he might have thought about taking some flowers home for *his wife*. (Six weeks, and he still liked saying that.) A wreath of buttercups and daisies, as fresh and sweet and unspoiled as she was. Roses, to spread beneath her feet.

- Strawberries, if he could find any, in this lavish garden of the West Country. Though, the darling girl, she said the one thing she really fancied was slices of salt belly-pork, fried crisp in a griddle over a wood fire in a field in the middle of nowhere, washed down with icy cold water drunk out of a nearby brook out of your two cupped hands. She reckoned black-powder was the only seasoning she needed to her breakfast. There were times he suspected that his sweetheart was possibly *not* the most romantic of lovers.

He was still about a mile shy of Clifton, when he heard hoofbeats on the road. No wheels, just trotting hoofbeats. One set. He hopped neatly off the road into the ditch and lay in the grass with the insects buzzing about his head, hoping without his hat his hair and the sun-bleached tassels of grass were of a close enough colour not to draw the eye. He had no sword, he had no plate or buffcoat. He had a pistol shoved into his belt and a pouch of shot at his waist. He'd been told often enough that he might be daft but he wasn't stupid. Frightened, his heart fluttering up into his throat like a hedge-bird, but at the same time excited, and rather unaccountably, *happy*, as he cocked his pistol and waited. With the oddest feeling that he might be about to do something daring, something heroic, something that would change the future -

"Oh for God's sake Hollie, do you know I could have shot you!" he yelled, sharp with disappointment as he straightened up out of his ditch. Hollie's raking brown horse took one look at the dishevelled heap of hay erupting from the undergrowth and went skittering across the track in a state of panic. "What the hell do you think you're *doing*?"

"Going home!" Hollie yelled back, yanking the horse's head up with a most uncharacteristic force.

"What - is it - Hollie, is it *over*? Have you had news? Tell me! That's marvellous!" And Luce was at the brown horse's head, wanting to stand in the road and hear all about this most marvellous of developments, his face splitting into a gigantic grin.

Finished. All over. "What happened? Has Rupert - what - the King -"

"Fuck the King, and fuck Rupert," Hollie said, and his voice was tight and shaky, "*twice.* Stand away from the horse, Pettitt. I'm going home. And Fairfax can shove his commission up his arse."

"What?"

"If you don't give over standing there quacking at me like some kind of benighted duck, sir, I will ride you down. Now get away from my horse." He gave the horse's reins a vicious jerk, and Blossom went half up on his hind legs, snorting with pain and distress, and then sprang forward like a clumsy ball from a cannon. Luce fell back, more astonished than afraid, stood blinking for a few seconds -

"You will *stand,* Colonel Babbitt!"

And just in case Hollie either hadn't heard or wasn't answering to his title any more, Luce took the pistol he'd been waving aimlessly around earlier, aimed it as high as he could over the brown horse's ears, and fired into the air.

Blossom went shying off into the ditch, with a lissom twist that was most alien to that lolloping great beast. Blossom wasn't expecting a ditch, and Hollie wasn't expecting his horse to acquire a sudden grace, and there was a brief moment when the big brown horse was perched almost heraldically on the lip of the overgrown gully before the bank gave way beneath his hoofs. There was a deal of squealing and thrashing, a flash of paler chestnut underbelly as the horse overbalanced, rolled, and righted himself.

It was over in a matter of seconds. Blossom heaved himself up onto all four legs, looking woeful and shaky. Hollie came up shortly afterwards, hatless and filthy. He looked fairly shaky himself, but there was a light of wild hilarity in his eye that made Luce brace himself for fireworks. "You little bugger," he said unsteadily. "Lucifer, you little - *bugger*. That is the second time you've pulled that stunt on me, you little sod."

There was a great streak of mud down the brown horse's sweaty shoulder, and he was standing with the tip of his hoof just resting on the grass, his head hanging to his grazed knees. Hollie heaved himself out of the ditch and ran his hand down the horse's leg. "Second time you've done *that*, as well, brat. I'll not have a sound horse left in the troop, between you and that bloody wife of yours."

But he was laughing, even if it was with an edge of hysteria.

"Are you all right, sir?" Luce said again, and he meant it, he wanted to know, because Hollie did not sound all right, he sounded right on the perilous edge of losing it altogether.

"No, I'm bloody not all right, brat, I've a bruise on my backside the size of bloody Somerset. Ah, Christ, Luce, I want to go home. I've had a bellyful. I just want to go home. I wish to God you *had* shot me. Not, you know, terminally. Just sufficient to get me home." He sat in the grass with his hair hanging in his eyes, and the brown horse took a shuffling step forward and lipped at the top of his head apologetically. "Sod *off,*" Hollie muttered, waving a hand at the beast's investigating muzzle. "I'm trying to be -"

"Malcontent," Luce prompted. "Or d'you mean choleric?"

Hollie looked up through a veil of tangled cinnamon hair. "God knows, Lucey. There's plague in Bristol. They say. And Rupert won't let 'em out.

That's all right, though, because all the nobs are out already. Apart from the bloody knob who's holding the place. *He* can come down with it, for all I care. But. They're just people, brat. They don't deserve this. At least at bloody Bridgwater I could go in and *help*. I might be big and cack-handed but if you tell me what end of a hammer is which, I can put a nail in straight. They're just - people. Even the bloody Malignants. I hope to God you've never seen the plague, close to, like I have. It's too hot. At least at Nuremberg it was cold and the bodies didn't stink. Well, not for the first couple of weeks, anyway. It's going to get ripe in there, lad. And once you've got the plague inside the walls it'll go through the city like a dose of cascara. I am too old for this shit. Or too soft. There's people in there, Luce, and we're going to wall 'em up alive to die just because His bloody arrogant Majesty won't be told no for an answer. And I can't. I just can't stand here and do nowt. I can't turn my back on them lot in there, and I can't stand here and watch *you* lot out here come out like the plagues of Egypt when we finally get in."

"But surely Fairfax is a good Christian man -"

"Fairfax, Lucey, was distracted when I asked him what he planned to do. And after the third time of asking, he looked up at me and he said, well, man proposes and God disposes. And I could've hit him."

Plague. Just the word made his belly squalmish. Plague in the heat of late August. Luce swallowed something bitter that seemed to have got into his mouth. "He plans to do nothing?"

"He plans to do but plenty, with a few bits of well-placed thirty-two pound shot. He's very sorry, but they should have chose their sides better. Made their beds and they must lay on them, the damnable

Calvinist bastard. Reckons it might shift Meinherr Rupert quicker, if he's sitting to his meat with a sauce of rotting flesh on the side. That is the correct military perspective, Luce. It's me that's gone soft, not him. I want to go home." He sounded like a forlorn child. "I want to see my girl again, Luce. I forgot what it's like to be clean, and civil. Not to sit across a table from someone wondering how long it's like to be before my estimable sire reads the Offices for the Dead over 'em."

Luce looked down at his hands, clasped rather uselessly on his knee. It was a funny thing. He didn't consider himself vain – Gray seemed to consider him well-favoured, and that was sufficient – but he did flatter himself that he had competent, deft hands. A little scarred about, a little callused perhaps, but gentle, and strong. He'd got quite good at mending, this last two years, he and Witless. Witless was yet a stuttering incompetent on the field, and he still managed to be fat, which took some achieving under siege conditions, but if you set him to a wound he was as gentle as a sucking dove. Luce had learned a lot from watching him.

What he had mostly learned was that if you had the skill to help, and the Lord gave you the capacity, it was a black sin to turn aside. He'd also learned that duty wasn't just obedience to orders. Parliament ordered him to oppose the King's men, and he did that, to the best of his limited ability. He remembered once furiously turning on his uncle Essex, when Essex had been Commander-in-Chief of the Army, early in the war. In the first wary days of friendship with Hollie, when the big redhead had been hurt almost beyond bearing by the loss of his best friend at Edgehill, and he'd gone to Essex and begged his uncle to give Hollie back his command.

You broke him, he'd said, *you* fix him.

And that was how Luce felt. He was, in part, responsible for the breakage that went on round him. (Not Hollie, not now. Hollie was almost wholly mended, almost all of the time. Auntie Het was the mending-est lady in Essex, and the neatness of her seams was legendary.)

Even though the thought of it made him feel sick and hollow inside, he couldn't leave those people to die untended. Not while he might be able to help.

It was his duty to do the mending, and he couldn't stand by and not do it.

"Er. No," was Hollie's considered response. And then, "Luce, I said no. It's my troop, and I don't often get precious about it, but I'm buggered if I'm going to go home to your auntie Het and tell her I let her nephew deliberately infect himself with a contagion. *No*."

"But –"

"*But* you have been married for less than two months. And you want to make her a widow already? What's *she* going to do, brat, if you end up boarded up in some bloody slum in the backside of Bristol? Who's going to take care of her then, Lucifer – me? I'm married already, I can't take her on. Venning's spoke for. Her and Toogood'd mar another couple. Cullis is too old. Reckon she could change her mind about Russell – that's if he's ever fit for active service again, and in any position to look after the lass? *And* we're assuming she's not already got your babe in her belly, Luce. Which the way you two go on, would not be beyond the bounds of possibility –"

"All right, all right, you've said your piece," Luce muttered, blushing furiously, "point taken, stop going on about it. But *you* said –"

"I said, Luce. *I* said. It's *my* job to make shitty decisions. Not yours. If *you* want to agonize about the fate of the rest of the bloody Army, get promoted, and then you can come back and sit wringing your hands over the buggers. Till then, how about you leave the agonizing to me. I get paid for it. *When* I get paid," he finished darkly, and Luce recognised that sudden grim expression and decided to leave well alone.

He also recognised Hollie bored and restless and rattling like a loose board in a gale, prowling the horse lines seeking for whom he may devour and springing unannounced inspections on the troops just to occupy himself. He quietly tipped the wink to both Toogood and Venning, who made sure from that point onwards they might be untidy but they were never unprepared. It teased Hollie almost to the point of madness, that the worst fault he could find with Venning's troop was that Tinners was flopped on a trooper's coat gnawing industriously on an elderly bone, and the offending trooper in his shirt sleeves in the late summer heat equally industriously buffing a burr out of his sword blade.

"He's looking for trouble," Venning said.

"He'll bloody get it, an' all, if he keeps this up," Toogood muttered. "D'ee know what, I thought I liked Rosie Babbitt. But he's one o'*they.* He's no different to all they other stiff-necked arseholes strutting around in charge – do this, do that, get your head shot off while I sit down over this way in peace and quiet. *Tosser*." He mimicked a limp-wristed officer's point, waving a languid hand in the direction of the walls of Bristol. "All right for he, ent it? Don't 'ee worry, my 'andsome, you leave it to Rosie, he'm *well* tight in with Black Tom and Old Noll."

"What?"

Toogood stopped with his mouth open. Hollie Babbitt might be big, but without plate, without harness, and without spurs, he was bloody quiet. And he was about two feet away, with his elbow on the backside of the big fleabitten grey Rabbit, where he'd been checking the horse's feet.

Tinners raised his head from his bone, his tail thumping against the baked ground.

"*What* did you just say?"

"Nawthen," Venning said, grinning hopefully. "We was just talking about –"

"Captain Toogood. Me and you need a word, my lad. 'S all right, Drew. It's in an *informal* capacity." Hollie tucked his hair behind his ears and grinned. It wasn't a reassuring sight. "If I need seconds, I'll take Luce. Not you. You can stand for *him*."

"I ent said nothing I don't stand by," Toogood said furiously.

"Sure of it. Now form your men up. No, captain, not in five minutes - now. You know what a forlorn hope is, don't you?"

"What?"

"You heard. Well tight in with Cromwell, am I? Well then, big gob, you can come along wi' me and see how well tight in I am. I want that god-damned rabble you call a troop ready for action. The rest of you lot are stood down. We're going in, Captain Toogood. Tonight."

It was a matter of pride that Toogood should have his troop formed up and ready before Babbitt had saddled his horse. It was touch and go, because the big grey gelding was picking his way carefully across the camp when the last of Toogood's men slid into place, wriggling his shoulders to settle his plate more comfortably and panting with exertion.

Hollie grinned again. "Well, well. So you had them form an orderly heap, then?"

"Order your ranks," Toogood snapped, and there was a snorting, squealing shuffle as eighty men tried to form themselves into an impeccable body.

The Rabbit tossed his head nervously as Toogood's colours flapped in a rising breeze, a badly-drawn white bird on a black background. "Company sparrow getting lively, is it?"

"That. Is a chough. Sir."

"It's a dead duck, Captain Toogood. Is what it is."

"You will treat my colours with respect, sir –"

"Will I? Going to make me, captain?" Hollie wheeled the fleabitten grey horse, leaning from his saddle till he was almost nose to nose with the Cornishman. "Withdraw your colours, sir."

"What?"

"You heard me. You'll be going in under mine."

Toogood looked round wildly, did not see Luce Pettitt. Possibly because Luce was biting his tongue at a distance of about a hundred yards, absolutely furious with Hollie and knowing that pig-stubborn judas-haired creature too well to push his luck. "*Yours*?"

"Mine, captain. It would appear that we make attack proper under cover of darkness. I have been tasked – by my *bosom companion* Lieutenant-General Cromwell, you understand – with a little bit of what I do best, Captain Toogood. A spot of light vexation. Since you seem to be in the business of pissing people off tonight, you would appear the most suitable candidate for the task. Now. You – you, trooper in the middle, grey horse –"

"Me?" the trooper in question squeaked.

"Your carbine is bloody filthy, boy. What'd you do, let Venning's dog have it? Twelvepence. And you there at the back – scruffy bastard in the dirty coat – same goes for you. I'll not have no bugger in my company turned out with harness in that state. Twelvepence."

Toogood went to protest. He got as far as calling Hollie a damnable hypocrite before he felt the stinging slap of a bridle-gauntlet across the cheek, and broke off with a yelp. "Because, gobshite," Hollie snarled, "mucky kit is ill-kept kit, and that's what's between you and six foot of West Country earth, d'you understand me? Fucking amateurs! And Venning – leash that fucking dog!"

29 - Red Sky at Night, Town's Alight

He knew it was coming for two in the morning, because in the still, sleeping, and possibly dead town of Bristol, the clock had just struck the three-quarter.

Toogood thought he'd got away with it. Cocky little bastard, thought because he was still here and strutting around unmarked, that he was back in Hollie's good books and he wasn't, he wasn't nothing like, just that the planned bit of poking-up hadn't taken place in the end because Fairfax had decided that he was bored with *Meinherr* Rupert's increasingly sniffy letters out casting aspersions on Fairfax's honour in the most dignified and respectful terms, and that instead he was just going to blow the damn' place to bits, starting round about now.

It was September, and that meant there was a bright, full harvester's moon hanging low in the sky, round as a cheese. "D'you reckon he's awake, then? Rupert?" Luce hissed, looking down into the lightless city, and Hollie smiled without much humour. "He fucking will be, in about fifteen minutes."

His palms were sweating. That was daft. He'd been a fighting man for almost twenty years, when he came to think on it, almost as long as Luce and Russell and possibly Toogood had been alive, which was a sobering reflection. He wished for Tyburn under him, remembering the restless power of the big black stallion between his knees, leashed taut as one of the old warbows some of them Welsh buggers from Bridgwater had talked about so fondly. Christ, *Tibs* was almost as old as Lucey. Well, the black horse deserved his retirement, then. Just meant that Hollie was stuck with the lolloping Rabbit, while Blossom was still laid up. There was only Blossom could fall into a ditch half way up the Clifton road - thank you, Cornet Pettitt - and strain a tendon. And there was only the Rabbit, who must be nigh as old as Tyburn now - overdue for his own retirement, or for the knacker's yard - who was big enough to take lanky Hollie.

He'd had a brief and stupid set-to with Disbrow, not an hour back, over something as stupid as Hollie wearing his bridle-gauntlet on the wrong hand. Disbrow had took exception to the way Hollie had it on his *right* hand, and not the regulation New Model issue left hand, to which Hollie could only say he was quite well aware he was doing it cack-handed but since he'd broke his wrist at Edgehill he was heartily sick of having to swap hands halfway through a battle because his right hand wasn't always reliable. And that if Disbrow used his eyes that was why he'd notice that Hollie tended to be way out on the left flank of his men, so he didn't take anybody's eye out fighting left-handed. And that it had took one of his lads bloody hours to swap the regulation issue armour over so it worked on Hollie's right hand, thank you very much, and he didn't care what it said in the bloody Soldier's Catechism, he wasn't going to get his damn-fool head shot off just so Noll Cromwell's eye was not offended by one of his cavalry officers fighting left-handed.

"You are independent-minded, sir," Disbrow had hissed, making it sound like an insult, and Hollie could only nod obligingly and then scratch at the gall on the back of his neck where the collar of his buffcoat rubbed him.

"And probably lousy," he said, just to annoy Disbrow, who'd gone poker-stiff and quivering.

"Be assured I will make a report of this to Sir Thomas!"

"What, that I'm cack-handed with a blade? Aye, and tell him summat he don't know. So unless you want the point of my sword up your nose, lad, I'd stop out of t'way."

That was the other thing, that gall on the back of his neck. It hurt. It didn't usually hurt, it was just a vexation, but in this heat, under a yard of most un-officerly-looking russet hair, it was wet and raw to the touch and it hurt like hell. It wasn't improving Hollie's temper, that every time he turned his head he had to stifle a yelp of pain. The Rabbit's head came up sharply, his stupid long ears pricked. There was something moving in the darkness.

What was moving in the darkness was a wholly unexpected barrage of artillery, which no one had expected, and which had most of the horses in Babbitt's troop panicked and squealing, put Gray on her arse and her grey gelding fifty yards away and bolting for home until Venning headed it off, and if Fairfax had been expecting a stealth attack he wasn't going to get one. In between the shattering thumps of the artillery pieces taking chunks off the walls of Bristol, and shouting and yelling from both sides of the wall, and Drew Venning's benighted dog yammering at being tied up out of the way, and Gray swearing prodigiously, and Lije Babbitt howling godly exhortations in his customary indiscreet roar - "Shut *up*, for Christ's sake!"

Oh, and Hollie Babbitt standing up in his stirrups yelling at his own troops to shut the hell up and let a man *think*, while the Rabbit went bouncing round in panicked circles whinnying. The temptation was strong to send one of the lads - probably Toogood, in the hope that he might have his head took off by an errant thirty-two pounder - to go and ask Fairfax what the bloody hell he thought he was up to, pulling that stunt without warning. Hollie had been stood at that council of war and nobody had mentioned unleashing hell on Bristol like *this*. Not for another half-hour. The city was beginning to be slightly better illuminated, lit up now from within by a deceptively homely dawn-like amber glow. Might have been a nice place, Bristol. Green and pleasant, probably, when most of the walls were still standing. As it was there was a very distinctive sound to a wall coming down, a sort of whispering, hushing roar. And Hollie hated it. There was someone screaming inside the city. Shouting. He didn't mind the shouting, but not -

"Red sky at night, town's alight," Venning said happily, and Toogood, thirty yards away in the dark, chuckled. "Red sky in the morning, town's still burning?"

A lot of screaming, now. And the smell of burning, drifting down on a soft late summer breeze that smelt homely, like woodsmoke and harvest and of roasting meat, and Hollie was aware of Disbrow's eyes on him and so he did not lean his face into the Rabbit's mane as he wanted to, he did not dismount and retch till he tasted *anything* but that greasy smoke in his throat. He rubbed his nose with his bridle-gauntleted left hand, inhaling the scent of sharp steel and sweaty horse and leather instead, and set his teeth. Not that anyone would hear his teeth chattering over the sound of Fairfax's siege guns laying Bristol flat, but that was Disbrow, twenty yards away, and nothing would give the Major more pleasure than to see Hollie Babbitt brought low.

"All right, sir?" Luce said at his elbow, and he turned his head slightly.

The colours hung limp in the brat's grasp, unmoving in the suddenly still warm air. "I'm all right," he said, and didn't mean it.

Something in Bristol collapsed with a sound like stiff paper crumpling, and a great shower of sparks flew dancing into the air, horribly festival. He forgot Disbrow, forgot Toogood's insubordination, and reined the Rabbit a stride back, as if that might take him further away from what was happening in the city at the bottom of Truebody's Hill. "Luce -"

"Sir." Not a question, more a statement of faith, the brat's knee against his own, and the brat's roan stallion solid and four-square against the Rabbit's flank. Hollie put his hand out blindly, touched the staff of the colours - a warm breath of air stirred the silk against his fingers and he swallowed a mouthful of bitter bile at that soft brush, soft as skin, soft as a dead woman's hair -

"Luce in all mercy shoot me."

"Er - "

"Lucey I cannot do this. I *can not do this*." Now his teeth were chattering, and there really was nothing he could do to stop it. The Rabbit was sidestepping anxiously because Hollie's hand was shaking on the bridle and the horse didn't know what he was being asked to do. "In God's name, Luce, put a bullet in me. I *beg* of you -"

Blood. And fire. And plague. And Margriete dead at the end of it, and a worn letter with his name on it, following him as inexorably as Nemesis -

- And the brat's white face turned to him in the dark, his pale hair loose on his shoulders, eyes as level and dark as the empty pits of a skull. "It's all right, Hollie," he said softly. "It's now. It's not then. I - we - *we*'re with you. She's fine. She's good. Russell's there, he won't let harm come to her." And then he smiled faintly, and the suggestion of a death's-head about his face vanished. "Or she won't let any harm come to Russell, one or the other. We are all good. We'll come about."

Hoofbeats, a wild yammer of voices, and a pagan yell of delight from Toogood. "He'm in, lads! Brace up!"

Noll Cromwell, his Fenland burr distinctive in the roaring confusion, coming down the hill at a tidy gallop. "Babbitt, is 'ee fit, lad? We're in!"

No. No, he wasn’t fit. And if it hadn’t been for the thought of Het and the girls, that small bright flame in the corner of his mind that still saw daylight, he'd have gone in with the intent of finishing it, just to have it over and done.

Or he'd have done it at his own hand. "Thee and Russell is not so unlike, in the end," he said aloud, and laughed shakily, and pulled the Rabbit's head up, and whistled his lads up like hounds to the hunt, to be about his business. And pray God, one day soon, it should be the last time.

30 - A City That Is Forsaken

"Hello," she said cheerfully at his elbow, and Luce jerked as if one of the flying splinters of Bristol masonry had caught him, and glanced round.

There was something mildly strange about being greeted by your wife going downhill at a collected canter, heading for a breach in the city wall where you could see black figures running and flames leaping. Even now, he still couldn't quite merge that lovely mental image of Gray as naked as a needle, dappled with shifting sunlight under the willow-trees on the banks of the Wagg Rhyne, with his current vision of her in buffcoat and boots, grinning fiercely at him over her shoulder as her iron-grey horse tried to get his nose ahead of Leo's on the downhill straight. "Gray, *will* you -"

Be careful. Slow down. Go gently. Luce thought he must be the dullest man in the Army of Parliament, betimes, and Gray never listened anyway as she pulled the Pig's blunt grey nose up and headed him for the tumbled stones of the breach in the wall, whooping joyously. She was one of the few people he knew who could ride competently enough to fire a pistol at the gallop. She did most things more competently than most men. Leo stumbled as the turf started to give way to broken masonry, his hooves clipping chunks of shattered stone out of the way. There was someone with a strong Fen-country accent yelling, his voice echoing from the broken walls. Cromwell, or Drew Venning? He never could tell the difference between those two -

Gray was gone, on her grey horse, clattering between the whining shot and the crashing masonry, and he could swear she was laughing. Someone behind her on a white-stockinged chestnut, a distinctive beast, one of her own troop, not his, Venning and his big black coming up at a skating gallop behind.

Babbitt with the reins round his wrist, a great black smear of blood down the side of his face from somewhere, looking wild-eyed and shaky but at least he was reasoning and responsive, or as he might put it himself, upright with breeches on. Luce couldn't help it. He did a quick, automatic head count, who was missing, who was hurt, who might need attention. He did it every time. He did it in his sleep, some nights. Toogood, dark eyes and white teeth flashing in his tanned face, reining his horse in with a quick glance of query - everything all right, is it? - before thumping his heels into Charles and sending the bay off at a clatter after Venning.

That benighted dog, yelping, with a frayed tag-end of rope at his collar where he'd bitten his tether through, scampering in the vanguard.

"He's fucked off into Bristol Castle, the little bugger," Hollie yelled above the whine of shot.

"Best fuck off after him, then, hadn't 'ee?" Venning yelled back. "Tinners - go home! Home, I say, boy!"

Tinners ignored him, leaping up at his master's boot as if he was just off out for a day's hunting, and Venning was grinning and trying to look disapproving and failing miserably.

Leo was a good horse, a sensible, good-humoured, reliable beast, but he wasn't fast, and Luce and the roan stallion were at that stage of their acquaintance where Luce might ask, but he might not always get. And that was fine, because when he dug his heels into the horse's flanks, Leo's head came up and he looked startled but after a second of bemusement he realised that he was being asked to pick up his speed into the mass of tumbled masonry and burning spars, and he went willing, his nose at The Rabbit's ragged tail as the troop plunged into the wreckage of Bristol.

There was a noise. Luce thought, afterwards, it was more of an absence of noise, a sort of waiting silence, a heartbeat between the soft roar that sounded like the distant sea, and the clattering, crumpling thud as the wall came down on the troop. Something hit him on the shoulder with a force that nearly had him from the saddle, and for a second he was capable of nothing more competent than hanging on to the rearing, panicking horse, seeing constellations of bright stars behind his eyelids. And then there was someone screaming - a woman screaming - a great cloud of thick, choking dust, tinted rose by the rising sun, that tasted of burned wood and old stone and clung to his throat so that he gagged. The whole of his left arm was one fierce yowling agony, but it wasn't broken, it served. His hand on the rein was steady, and Leo was settling, shuddering, his coat twitching as if he were bothered by flies, but settling. And the screaming was settling to a confused shouting, swearing, groaning, but whoever it was might be hurt but he had sufficient breath in his body to be calling Hollie Babbitt a ham-fisted bloody arsehole. And Hollie was whole enough to be swearing back at him, that North Country burr was distinctive enough to be reassuring.

There were still shots being fired, whining and zipping somewhere within the walls. But that was all right, and he was aware of a sense of rather shameful relief, because this troop was now out of commission, safe, intact on this side of a jumble of tumbled masonry, the battle was going elsewhere -

"For fuck's sake, Lucifer, are you just going to sit there gawping, or are you going to get down off that god-damned horse and *help*?"

Hollie at his knee. On foot. Covered in dust, his helmet off and a great bloody gash at his temple, streaked with blood and looking even more like the fifth horseman of the Apocalypse than he usually did. "Toogood's down. You're a bloody medic-apprentice - earn your pay!"

"Me?"

He dismounted, blinking. "What about Witless? He -"

"Witless, and the rest of the bloody company, are chasing after Rupert and probably in Bristol Castle by now, now stop asking dumb-arsed questions and *help him*!"

Head count. Automatic. Probably about twenty of them, this side of the rubble. It wasn't Toogood screaming like a woman. It was one of the horses, down. Toogood was sobbing, now, praying and swearing and crying by turns. Luce knelt at his side, feeling slightly sick as his fingers probed the jagged break in the Cornishman's forearm, splinters of bone sharp through the blood-soaked leather of his buffcoat sleeve.

"Hurts, then," Hollie said laconically, and the Cornishman gave a shaky laugh.

"Hurts like arseholes, my handsome."

"You start calling *me* handsome, mate, and I'll start reckoning you're fevered as well."

"Stay still," Luce said, "while I -"

"You got to be out of your mind, boy, you think I'm going to sit here and let you -" He sat up anyway, grey-faced and sweating, and then collapsed back against Luce's arm. "Ah, Christ, I can't -"

"I know you can't, you daft southern bastard. Shut up and do what the lad tells you, or I'll have you knocked on the head."

"Brandy," Toogood suggested, hopefully.

"In your dreams. When Luce's finished with you."

"You're a hard man, Colonel Babbitt." He grinned. There was blood at his mouth, and Luce must have blanched, because the grin widened. "'S all right, Lucey. Bit through my tongue when this bawky gret roust-about was hauling me out from under."

He struggled up again, whimpered like a child, and turned white under his tan. "Charles -"

"He's good. One o' your lads has got him. Sound as a bell, don't fret. Bit dusty."

The Cornishman's dark eyes turned to look for his horse. Came to rest, instead, on the freckled white bulk, heaving fitfully atop the fallen stones. "Rosie, thass -"

"Aye. I know. I'll *deal* with it, Kenelm. D'reckly, as you might say. Luce - you good?"

"Perhaps not the word I'd use, sir," Luce said faintly. Toogood's broken arm was swelling almost under his fingers.

"Don't 'ee cut that coat off, boy," the Cornishman warned him, quietly. "'Tis the only good one I got. I'll take it off myself."

"You are a brave man, Captain Toogood."

"I'm a poor one, Cornet Pettitt. Now. Heave-ho, me buck, and do your worst."

He grinned again, his eyes screwed shut in an agony that belied the brave expression. Wordlessly, Hollie shrugged off his sword hanger, handed it over. "Bite," he said. "Set your teeth in round about the middle - 's where *I* always did."

And leaving Luce staring at the dimpled leather, he got up and crossed to the shuddering bulk of his old fleabitten grey horse. The unwanted, dislikeable, perverse Rabbit, with the bones of his foreleg caught between two great slabs of fallen stone. The horse heaved again, rolling his eyes piteously. There was little more pitiable than a horse mortally hurt. The Rabbit grunted, almost had his quarters underneath himself to try and haul himself clear of the stones, and then collapsed against the broken masonry with a groan that was almost human.

The grey horse whinnied again, his head coming up to look at Hollie in mute agony.

Hollie sat in the dust at his horse's head, unbuckling the bridle. It was stupid. He caught one of Toogood's lads looking at him oddly. "Don't want to waste the harness," he said gruffly, but it wasn't that, it was something about not dying in your harness. As yourself, as a free thing, not as an agent of someone else's will. He stroked the big horse's bony, ugly nose, straightening the coarse grey forelock. Rubbing the whorl of hair between the horse's eyes.

Very gently placing the muzzle of his pistol against the place.

"Thee was a good horse," he said softly. "When thee chose to be."

And closed his eyes, and pulled the trigger.

31 - She Stains the Time Past

"You be bloody mindful of that horse," Toogood said wanly, as Hollie mounted the Cornishman's much-prized mount. The bay horse eyed him warily, made fractious by the smell of blood, but didn't argue - evidently recognising that Colonel Babbitt wasn't in the mood to play silly buggers.

Hollie gave him a stern look. "You - shut up and get your arm seen to. Properly."

"Lad's done me -"

"Lad's done a bodge job," Luce said firmly. "Enough to keep you comfortable for long enough to let Witless see to it. I am *not* a proper surgeon, captain. I am a half-trained one at best."

"Half a loaf's better 'n no bread."

"You'd know, you bloody peasant," Hollie said wryly, and Toogood smiled shakily.

"Go on then, you bloody *Northern* peasant. Sod off. Go and give Rupert his bloody nose. And give him one from me, hey?"

"It's all over, sir," Luce said. "Listen. All done."

The city was settling - in the first full sun of the early morning, you could see the lush green hills surrounding Bristol, quiet and peaceful as though nothing had taken place. (Seeing them through a thin haze of dust and smoke was something of a giveaway, though.) It was quiet enough, at that moment, to hear the thin, piping see-saw of a chaffinch.

Then someone fired a shot off about half a mile away, and there was another clatter of hooves, and Luce shrugged. "All right, mostly all done. D'you want to see if there's anything needs mopping up?"

"Reckon," Hollie said, squinting through the sticky blood running down the side of his face.

"Or d'you want me to stitch that for you?"

"This?" He touched a finger to it, raised his eyebrows, regretted it. "Ach, no. Het's spent the last three months looking at Hapless Russell's marred face, she won't mind if I have a like scar."

He touched his heels to Charles's sweating flank, and the bay horse jerked into a trot. "I'll be careful, Toogood," he called over his shoulder, grinning.

They rejoined the rest of the troop without event. Luce's shoulder was throbbing, but Leo was such a good horse. Head count. Venning. Venning with his cheerful blue eyes dark and shadowed, and the freckles standing out on his white face like nutmeg on a custard.

Cullis blood from waist to shoulder, his rough grey hair standing on end where he'd run a bloodied hand through it.

Betterton, limping, with a bloody rag tied round his wrist, but - "Upright wi' breeches on," he said, blinking hard.

And Witless. Witless scanning the faces of the rest of the troop as they came in, as if he were looking for someone, and that made Luce's heart drop like a stone, though he had no reason to think -

"Luce. Lucifer, may I - could you -"

"Me?"

The fat young man's eyes were steady, and very kind. "I hope you were proud of her, Luce. She was one of the first into the castle, after Rupert. I am sorry."

He shook his head, not understanding. "For what?"

And Witless touched his arm, very gently. "I'm sorry. Look - come this way. No - alone, Colonel Babbitt. Please."

He had done the best he could. He'd put a clean linen pad over the shattered ruin of her left eye, and he'd made her decent. Her face was clean, what he could see of it. Her mouth hung a little open, the gleam of her teeth showing just below her top lip. She was breathing. Slowly, and wetly, but she was breathing, yet, and -

"Is there nothing that you can do? Surely - " she was breathing, and whatever lay under the linen pad, she could be healed, surely, she would look most distinctive and endearing with an eyepatch - "Russell, at Naseby - we thought we should lose him, and yet -" Witless was shaking his head and he looked as if he might cry. "There is so little blood," Luce said weakly. "Surely she cannot -"

"The ball is lodged -" Witless flinched, his mouth twitching as it often did when he had to say something harsh, and his hand fluttered at his temple, and Luce understood, and did not want to hear more. "She will not wake, Luce."

"She will not know me?"

Witless dropped his eyes, and his mouth jerked again.

Someone else in the church groaned pitifully, and Luce swallowed. It was a church. It had no right to smell of spilled blood and shit. Gray had no right to have to die here, in public. "Would she - will it hurt her, to carry her to my quarters?"

"I would not - no -"

"She's like to die anyway, Witless," Venning said grimly, looming up in the shadows. "Now, or later, d'rather she'd die at home with a bit o' peace, than -" his eyes gleamed in the half-dark, glancing awkwardly at the writhing body of the pikeman with the burst belly in the aisle. "I'll carry her, bor. She'm one o' my troopers."

Luce put a hand to his mouth. Bit, hard, on his knuckle, till he tasted blood, because he would not cry for Gray, not in front of all these people, and he would not cry for kindness. Not here. Not now. "If anyone will carry her, I will. She is my wife." His teeth chattered together, and then he set his lips again. "*Please*. Anthony."

Witless was so rarely called by his own name that he didn't recognise it for a second, and then he nodded. "Be gentle -"

Venning rounded on him, glowering. You forgot, with Drew, that under the placid good humour there was a core of implacable purpose: slow to anger and slow to grief, but when moved, he stayed moved, simmering. "D'ee think we'd be owt else, you sawney fule? Get back to hacking limbs off, will 'ee, and do suffen useful -"

He helped, of course, because Gray was so little - had always been so little, and seemed smaller, unconscious - that tall Luce should have had to stoop to lift her, and he couldn't bear to do that, and so Drew lifted her frail little body and settled her head against Luce's shoulder, and her arm loose over his neck, and then he turned her face a little so that the stained linen pad didn't show. "Lil' mawther might just be asleep," he said stiffly, and then he bit his lip, hard. Shrugged off his worn soldier's coat and laid it across her. "Wouldn't want her to be cold, bor."

32 - The End of Days

Luce had always thought he would carry her so over the threshold of their house of dreams, or to their bridal bed. Gray's bridal bed would be six feet of Bristol earth. Her breath was warm against his bare throat, the limp deadweight of her pulling his shirt collar askew so that she seemed to be nestling her face against his shoulder. "Do you know where Hollie is?" he said to Drew, standing in the street outside his quarters, sounding perfectly conversational, he thought. He hoped he did. There would be time enough for the world to end, afterwards.

Drew blinked at him. "Not a clue. D'ee want me to fetch him?"

"No, no, I think she and I will be fine. We will be fine. I just should not like him to come home unexpectedly and find us - her - well. I don't know how long it will be, Drew." And then he turned his face and kissed her white forehead, feeling the grit of the road under his mouth where Witless's cloth had missed a little. Her face was wet. He didn't understand that. It wasn't raining, and yet her poor face was wet. Bent his head over her, and kissed her again, though she was as unresponsive as a marble statue, and realised that the wetness was his own tears, running unheeded down his face. "I would not forbid the colonel his own quarters, you see. Not for me. Us."

He laid her down on the bed, and folded the covers over her, gently. Her little hand lay upturned on the blankets, fingers curled as if she held something precious. (His heart. Always.) Her nails were dirty, bitten, dirt ground into the creases of her palm. Someone had stood on her hand, where she'd lay, after the fight. There were the marks of hobnails

purple on her palm, on her fingers. A cool and clinical part of Luce's brain assessed the damage. Little finger broken, the little bones of her hand cracked. She didn't mind, as he felt it. She didn't move at all. He put his head on the blankets beside her and lifted her hand and put it on the back of his neck -
like she'd used to when she was alive -
he shook his head, no, she *was* still alive, her chest was still rising and falling, she was still warm, her heart, *his* heart, was still beating. The Lord may yet give him that miraculous gift.

But she didn't feel alive. She didn't ruffle her fingers through his hair, she didn't roll over and grin up into his face, the way she had when -

"Luce."

Hollie Babbitt was panting as if he'd been running. Perhaps he had. He was holding something. "For - her," he said, holding the bundle of linen out. "Not - have her - shamed."

"What -"

It was a shift, or a nightgown. Linen so soft and fine it was almost like gossamer, and trimmed about with panels of intricate lace. "Don't know - what- she'd prefer," Hollie said, and took a deep breath, hands on his knees, wheezing. "Give her - choice."

"To die as a woman?"

"*Lady*."

To die as a woman, or as a plain cavalry trooper. To die as Mistress Pettitt, and be buried in her silks and laces - she never had had her ears pierced. She never had worn the earrings he'd bought for her - the skirts she always said she'd wear at home, after the wars, when she was Mistress Pettitt. Or to die as Gray, that irascible little terrier of Venning's troop. In breeches, with her freedom. "I'd rather she didn't die at all, Hollie," he said mildly.

"Don't reckon you get a choice, brat." Luce looked up into his commanding officer's face for the first time. Streaked with blood and dust and - tears. Hollie rubbed the back of his wrist across his eyes and looked defiant. "What?"

"Where - *did*- you get the shift, sir?"

"Not Griete's, if that's what you're asking." He caught his breath shakily. "Wife of the governor of Bristol, Luce. You know Fairfax agreed no looting?"

"Ye-es....?"

"It wasn't, precisely, looting. More like, uh, armed robbery. And if Fairfax objects Fairfax can fuck off. She deserves it."

"Hollie."

"Mm?"

"If you make me laugh, sir, I might begin to cry. And I'm not sure that at the moment, I could stop. Please don't."

Hollie inclined his head gravely. "I'll be outside, lad. I'll stop outside till -. Till you need me."

33 - Heaven Fashioned Us of Nothing

Hollie sat on the stairs with his eyes closed, feeling that old familiar gritty sting of too many tears under his eyelids. Watching the sun dropping down below the rooftops, covering the city with a kind rosy blanket, and listening to people being alive in the world. About their business - beginning to stir again, after almost a month under siege, beginning, shyly, hesitantly, to be unafraid. Someone singing in the kitchens below and for Luce's sake he wanted them to be silent - how could they sing when a man's wife was dying in his arms? - and then he shook his head, no. The Lord giveth, and the Lord taketh away. Blessed be the name of the Lord.

He hoped Luce was strong in his faith. He hoped the lad would believe most firmly that he would meet her again, in a better world than this, and that it would comfort him in his adversity. Hollie had remained uncomforted in his for the better part of ten years, seeking comfort or extinction by turns. Had lost his hope, his career, his faith, his good name. If it hadn't been for Het, his bright pole-star, he'd not have come back. The September sunset was warm and mellow now, flooding the landing with a golden tide, and the singer in the kitchens had fallen silent. The *city* was silent, an odd moment of stillness, almost as if the world were enclosed in a fragile, hollow soap bubble. A blackbird, singing, in an apple tree, the liquid notes falling clear into the dusk.

He could hear Luce, talking to Gray, through the latched door. Couldn't hear the words. Just Luce's happy, bright conversational voice, talking to himself. Talking to a dead woman who was still breathing.

Saying, God willing, all the things he hadn't had time to say in six weeks of marriage, and should have had a lifetime to say. The lad was barely twenty-two, he was a boy yet, it was *wrong* that he should be made to suffer so. It was bloody wrong and any God that thought it was fitting to put a pistol ball in the brain of a living, feeling young woman with so many years of useful life in front of her, and then to leave her husband to lie alongside her on a narrow bed in a strange town and wait for her breath to stop - ah, Christ, no, that kind of God was a vengeful arsehole and Hollie Babbitt would look Him in the eye on Judgment Day and bloody well tell Him so, and the hell with the consequence.

It was nothing to do with Luce. He knew that. It was thinking of himself and Griete, all those years ago, that made the tears come again. Thinking he knew what Luce was feeling, though he didn't, God knows he couldn't, they were as unlike as flint and cheese, but - even so. Hollie knew what it was to love and then suddenly to find yourself cut loose and desperate. He'd not let Luce go into that darkness. Not alone.

He put his back up against the door and sat with his head on his knees for a while, listening to his own breathing. Thinking of his own girl. Loving her twice over, loving her for Gray's sake, for still being alive to *be* loved while Gray was leaving this world. Crying again, silently, for he had no right to mourn another man's wife, but he mourned the loss of Luce's first love and the lad's innocence and, for a while, his joy, and that was a death in itself for Hollie would never have his brat again. Luce the brat was gone. Luce the man was being born in the chamber behind him, and probably Luce the man and Hollie would be closer friends than ever for that common grief, but -

He'd miss the daft, dreamy little bugger. He could only hope the man was one day going to be as full of hope and dreams and cockeyed romanticism as the boy.

The moon was rising. Would go on rising, this day and every other day, as though nothing had happened. In the room behind him, Luce's voice was growing hoarse, but still steady, still constant. That was Luce for you. Fond of the sound of his own voice - but steady. Constant. Worn out with war and grief, Hollie slept, with his naked sword to one hand and one of Het's faded silk ribbons clutched like a child's comforter in the other.

It was shortly after dawn the next morning when Luce opened the door. Pale, but neat and dry-eyed and calm "She's gone," he said softly. "Would you be so kind, sir, as to fetch - fetch your father?" .

34 - The Garments of Vengeance

They buried her as Gray Pettitt, which seemed a suitable compromise, with full military honours. Fairfax had protested. Once. Oddly, Hollie had had to say nothing in argument. Luce had simply lifted his head with a thoughtful expression, met Fairfax's dark eye, and held his gaze without a word, and nothing more was said.

The iron-grey gelding seemed bemused by his empty saddle, but at least his bemusement kept him civil. Luce carried the colours and walked by his wife's side, a hand on her coffin, talking to her. He'd not stopped talking to her since the night she'd died. Sometimes he was quiet, though Hollie knew the conversation was continuing on in his head, and sometimes he just stopped pretending and talked to her aloud. He said he was quite aware she was dead. He wasn't mad with grief. He just talked to his wife. Did they take issue with that?
- and Hollie, who *still* talked to his first wife at times, said no, they didn't.

It was a funny thing. Hollie had thought there'd be a moment where he and Rupert would finally meet. Their eyes would meet across a crowded room and it would be a significant moment. Rupert would recall him - and Hollie would feel a sense of vengeful satisfaction at seeing him finally humbled to the dust, after all these years. Years of being in Rupert's shadow - of being the *other* two-yard high cavalry commander with a habit of hit-and-run raiding, the less well-known one. Years of - oh, *Rupert's* tactics, and having to bite his tongue and say, politely, no, Gustavus Adolphus's, actually. And their paths had kept crossing - little silly petty things, the humiliation of spending the night in a damp prison cell in Amsterdam and being bailed out by a furious Margriete in the morning, after punching one of Rupert's piss-proud mates. Slumming it, they'd been, a gang of them drawling and brawling and haw-hawing in Margriete's tavern, and he happened to have been to home at the time and on door-duty, and he'd took exception to the boiling lot of them and out they went. Rupert had ended up in the gutter, wearing a pisspot for a hat, and he hadn't took to it. Hollie had ended up with a black eye and a very cold bed for the better part of six weeks, as a result of *meinherr* Rupert's interventions.

He'd had ten years of knowing that the reckless little prick had lost Hollie his first commission, after the battle at Vlotho - or Hollie's bad temper and drunken lack of caution and just not caring any more by then what he said and to whom, had lost him his commission. Hollie might have been mostly drunk and self-destructive and desperate after losing Griete, but he never planned to take any other bugger with him, and Rupert's self-indulgent, ill-disciplined charge had backfired, horribly. Lost a good fifth of Hollie's troop - he'd been bloody furious about that, and quite drunk enough to go after Rupert with the intent of punching his lights out. Which, since Rupert had been taken prisoner already that day, achieved nothing, but Hollie had offended enough people for his commission to be taken off him, and given to Rackhay. Which he would not forgive Rupert for. Ever. It had been a stupid, flashy boy's trick, and it had lost good men, and it had lost Hollie's good name, and it achieved, in the end, *nothing*.

And then there'd been Edgehill, and Rackhay's death in Rupert's first cavalry charge, and the humiliation of Powick bridge, and all the other needling little incidents he thought he'd bear a grudge for ever for, and then Fairfax had asked him to attend when Rupert signed the Articles of Surrender and all he could think was Christ, I don't want to leave Luce alone for that long. In case. Luce had said it was fine and he would be fine. Venning kept muttering darkly that it hadn't hit him yet, to which Hollie could only think that whatever *it* was, it might oblige and hurry up and hit Venning if he didn't stop telling Luce how he should feel. He had been fine, too. He'd been sitting at the table in their quarters when Hollie left to take Rupert's surrender, and he was still there when Hollie came back, studiously writing letters in the dark with a dry inkpot. *Said* he was writing letters. There were three on the table. One to his mother, one to Het, one to the Earl of Essex. Nothing untowards. Just that it didn't normally take a man a full day to write three letters.

The only time Hollie had been, briefly, distracted, was when Rupert rode out with his officers. Back to Oxford, to take his lumps from his uncle. Hollie had very politely held his horse's head when he mounted, and then he'd looked up at the prince, squinting into the sun behind Rupert's head.

"Was it worth it?" he said, because he wanted to know.

And Rupert had looked down at him. A handsome lad, if you liked that sort of thing, which Hollie didn't, and if his daughter had come home with a Bartholomew-baby like the Palatinate Pest to husband he'd have sent her to bed with a warm bum. A sullen, mutinous looking lad with a bottom lip like a baggage-mule when he was sulking, and he was definitely sulking now. He'd looked down with that pendulous lower lip flapping (an expression which reminded Hollie quite irresistibly of the Rabbit when that awkward beast was about to dig his heels in) and he'd looked Hollie over, taking in the mended linen and the absence of lace and the plain cut of an old-fashioned dark doublet and narrow breeches which cried out Puritan. And then taking in thirty-six inches of very well worn and well kept munitions quality Birmingham steel hanging at his side. "It was not," he said stiffly. And then he pulled his horse's head up, and clicked his tongue to the big overbred white stallion - did not use his spurs to engineer a flashy departure, Hollie noted with grudging approval, but urged the big white horse into a swinging walk to catch up with his own officers, kicking up the dust on the road. And was gone.

Three shots over the grave. Bloody Venning managed a misfire, twice. Luce laughed, and said she'd have liked that. He'd taken to target practice again, and that scared Hollie, a little. Coming across Luce at all hours of the day practising trick-riding with that big roan horse of his and it wasn't that Leonidas wasn't competent or willing, it wasn't even that *Luce* was unfitted for the work, it was just a little disturbing to find your gentle, dreamy cornet suddenly training himself to fire a pistol at the gallop. He was getting hell of a good, too, and that was in under a week.

Someone put the first shovel full of dry earth on top of the narrow, raw wood box that was the best they could find to hold the beloved mortal remains of Gray Pettitt, and Luce looked down at his feet, at his dusty, unpolished boots, and bit at his lips.

"God bless her and keep her," Venning said grimly.

Toogood blew out his breath, shaking his head. The Cornishman had risen from his bed for Gray's burial, though he looked bloody awful, and under his tan his skin was the greenish-white of spoiled bacon. "Any of 'ee want a drink? For I'd raise a glass or two for that maid."

"I had not known she was so much loved," Luce said softly, and Toogood looked at him levelly.

"She'm one of ours, Luce. We don't forget."

"Tell 'ee who we have forgot," Venning said. "I don't envy him as has to tell Russell. *He* was sweet on her the one time, wasn't he?"

And Luce - calm, composed, polite Luce, so neat and placid, still - looked at Venning blankly, and then, with a horrible slowness, fell on his knees at the side of her grave, his shoulders heaving silently.

35 - All Delight Doth Itself Soons't Devour

Luce didn't feel any great agony of soul. Hollie seemed to think he might, which was disconcerting, the idea that cynical, spiky Colonel Babbitt might be possessed of more sensitivity than he was himself. Luce didn't feel anything, very much. He found tears running down his cheeks at times, and that was a surprise, because he hadn't known he was thinking of her, or indeed weeping. He didn't think it was his fault, he didn't think it was because he hadn't loved her enough or he hadn't taken care of her, he didn't think it was the Lord's judgment on him. He just wanted to be left alone.

He'd expected a great romantic tearing grief, and he didn't get it. Everyone was very kind, and he was a little bemused by it, because surely he should feel more than this? But he didn't, and he went on walking and talking and eating and sleeping as usual, feeling as if he was wrapped in a fuzzy grey mist.

He looked up. He'd gone somewhere else again, for a while. He seemed to be doing that a lot, this last week. Looked up, squinting into the sun, closing one eye to peer into Lije Babbitt's more-than-usually grim face.

"Thank you," he said automatically, seeing the regimental chaplain's lips moving. Not listening. "Very kind." Smiled. Knew he was smiling because he felt the stiffness in his cheeks - so *that* was how Russell did it - kept nodding, attentively. Looking at his hands, at the dirt under his nails where he'd scrabbled in the earth of her grave. Remembered doing it. Remembered the splinters of the raw wood under his fingers. Didn't remember what he'd been thinking, at the time. Had he not washed in over a week? It didn't matter. They were all dirty -

"Lucifer. *Mind me.*"

A little bit of the grey fuzziness parted. "Why? I mean - what is it?"

"I'm worried about my boy."

"Are you? I'm sure he'll be fine."

Lije glowered at him. "Has thee not noticed? Out all hours of the night - he looks like death, cornet."

The which made Luce wince, and then look up furiously. Hollie Babbitt was distinctly alive and breathing. Elijah had no right to remind Luce of that, none at all, to rub it in that his boy was whole and in the world while Luce's fierce bright girl was dead - And then he stopped, horrified with himself. It wasn't a competition. "What's he doing?"

"I thought you might know, sir! Given that you and he share quarters, and you count yourself his friend!"

He did. Of course he was Hollie's friend. He didn't share quarters with the redhead, not for a week and more, not since - not since he had started to find the sympathy unbearable, and had sought accommodation elsewhere. "I shouldn't worry. I am sure he's fine. He's not out drinking every night, at least." Because someone would have said, or Fairfax would have haled him in, or something. There would have been *talk*.

Elijah sat down, uninvited. He clasped his hands at his mouth. He looked afraid. That was not like Elijah. He glanced sideways, those mad hawk-yellow eyes wary, looking frighteningly like his son in one of his less approachable moods. "'M scared, boy," he said eventually, and unclasped his hands to hang between his knees, beginning to rock to and fro on the bench. Almost imperceptibly, though his worn buffcoat creaked. "Afraid almost beyond the Lord's help, and that -" he grinned, showing a snapped-off yellow canine tooth that hadn't been missing before, "that's not like me."

"Trooper?"

"Lije. I told thee before. Call me Lije. The boy is dabbling with ungodly things, Lucifer. They say there's plague in the city, aye? And I seen it with my own eyes - seen the marks of the pestilence, as they was burying the bodies. I *know,* lad. I read me Leviticus and I know what pestilence looks like."

"Yes." Yes, there was plague in the city. Had been. It was burning itself out, now, after the siege had lifted. Luce had thought, for a while, that his duty - as a surgeon, even as a half-trained unlicenced whelp of a surgeon - must be to those people who suffered within the walls. He wasn't sure he cared, now. He looked at Elijah. "Your point?"

"You seen my boy of late, trooper? Today? Yesterday? He looks -"

"You said."

"Aye. I said. You seen his neck?"

He remembered Hollie, irritably picking at something under his ponytail. Wincing as he did so. Luce remembered seeing the dark stain on the collar of his buffcoat, and thinking nothing of it. His mouth went dry. "What do you mean?"

"I mean, I reckon that bloody soft-headed boy of mine has been poking his long neb into business that don't concern him. You know what he was like at Bridgwater. Couldn't keep him out o' the place, when he thought he might be of some use, setting the town to rights. I reckon he's at it again, Luce. I reckon he's been down at the docks. Helping." He laughed, and his voice cracked, and Luce realised with a prickly feeling that went all over his skin, that Lije Babbitt was on the verge of tears. "What'll I do, lad? I can't stand and do nowt and let my boy die o't' pestilence. It's a hard death. He seen it - there was plague at home, just before he left - he must ha' been all of fifteen, he was grown enough to remember. His bloody *mother* died o' the sweating sickness. He *knows* what it'd do to me, to lose him so."

The hell with Elijah. Luce knew what it would do to the rest of the troop, if they lost their firebrand colonel. And, probably, what it would do in a very real and physical sense, if a man they had sat to their supper with every night for the last week, had broken bread with and drunk with - ah, Christ, had drunk with, passing a leather bottle of warm brackish water from hand to hand in a dusty street - breathed the same air -

"Watch," he said, and a trickle of cold sweat ran down his back. "And pray."

It didn't matter, and so Luce moved his things back in with Hollie within the hour, because it wasn't important if Luce picked up a contagion, not now. Which wasn't to say that he wasn't sick-shaky at the thought of it, and it kept sneaking all unbidden into his head - sweating, Lucifer? Is that the heat, or the plague, from being in a chamber with Hollie Babbitt's unmade bed? Bowels turning to water - sheer unmanly terror, or the contagion?

And of course there was no answer to that, other than to watch and pray and try and read a book, wait for Hollie to come back from whatever mission of stupidity he was on. To know your mouth to be dry with miserable fear, and not to be able to swallow for the great lump in your throat. (Fear, Lucifer, or contagion?) To want to walk up and down the crooked boards of the little chamber that looked over the docks, and not to be able to stand for the weakness of your knees.

Some bloody surgeon *he* was. (But that was all right, because if his friend was as sick as Elijah feared, they'd both be dead by the Sabbath anyway.) He experimented by rolling a sheet of Hollie's correspondence into a cone - holding it over his face, feeling like an absolute fool. That was what they did, proper, real doctors, they wore masks, breathed in fumes to clear the tainted air. This stifling little chamber was mostly tainted with the smell of unaired linen and stale beer, left in a jug on the windowshelf with a thin film of dust on the top.

And he was stuck with it. He could not and would not go back downstairs, not having been in this tainted room, not and carry the contagion on his clothes to innocent men. Such as you could describe any of Babbitt's troop as innocent.

He wiped his sticky, sweaty palms on his breeches. Gritted his teeth and went for a walk round the room, just to be doing something. Sat down and started to write to someone, a letter in the event of his death, to be opened by -

But he didn't *have* anyone to open it, because Gray was dead, and if he died here in this airless room he could be buried with Gray, and that was good, surely, that was right and fitting -

And his poet's soul was arguing the toss, and his sensible, respectable merchant-glover's-son head was arguing that he was not yet twenty-two and he had a lot of living to do yet. And he had both parents living, and three healthy sisters, and an auntie - hardly *nobody*, to cry for him -

Which made him think of Auntie Het, away in Essex, waiting like Argos, that poor faithful dog who'd waited for ten years for Odysseus to come home. And they never would, neither he nor Hollie, they'd both die in Bristol, alone and suffering and friendless. He put his head down on the desk and he was having a lovely howl to himself when the door came open with a most uncharacteristic gentleness.

"Brat, 's that you?" Hollie said, and without waiting for an answer came in and dropped on the bed. "Glad you're back," he said muzzily, put his arm over his eyes against the sunlight, and fell asleep. Luce could tell he was asleep, because riddled with contagion or not, he snored as badly as ever. (*Worse* than ever? Was it a sign of the disease?)

He hadn't even taken his boots off. That could not be right. Luce went over and peered at his friend. A little flushed, but that could be sunburn - a little sweaty, with his loose hair sticking to his face, but it was summer, and it was hot. It could mean nothing. It could mean everything.

Hollie opened one eye. "Lucey. I'm delighted to see you, brat, but will you give over *hovering* over me. You're not my bloody mother."

And his mother had died of the sweating sickness, Elijah said. Was that significant? Was he wandering in his wits?

"Your father is worried about you," he said feebly, and Hollie rolled over and thumped his pillow with a snarl.

"Is he. Can he do it quietly? I'm bloody knackered, Luce. Been shifting timber half the day and my shoulder's giving me hell."

Pains. That was another sign. "May I see?"

"No you may not, you may fuck off and haunt someone else and let me get a bit o' shut-eye! Jesus...." He growled, buried his head in the pillow, hunched his shoulders. Rolled over again shortly afterwards. "You're fretting as well, whelp. I can *hear* you. What's up?"

Luce flexed his fingers, because now came the time to screw his courage to the sticking-post, and he wasn't sure he could do it. "Your father - Elijah -"

"I know who he is!"

"He thinks you may have been - at the docks, sir. Being of assistance. These last few days."

Hollie sat up. "How old is that ale, Luce? I tell you what, I could do with a drink. I - what are you looking at me like that for?"

Deep breath. "Because he fears you may have been infected with the plague."

"You're putting me on! What's he worried about, that it'll kill me before he does?" He lay down again, grinning. Said nothing. Came over onto his side, abruptly, with a creak of bed. "You're serious, aren't you? *You* think I'm diseased?"

"I - yes. Possibly. Let -" moistening his lips again, "may I look at the back of your neck, sir?"

The redhead flinched as he touched it - a raw, wet, open sore just at the nape of his neck, sticky and crusted with yellow. A bubo? How could you tell, when the thing was in such a place? "It's where my buffcoat rubs me," Hollie said fiercely, and even he was beginning to sound frightened. "You know that, Luce. I've been muttering about it long enough. That's all. It's nowt -"

"Then we shall have to see, sir."

"What?"

"Watch. And pray. And hope that it is, that, and no more."

Luce crossed to the door. He had his eyes closed, but he didn't think Hollie would notice. He wanted to cry, not for grief, but for misery, and that felt worse, that was sore and headachy and tight and shameful. He rapped on the inside of the door, hard. "Sergeant Cullis?" he shouted. "*Cullis*?"

"All right, all right, I ent entirely deaf," Cullis yelled back from the kitchen downstairs, "give us a minute and -"

"Don't come upstairs! Just - put some provisions. For." He gulped. "Hollie and I. In a basket. On the stairs. And Sergeant Cullis - if, if you could quarter yourself and Captain Betterton - elsewhere. I'd be grateful. For now."

He came away from the door, feeling as shaky and weak as if he *was* sickening. Hollie was looking at him with a faintly comical expression of disbelief. "What -" The redhead was shaking. The hand he lifted to push his sweat-limp hair from his eyes trembled like an aspen leaf in a high wind. "Luce, you reckon I might have a contagion, and you just shut yourself up with me? You out of your mind, or what?"

"Oh, I imagine so. But look at it this way." For the first time since Gray's death, he wanted to laugh. Wildly, for sure, but - laugh. "I've been working on an epic poem on the battle at Marston Moor, in honour of my lord Fairfax. I imagine if I have a week clear of my duties to work on perfecting it, and I have you as my - critic, sir, that's right, I can read you verses while you're also relieved of your duties - imagine, Hollie, our fame is assured!"

Hollie didn't look convinced. On the other hand, he didn't look as if he was going to cry or throw himself out of a window, either. "Jesus," he said faintly. "A fucking literary critic. Me. Jesus. My mother would turn in her grave. Jesus." He looked up at Luce, wide-eyed. "I reckon I'd rather have the contagion, if it's all right with you?"

36 - Cease From Anger, and Forsake Wrath

It took almost a week, in the end, in which Hollie's perception of great art took a battering, and Luce came close to taking several. But in the end, it was nothing. Seven days without that heavy buffcoat, and the sore on the back of Hollie's neck had turned to a scab. Seven days of nothing to do but sleep and eat and swear at Luce Pettitt and although his temper was nothing to write poetry about, his body was fit and well-rested.

Luce was a pain in the arse, and there was no getting away from it. Even apart from the epic poetry - which was grim, and somewhere about the sixteenth stanza Hollie had dropped the whole boiling lot out of the window, which had led to some harsh words around the nature of philistines who didn't know art when it sank its fangs into their leg, and dithering verse-mongers who used up all the ink - even apart from the fact that for the first night the brat had the squitters something diabolical, which he put down to distress and Hollie put down to a meat pie with more whiskers than he had himself. Even if you didn't mind that every conversation mentioned her name, or that she liked something, or didn't like something.

Even if you didn't mind that after less than a fortnight the brat had mentally transformed that fierce, scruffy fighting terrier into an alabaster angel, it was hard work, and he couldn't wait to get out and find out what a bloody lash-up Messrs Venning and Betterton had made of his troop. And if Toogood still had his arm - the memory of Mattie Percey at Marston Moor was still too strong for Hollie to pretend that such things did not happen. Them three had took to haunting the stairs, after a few days: loitering and passing the time of day, despite Luce's sterm warnings about foul air and pestilence. Venning reckoned there was yet plague in the city, but that it was contained. Which was reassuring - if, coming from Venning, not necessarily reliable.

And he was a bastard at times, Drew Venning. If he'd sat on them stairs once noisily munching on something and telling them how good it was, he must have done it a dozen times. "Tell 'ee what," he'd say, cheerfully and indistinctly, "tell 'ee what, has 'ee tried them mutton pies from the bakehouse on Fewter Lane?"

To which the usual answer was no, you selfish bastard, and we just have to sit here on the other side of a bolted door snuffing like a pair of benighted bloodhounds till one of you remembers we're up here, by which point the pies are long cold.

But they came through. Possibly verses sixteen to twenty-five would never be quite fit for publication after Hollie had screwed the page up and dumped it in the brimming chamber-pot, though he thought his friendship with Luce was possibly the better for it. There were certain limits beyond which his tolerance could not be pushed. But they were whole, and hale, and alive. And Hollie was going to head straight for that bloody bakehouse and he was going to have not one, not two, but *three* of those bloody pies that Venning kept maundering on about, and he was going to take Luce with him, and then, after a week of more or less total abstinence, he was going to find the nicest pot-house that'd serve the scabby pair of them and he was going to get the brat right royally rat-arsed.

But he never got the chance. Luce had washed and shaved and changed his linen and looked as nice as ninepence. Hollie stuck his head in a bucket of very cold water in the stable-yard, shaking wet hair out of his eyes with a sigh of shameless bliss. Cold water. *Fresh,* cold water. He'd been able to think of nothing else for the last week, but stripping to the waist, and not caring who saw his scarred back, and washing in cold - *really* cold - water. Cold enough to raise the goose-bumps on your arms. And then parking himself comfortably in the sun with his legs stuck out in front of him and Blossom's muzzle investigating his hair, idly mending a noseband where the stitching had started to come adrift.

Toogood wandered past with his broken arm in a raffish sling. Hollie was trying not to think too closely about that, because it looked as if it might have begun life as part of a square of scarlet silk with a white device on it, and that might have been the bottom corner of Prince Rupert's colours, and that would be *really* embarrassing. He wondered, without being that bothered, if the Palatinate Ponce had made his way back as far as Oxford yet. No, Hollie was just - content, with the sun making patterns on his closed eyelids, and the familiar feel of clean leather under his fingers, and the smell of warm horse. Blossom, having made sure that Hollie was who the horse thought he was, returned to cropping the grass at his side, not straying too far, just in case Hollie went away again.

"Useless soppy animal," he muttered, and the rangy brown gelding swung his head questioningly and blew down his nose. "Yes, you. Great lolloping beast. Thee is more like a dog than a bloody horse -"

"Aye, but you're fond of him."

He hadn't expected company. Most of the troop had put the word out that Rosie was released from captivity and sat in the yard soaking wet and grinning to himself with no shirt on, whilst cleaning tack *by choice.* Of such minor eccentricities was his reputation for unpredictability made. He opened one eye. "Oh it's you. What you come back for?"

Kenelm Toogood shuffled. "Come to say sorry, see. I was out of order, before Bristol, and if you'd said to me what I said to you I wouldn't of pulled you out from under no walls. And I wouldn't blame you if you said you wanted me cashiered, or - whatever 'tis. But. Drew reckoned you might hit me instead?" he said hopefully, and Hollie couldn't help but laugh.

"Might stop your pay -" He meant it as a feeble joke, and he hadn't expected the Cornishman to go stiff and shaky.

"Can if 'ee wants, sir, 'tis not my business. I mebbe deserved it anyway."

And Hollie closed his eyes again, not wanting to see the darned patch on the cuff of the captain's coat where the blue was a slightly different shade, the much-mended sword-hanger, the cracked boots. A young man with pride and dignity, and weren't they all, all principle and no pay. Piss-poor in Cornwall, so they said. Stripped of their arms and harness and made to leave Cornwall naked, after Essex's abortive campaign two years back, they said, set on and jeered at by Malignants and women. Killed, some of them. Robbed and murdered. And he *was* a Cornish lad, young Toogood. Bodmin? Launceston? Somewhere that was nearly not Cornwall - Callington, that was it, the lad was Callington-bred. A Cornish Parliamentarian. That made him about as rare as hen's teeth. "Don't be so bloody daft, Kenelm. Me and the brat is going to have a wet, later on. By way of that bloody pie-shop of Venning's. My shout, I believe. You coming, or no?"

The dark-haired captain pulled himself up straight. "No. No, sir, I ent, and I'll tell you for why, and it's not cos I don't like 'ee. I come to look for 'ee because someone had to say about your father, and Drew reckoned you wouldn't go for me, not seriously, not with a bad arm."

"What?"

"Your - Trooper Babbitt, sir."

"I know who he is!"

"He - well, when you and Luce got shut up, sir, I d'hardly like to say, he said, he got up and made a big lot of testifying and preaching and - you know how he is, sir, he -" Toogood spread the fingers of his good hand awkwardly, "he said, as how if the Lord was asking him to sacrifice his boy like Isaac, he'd offer up his own service instead. He gone ministering to the sick, sir. Least, he *was*, before he - " the Cornishman's dark eyes lifted, and he licked his lips, "he'm shut up, sir, like you two was, except they say there ent none want to go near him, for fear of the contagion. Slap in the thick of it, sir, he was. Preaching like hellfires, even with the door nailed to, till his voice started to go."

"When -" Hollie shook his head. Because it didn't matter. Stood up, patted Blossom's shoulder with a sudden fierce affection, and shrugged his shirt back on. Feeling the worn linen catch, as it always caught, as it had caught every day of his grown-up life, on the raised finger-thick weals of scar tissue that his father had put there with the buckle end of a stirrup leather, when he'd been insolent, or disobedient, or irreverent. Every day of his grown-up life, till he ran away from home.

And there was little more he could say, was there? Apart from to sit with his back against the door, where the painted red cross was still fresh and as shiny as new blood, and say, aloud, "You *stupid* old bastard."

Not expecting a response, after three days without food or water, and that was what they said - there'd been no one near him in three days. Not expecting the cracked voice from just behind him to say, "Holofernes, is that thee, boy?" in a voice of disbelieving joy.

"No, you old fool, I'm a figment of your imagination, who the hell else would it be?"

"I feared thee might be, boy."

Hollie banged his fist on the door. "Believe me, you stupid old bastard, a figment of your imagination would not be half so inclined to break in there and wallop some sense into thy thick head. What *possessed* thee?"

But in the shut-up house behind Hollie, low down, as if he were crouched on the floor, and close to the door, as if he were as near as he could get to his boy, Elijah Babbitt was sobbing, and that made Hollie spook like a horse scenting flames. Not praying, not preaching, just sobbing. "The Lord has preserved thee, boy," he said at length, "the Lord has heard my prayers -"

"I never *had* the bloody plague!"

"It is a miracle, Holofernes, God has granted me a miracle, a most complete miracle -"

"Will you pack that in, you old fool! I do not have the plague! I have never had the plague! Neither me nor Lucey have been anywhere *near* the bloody plague! I had a sore on the back of my neck, that was all, not some great festering bloody - " He stopped, but the sobbing continued. "Father," he said warily. "*You* are clean, aren't you?"

And there was a long pause. "No, boy. No, I - I fear - I am very much afraid - no."

He was on the other side of a door. He could do no harm. He was alone, and afraid. Hollie put his hand flat on the sun-warmed wood, close to where he could hear his father's rattling breath. Heard him whimpering, pitifully, alone in the stifling dark. Without food. Without water.

There was no one around. He shot the bolt off the door. Not with the intent of breaking his father out, he wasn't that stupid. Just to hold his hand. "Pray with me," Elijah whispered, shortly before dusk, and turned his face so that his cold, stubbly cheek brushed Hollie's fingers. A kiss? He didn't know. The feel of it almost made him retch. But even so. He closed his eyes, though the old man couldn't see him through the splintered hole in the door, and he set his teeth and he prayed, for one of them or for both of them, prayed till he was shaking with it and his father was quiet, on the far side of the door.

They came for him at curfew. His father had neither spoken nor moved since dusk. It meant nothing. He was glad, in a way. He wasn't sure he wanted to see. He had money, God knows he had money, he'd hardly been profligate, locked in a garret overlooking the dockside this last week. There was a woman. There were several, but he picked the one who looked clean, and at least slightly respectable. Gave her a gold piece. (It was the only one he had, but she didn't need to know that. He had good linen, thanks to Het, and his boots were intact, and that would be sufficient evidence of his respectability.) If the old bastard was alive, it would pay for his care. And if he wasn't, it would pay for his burying.

He scrubbed his hands, to get the feel of that cold caress off his skin. Scrubbed with lye-soap, begged from the laundress in the inn, until his hands bled. And then he mounted Blossom and he whistled up his lads like a pack of hounds - and Fairfax gave him that customary disapproving dark-eyed glare at such impropriety but he didn't care, not now, not any more. There was a thin sea-mist starting to creep up from the river, wrapping round them like wool. Autumn was in the air.

Moving into Devon, they said, pressing the King's men, what was left of them, back and back into the West. The Prince of Wales in Truro, still loyal to the last, struggling to hold the Western Army together. Not against Thomas Fairfax and Oliver Cromwell, he wouldn't. The poor bugger hadn't a hope.

It was over. It was done. By the New Year, he would be home.

Luce - he glanced at his friend, lost in thought, not looking back as they rode out of Bristol - *he* could go home. He could go now. Hollie could do that much for him.

For himself?

He looked at Venning, who looked innocently back. (Plotting something, then.) Toogood, with his shattered arm mending, and hurting. Betterton, a thousand miles away from home, from a farm on the Tyne and a nice wife and God knows how many children, the number seemed to increase with every letter. Cullis, who'd been with him since the first.

Thought of Russell, almost-whole and dazed by his good fortune at White Notley, almost unrecognisable in his happiness. Mattie, married now to the children's stour Doraty. Of his girls, one of whom he'd not so much as set eyes on since her birth, though he had regular stories that she was a prodigy of beauty and wit. His wife said much the same, too.

Of his Het, waiting for him, at home.

Of how disappointed she would be, did he not see it through to the end, and see his lads done right by. He scratched the back of his neck - winced, as he caught at the healing scar.

"Westward it is, then, lads," he said. "Mount up."

37 - Glory In Tribulations Also

Essex
December 1645

The roan horse dropped his head, stumbling with weariness, and almost without thinking about it Luce gathered the reins up and dug his heels in sharply to Leo's muddy flanks.

The horse wasn't distressed, just wet and dirty and tired. Well, Luce was wet and dirty and tired too, such as it mattered, and he expected no more from his horse than he expected from himself. It had been raining all day, and that was fine by Luce; the thin white drizzle suited his mood, and it mattered little if he was wet, dry, cold, hot, alive, dead –

Auntie Het seemed to have acquired a new labourer. There was a tall figure in a shapeless old coat crossing the yard, a disreputable knitted cap pulled down over his eyes. The impertinent rogue stopped at the front door and kicked the mud from his boots, and then lifted the latch as if he owned the place. "You, sir! What the hell d'you think you're doing?"

The labourer turned round, the light from the open door falling full on the livid scar on his cheek. "Going to my supper, Luce, and if you had any sense you'd get down off that horse and do likewise," Thankful Russell said cheerfully, without so much as a flicker of astonishment. "I take it the colonel's about a hundred yards behind you?"

Luce shook his head, and swallowed hard. He hadn't thought he would mind. He minded, suddenly, very much that Hollie was back in Exeter. He wasn't sure he cared for minding. It was a little too close to feeling, and he didn't care to feel, either, right now.

Mattie Percey came out of the stables – peered at him, raised his eyebrows, and said nothing. Mattie Percey was wearing a wedding ring. Probably he should ask about that, in all civility. Probably he wasn't going to. Leo went with Mattie to the foaling-box at the end of the block, with Mattie talking to the big roan like a nurse talking to weary child, and Luce wondered if it was the prick of a guilty conscience that imagined both horse and groom give him a reproachful glance before they passed into the shadows.

Not that it mattered, much.

"Well, then." Russell looked quite at his ease, by the flickering kitchen fire. "I apologise for my shameful appearance, by the way. I'd been helping Warriner at Lane End Farm, move his sheep to the top field. I'm told the river's nigh to bursting its banks at Witham, so we wanted to move them up out of harm's way. I do not care for sheep," he said distastefully. "I find them to be most ungrateful creatures. With sharp hooves." He pushed up his sleeve and glowered at a long, shallow graze on his arm. "Would you care for roast mutton at some point during your stay, Lucifer?"

"Where is Auntie Het?" he said. He'd heard Hapless, he just didn't care to answer him.

"She's upstairs, putting Joyeux to bed." His scarred face relaxed into a faint smile. "I wish her all joy of settling Zee. Some fool told her it wanted but two weeks to Christmas, and – well. Here we are. Would you be so good as to pass me that basket, by the way. Thanks." He settled a ball of rags in his lap, shaking it this way and that critically. "I have little facility with making, I fear. Does it in any way resemble a doll, or shall I put this one in the fire, too? I was beginning to flatter myself that my carving improved, but, ah –" He turned the little figure round hopefully. It was not an attractive sight. It had carved hair and a square, lopsided face, and someone – Het, most likely – had endeavoured to make it pretty with a little gown made of pieced scraps.

Luce said nothing, could say nothing, suddenly speechless with misery. He was not going to cry. Was *not.* There would always have been a place for Hapless at the hearth in Luce's house of dreams. Gray would have insisted. She'd been very fond of Hapless. He'd been very fond of her. Hapless could have – he *would* have – been as fond and doting to Luce's family, as he was of Hollie's. He'd not have that chance, now. Luce wasn't going to cry.

"My carving isn't *that* bad, Lucifer," the scarred lieutenant said indignantly.

Luce pressed the heels of his hands to his stinging eyes. "She's dead," he said. "Gray. My wife. She's dead."

38 - Through A Glass, Darkly

Het had not known he was married. How should she? And he told her nothing, would tell her no more but that he had been a husband for those six glorious weeks and was now a widower, sitting sobbing on the parlour floor with his head in her lap while she stroked his hair as if he was a little boy.

He hadn't felt any better for it. Had felt no better, and no worse, since September. He just felt – nothing: cold, and hollow, and empty, most of the time, as if he was watching himself going through the motions of living. Het was kind, but thought she could mend him, as if he could be pieced back together with a needle and thread. He couldn't show his pain with Hapless: how could he, when Hapless had loved her too, so far as Hapless was capable of loving anyone?

It wanted but two weeks to Christmas. He came with no gifts, he bore no good tidings. He had a packet of letters for Het from Hollie, which had tailed off rather abruptly about a month ago when most of the troop had started to go down like kayles, one after another, with that perpetual flux that just wouldn't seem to go away. That had worried her. Luce hadn't mentioned that the last time he'd set eyes on Hollie his commanding officer had been leaning stiffly up against a privy wall with his teeth gritted, swearing prodigiously, with his face the colour and sheen of spoiled bacon rind. He had just said that Hollie was somewhat preoccupied with regimental business, at the moment. Which he was. Most of the regiment were preoccupied with the same business.

Hollie had said he would be home for Christmas and he would be home for Christmas if they had to fetch him hence on a hurdle. He was nothing if not faithful.

He seemed to remember as a boy that Christmases were deep in glittering snow, and fragrant with good things. They didn't seem to be, any more. Belly-deep in sucking mud in the lanes, and wet. Perhaps he was getting old, at twenty-two. Perhaps he ought to go over to Witham, and see in the season of Christ's birth with his parents. A dutiful son should have gone before now, instead of skulking at his aunt's skirts demanding comforting, like a pettish baby. Of which Auntie Het had a sufficiency already. The new one – the dark roly-poly one, Joyeux, who had an engaging smile and a way of flickering her eyelashes at you, even at three months old – *she* was a handful. A contented handful, but a handful. She looked nothing like her sire, for which the Lord be thanked, and everything like her mother. Thomazine, on the other hand, was like a minute version of Hollie, if it was possible to imagine that lanky engine of devastation as a child.

Luce wondered if any child of his should have been dark, or fair. Would have had Gray's fierce, level grey-green eyes, or his own dreamy, mist-coloured ones.

Stopped wondering, because it hurt. And because Russell was standing looking at him with an expression of restrained impatience that implied that he'd been there for some time. "I *said*," he said, "I was meaning to ride into Witham on an errand, and did you care to come."

"It's raining."

"So I see. I suggest you put a coat on, then."

Russell was looking – not precisely smart, he hadn't broken out the lace-edged collar that normally came out on high days and holidays, but he had a ribbon in his hair and he'd shaved recently enough to be still pink in places. "...Thankful?" Luce said warily. "Are you – ah, are you all right?"

"Harrassed," Russell said, and the unmarked corner of his mouth twitched. "It will be Christmas in two weeks, Lucifer. In case you hadn't noticed. We've a little maid of rising two here in need of a new gown, and muggins here didn't run fast enough to get out of the way when Mistress Babbitt said she needed a bolt of wool to sew it. I've a fancy for blue, for Tammasin. Het says –" he broke off guiltily, and Luce saw an uncharacteristic blush flood his cheeks.

"*Het* says?" he prompted, with gentle malice.

"Het says that if there's a sufficiency in the draper's, she'd like to have a new suit made for Hollie, before he gets home. Something not black, she says. She reckons we are sufficiently like in size to use me as a pattern." He met Luce's eyes defiantly, and looked as if he might have said more, had it not been for Thomazine barrelling down the stairs in a fur-lined coat that made her as wide as she was tall, taking a flying leap from several stairs up in the expectation that Hapless would catch her. Which he did, with an ease that brought tears to Luce's eyes. Again. "Thee grows a great girl, Zee," the scarred lieutenant said tenderly, and she put her arms about his neck and pressed her cheek to his as though he were the dearest thing in all the world.

Which left Luce. Not dear to anyone, not any more.

Apart from his mother. And so, like a child with a skinned knee, to his mother he would go, to be kissed better.

39 - Joy Cometh in the Morning

He left Russell and Thomazine arguing in the draper's shop over whether the fair and elegant Russell would suit poppy-scarlet – Thomazine said she wanted her gown in scarlet and she wanted Russell to match – and stepped out into the drizzle. Smiling. It was downright comical to hear Russell being upbraided by a tiny termagant: Russell, who was the most officious and efficient supply officer this side of the Thames, very meekly and very tactfully trying to divert his little charge into something a little more discreet, more suited to his good Puritan background, and being routed, foot and horse. Luce prayed most fervently that Russell's indulgence might be tempered by a little more common sense. The lieutenant might be sweet on Het, and he might have once harboured some tenderness for Gray, but so far as anyone could be said to have made him a willing captive it was a bright-haired little girl who had him wrapped round her little finger.

And there, he'd gone a whole five minutes without thinking of Gray, not once.

He thought about it, standing in the rain, and then shook his head and sidestepped into the haberdasher's shop, hoping no one would see him. "Ribbon," he said flatly. "Scarlet."

Scarlet for Thomazine, though it'd not suit her. A length of lace for the new one, for a trim to her cap, or a gown – he had no idea how much lace went into an infant's gown, so he bought too much. Het could always use it to trim a kerchief, or something. A muted leaf-green for Het, who always wore soft colours.

A new collar, for Hollie, to go with his new suit. He was lingering over a set of cuffs, wondering if his mother might care for the width of the fine lace, or if she might prefer something narrower, when someone put their hand on the small of his back, and he glanced round in smiling surprise, expecting to see –

Someone who was equally as surprised when he turned round, that he wasn't who she'd thought he was, either. She wasn't Gray – she was a young lady with rosy cheeks and glossy brown hair and a very determined mouth, and she had mistaken him for Thankful Russell, seeing Russell's horse pass in the street earlier and then seeing Luce's fair hair in the darkness of the haberdasher's shop.

"You know the lieutenant?" Luce said faintly, thinking there was a whole heap he didn't know about Russell, including, apparently, an astonishing and hitherto-unsuspected ability to melt like butter for any breathing female within a ten-mile radius.

"I'm Tom Warriner's sister," she said, as if that explained everything. "Of course I know Thankful. Doesn't everybody? He's always running errands for Mistress Babbitt." She smiled. She had nice teeth – white and even, with a little gap between the front two. "He's a dear."

"Russell?"

"Why, where do you know him from?" she said curiously, and Luce shrugged. "Here and there. I'm Mistress Babbitt's nephew – as well as Colonel Babbitt's cornet."

"Gracious," she said. "At the same time? You must be busy."

He was saved from having to make a reply to that remark by the arrival of the man himself, with one bundle under his arm and another, in the shape of Thomazine in her bunchy coat, swinging from his hand. "You done, Luce? Oh –" he gave the dark-haired girl a sudden, delighted grin, which was not a look Luce ever recalled seeing on the lieutenant's face before – "Alice, what a lovely surprise."

"I might say the same, Thankful. And Thomazine." Alice Warriner bent down and kissed the little girl on both cheeks. "Well. Look at you, all snuggled up like a little squirrel. Have you been on an errand for your mother?"

"Apple bought this," she said smugly, tugging the end of the parcel open to reveal a small amount of the scarlet worsted, and both Alice and Luce looked at the lieutenant with identical expressions of astonishment. He had the grace to look embarrassed. "What harm was there in it? I have none other to buy gifts for."

"Mama make Zee a gown that red," the child said, beaming, and Luce suspected he dared not look at Alice for fear her expression might echo the thought in his own mind. That most flaming and wanton red. On a child whose hair could best be described, charitably, as a warm amber. The poor child would look ill.

"And you will look delightful, I'm sure," Alice said mendaciously, and the little girl's mouth drooped suddenly.

"Not 'nough for Apple, though."

"Such a shame," Russell said sweetly. "But the more for you, pippin."

She thought about that, kicking the toe of her shoe into the boards of the shop floor. And then she looked up, smiling again. "Hollups," she said, holding up her hands to Luce.

"She wants to be picked up," Russell explained, with a hint of smugness. "I am evidently fallen out of favour. And she *is* heavy, Lucifer. I suggest putting her on your shoulder, rather than attempting to heft her like a parcel."

"Go Nantie Jane's, please," she said. "Zee sit down. Uncle Lucey? Nantie Jane's?"

His quiet, dignified mother, Nantie Jane. Prim Thankful Russell flirting ponderously with the sister of one of the local farmers. Hollie Babbitt prised out of his customary shabby black, and wearing blue. The world was indeed turned upside down.

"Should I take your parcels, Luce? I imagine I may occupy myself for an hour or so, whilst you call on your lady mother."

"It is far too wet to go walking by the river, Thankful," Alice said sternly, and Russell grinned at her.

"I may have sufficient in my depleted purse to buy you a hot pie, mistress, if your reputation will stand the embarrassment of being seen with such a ragged object of pity as myself."

"Zee want pie!" Thomazine said briskly, and Russell cocked an eyebrow at her, before counting his coins. "All right, my tibber. No bun, though, not unless Luce is buying. Luce? You in?"

"*Me*?"

"Thankful may act as my chaperone," Alice said grandly. "You may accompany us, sir."

And he found himself laughing, too. Assuring Thomazine that between the four of them they might scrape together sufficient coins for a bun.

"*Free* bun," Thomazine said.

"Three buns."

"Zee share with Apple, and Lucey share with Alice.

Thass noice," she said, beaming, in an suddenly and most alarmingly Buckinghamshire burr, and Alice grinned.

"Remind me again, sir, *whose* daughter is she?"

And then Zee changed her mind again, and since Russell was in the business of buying hot pies, she tucked her hand confidingly into his and decided to encourage him in the direction of the pie shop, leaving Alice with Luce. She shook her head. "Poor lamb, he hasn't a chance, has he? Not yet two and the child has found herself a husband already. Are you married, Master Pettitt?"

"No," Luce said, and strangely, he could say it without the words sticking in his throat, to this sensible, comfortable girl. "No, I'm not. She died. In the summer. I'm not married."

She ducked her head in sympathy. "Then I shall remember her in my prayers, sir, for she can have been no age at all, poor maid. God rest her." And then looked up, with her dark eyes sparkling with mischief again. "Quick, Master Pettitt, don't let them out of your sight, for once that child gets to her meat there'll not be a pie left in the shop."

40 - Lodge Here, That Thine Heart May Be Merry

There was a bitter wind lashing up off the Dengie peninsula, and there was hail lashing the windows, and Het was not sorry that almost everyone she loved was under her eye, and safe, under the same roof.

Almost everyone. But he would be home. Soon. It wanted but three days to Christmas now, Longest Night, and that was her unofficial anniversary, the night on which her baby nephew had first brought a weary, worn, cinnamon-haired captain to her hearth. And now she and her captain - her *colonel*, now, and a more sensible appreciation of a man's worth she had never seen - had two hopeful daughters, and her baby nephew had been married and he was a widower at twenty-two, after six weeks of marriage to a lady neither Lucifer nor Thankful Russell would discuss. And that was a sadness, and a mystery, but it was the way of things.

Surely Hollie wouldn't forget that date. Surely. Almost six months since she had seen him last - since the summer, when he'd arrived unannounced, with these two dear boys, and delivered Thankful into her care. She glanced up from her mending with a faint smile, looking over at her brood. Joyeux, in her cradle by the fire, snuffling gently in her sleep. Thomazine, curled like a hedgehog with her faithful Thankful, the bright sun to his pale moon. And her boys, her two grown-up boys, sprawled in a heap in front of the fire. Hers by love, if not by birth.

If she were to poke Lucifer with her foot, where he lay stretched out in front of the fire with his head pillowed on his arms, she suspected he'd claim to have been awake all along, despite the gentle purr of his snores. It was too wild a night to consider his returning to Witham. The river had finally burst its banks, and the ford was impassable. The wind was still rising, and her nephew's big roan horse was bedded down for the night in the foaling-box at the far end of the stables, at a respectful distance from Tyburn, who hated being kept in at the best of times. Lucifer wouldn't mind staying the night. She'd see to it there was frumenty for breakfast tomorrow - a good creamy one, stiff with plums and flecked with spices - just as if both Thankful and Lucifer had been her own boys, in need of good feeding. There was *always* enough that she could set another place at table for her own baby nephew.

The three of them looked like a litter of puppies, Thankful with his arm over Thomazine and Thomazine clinging to him like a little monkey with her head under his chin, the pair of them almost indistinguishable one from another. And Luce curled with his head pillowed on Thankful's hip and his arm over Thomazine from the other side, so that the little girl was held safe by her two guardians. The firelight gleaming on two smooth fair heads and one untidy russet. Het wondered, absently, whether it would disturb the two boys if she picked up Thomazine and carried her to her bed. If it would be better to cover the three of them with her old fur-lined cassock coat, tuck it around them so far as she could and bank the fire and leave them to it.

Bless them. All three of them. God bless them. Thankful and Lucifer *looked* like men, so stern and grown up in their military gear, and yet just for now, just for this one night, they were children again, safe and cherished and giddy as boys. Playing snapdragon, to Thankful and Thomazine's round-eyed astonishment, and Thomazine had been frightened by the flickering blue flames dancing over the shallow bowl of brandy till she realised there were raisins at the bottom of it for the snatching. It was a new delight to Thankful, with his austere upbringing, and he had very shyly wanted to play again, and again, until everyone else was thoroughly surfeited of raisins. And Luce had been almost his old self, lying on his back in front of the fire telling long and complicated fairytales till Thomazine crowed with delight.

She was glad he was here, under her roof, and not in Witham with his mother. Jane Pettitt kept wringing her hands over him, saying he was too thin and his linen was pitiable and he needed a haircut, and it was driving him slowly distracted. At least at White Notley he had Thankful for company, who was something like his own age, and a respectable gentleman by birth. (And both of them had the company of Alice Warriner - or, possibly, neither of them, since she was equally civil and indiscriminately fond of both of them.)

The rain was turning to hail, and she looked up at another wild spatter against the black glass, shivering. Wondering what the coming year might bring - an end to war, God willing. Peace and prosperity to the farm. A son. (She looked at the two sleek fair heads on the hearthrug. A son would be nice. But not essential. Not really.) Hollie, home safe and sound, to stay, forever.

The coming *dawn* would bring a busy day in the kitchen. Not a feast, and if Luce thought the table at White Notley would rival that of his elegant parents, he would have to think again, but - a soused collar of brawn, with mustard. Mutton pies, still hot from the oven. A chicken pie, from the white hen who'd stopped laying earlier this year and had been looking increasingly forlorn and bullied as the nights drew in.

Apples, the apples were still crisp and sweet and autumn-scented, but some of the pears were on the turn, might need to be baked. In a tart, with egg and cheese, or simply baked sweet? She'd see, in the morning, how soft they were.

Not ember tart. Not without Hollie. Not without it feeling like a betrayal to set his favourite dish on the table, with him who knows where, with who knows what put out for his comfort. No matter how much she loved these two of his most trusted officers - it might be *almost* as good as having him there, but it wasn't the same, no matter how much they talked about him. (Lied about him, in the kindest way, and she knew it, but even that made her smile.)

There was a great roar of wind in the chimney, and all the doors and windows rattled in their frames, and Het gave a little sob of sheer fright and clasped her hands to her mouth with a quick, helpless prayer.

And when she looked up again, her husband was standing in the doorway, looking at the four of them with a faint, dazed smile on his face. She thought for a moment he was a fetch, an apparition heralding news of his death, and she almost cried out but she didn't because her mouth was too dry for that. He looked at her. He didn't smile, or say anything sardonic, or clever, or funny, like he so often did when he was trying to make himself sound like he didn't care for anyone or anything much. He was thin. He was *miserably* thin, the bones in his face standing out through the skin as if they'd been carved from ivory. Not especially clean ivory. His hair was wet, and tangled, and dripping loose down his back. He just stood there, looking like death and blinking at her, with an expression she'd never seen before on his face.

He loved her. She knew that. He was a good husband to her, faithful and loving and kind. But that look of unguarded need turned all her bones to water. She came half out of her chair, holding her arms out to him, and he came skidding across the parlour and dropped to his knees in front of her, burying his head in her lap, and she thought - she'd have sworn - surely her Hollie wasn't *crying*?

She bent over him, forgetful of the child, forgetful of the two sleeping young officers, only thinking of her dear man, shaking in her arms, his teeth chattering with stifled sobs. Kissing the bits she could reach. Murmuring nonsense-words of comfort, as she would to Thomazine, as she did to Joyeux. Saying nothing of any import, none of the questions she wanted answers to - *what has happened to you, this last month, since I last read your words? How did you come by that scar through your eyebrow, and why did you not tell me of it? How goes the war, and who was Lucifer married to, and why will no one speak of her?*

She said none of it, and his hand tightened helplessly on her hip, relaxed, tightened again, hard enough to leave a tingling bruise. "I thought I should never -" he caught his breath, "never see your sweet face again, lass."

"Oh, husband. I am so glad to see you. I am - ah, Hollie, my dear and only love, I have missed you so very, very much -" And there wasn't much more she could say, other than to smooth his wet, rough hair on the back of his wet, rough coat, and then to point out, as he burrowed his face into her lap, "Dear - that's *not* my face. You know that, don't you?"

"I missed that too," he said indistinctly, muffled by folds of her skirt, and she startled - "What, dear, you missed - uh - well - country matters? Well, indeed, I am sure, but -"

"Thy good sense, lass," he said sternly. "Thee is less for sweethearting than *I* am. Though…"

"Ah, no, sweeting. If - *thee* - " it felt odd, to try and use his own North Country phrase to him, but it was the language of love to Hollie, she knew that now -"if thee would be my sweetheart, dear lad, I would not turn th- *thee* away."

"No matter how ill-suited I might be for t'job?" He looked up. Tired and unshaven but his dear bony face was radiant with joy. She pushed his hair out of his eyes.

"Never for me, love. Never for me."

He said nothing. He just blinked up at her, his lashes wet and spiky with tears. "Ah, God, I love you, lass," he said, and put his head down again, with something that might have been a laugh and might have been another sob. "Been a hell of a time -"

Hollie propped himself with his elbow on his wife's knee, and her hand settled on his neck, stroking with one finger just under his collar. His hair was wet and tangled, and his linen was damp and felt not too clean, but his skin was warm and so comforting and familiar, and yet so exciting. She didn't often get the opportunity to tickle the back of her lanky husband's neck. He wriggled contentedly, like a petted puppy. She wondered, as she often wondered, what my lord Fairfax, who was very stern and godly so they said, would make of Hollie at home. Underfoot in the kitchen, flirting for cake batter. Half-asleep with his head in his wife's lap, making comfortable, drowsy little noises.

And then sitting up abruptly so that Het's exploring hand slid to his shoulder. "Het," he said, sounding suddenly wide awake, "d'you want to enlighten me what Luce and Hapless are doing asleep on our parlour floor, with my - we got a leak in the roof, or summat? Can't you find these two lads a proper bed? And how come Luce's not with his mother? And -"

And then Thomazine came wide awake, sitting bolt upright with a whisper of, *"Daddy!"* that was too heartfelt even for her customary lusty expression of delight, and flew to his arms.

"He *was* in Witham, dear. But the river is in flood, apparently. Unsafe to cross at the ford. I am told." Her hand moved on his wet shoulder, thoughtfully. "I bid Luce stay here because it was too wild a night to travel safely," she said. She said no more.

He ducked his head awkwardly. "Neither fire nor flood would keep me from my lass this night. Anniversary of the night I first set eyes on you, d'you remember?"

"I could hardly forget," she said softly. "You and Mattie."

"Aye. Well. Who'd have thought? Me - " he tipped his head back and looked at his wife, unsmiling and loving, "never thought thee'd take me, lass. Not to keep."

She moved her hand from his shoulder, smoothed his hair. "I had to, really, dear," she said fondly. "You *were* in need of some attention. I couldn’t for shame leave your linen to go unmended, could I?"

"Dad-*dy*!" Thomazine, being ignored, fetched him a stern thump in the chest with her little fist. "Mind *me*, daddy!" And he held her tight, till she wriggled in protest, and then wriggled herself comfortable and went back to sleep with that frightening suddenness of the very young. In her cradle, Joyeux stirred and quacked drowsily, kicking out a foot from her wrappers, and Hollie tipped his head back into his wife's lap again. Saying nothing, but just looking up at her with an expression of cautious astonishment.

"That -" he said faintly, after a pause which was broken only by the wind in the chimney and the crackle of the dying fire, "that - it - you - " Had he not been holding his firstborn, he might have been able to shrug. As it was, he could only look comically stunned.

"Yes," Het said. "She. Joyeux Ruth. Thankful thought she looked - joyful." She leaned forward in her chair, mending and all, and put her arms round her husband - wet, draggled, and unlovely as he was. Edged closer so that she could snuggle her cheek against his hair. (He needed to bathe. *Badly*. She didn't mind.) Thomazine stirred in his arms, but did not wake. She clearly didn't mind, either.

He leaned back against the unyielding ridge of her stays, which must have been uncomfortable, and heaved a sigh of contentment. "Ah, lass, it's good to be home. There's been times these last few months I wasn't sure I'd *see* home again."

Het had no reply to that. He was a soldier. She knew that. They were hurt, or killed, in their duty. She knew that, too. He'd lost friends, good friends, in this war. He had scars. He had new ones - a new one that split his eyebrow, that was still pink and sore-looking. He was thin, and he looked tired and scruffy and somewhat worn, but then some people would say he always had, though she couldn't see it herself. But to hear him sounding so despairing was new, frightening, and her arms tightened round him as if she could save him from his own thoughts by main force of will. "I don't want to go back," he said, in so small a voice she almost didn't hear him. Laughed bitterly. "I have to, don't I?"

She wanted to say no. She wanted him not to go back. But yes - she thought he had to. For himself, for the sense of honour and duty he liked to pretend he didn't have, and which he was surreptitiously stiff with. Selfishly, she wanted him to stay here, with her, and breed his horses and see his daughters grow up. She wasn't sure he could do it. He wasn't a man who could walk away and leave a job half-done, her Hollie. Luce mumbled something, rolled over, propped himself on one elbow and peered groggily up through his hair. "Good lord," he said. And then, "Good lord," again, with joy and disbelief. "That's not you, sir?"

Hollie's mouth twitched. "Aye, well. What's left o' me, brat. What with the squi -"

"Squirrels," Luce said firmly, and very quickly, as Thomazine started to stir against Hollie's chest. "Terrible squirrels, in Somerset." He sat up, scrubbing his hair out of his eyes with both hands, looking like a little boy woken untimely, and gave his commanding officer a wry, sleepy smile. "Then I imagine I have to come with you, don't I?" He yawned. "Do me a favour though - not tonight, eh?"

"Not till I've seen my girls," Hollie said. "All my girls. *Awake*. I'd like the littlest to at least know her father's face. If." He didn't say any more than that.

Luce gave him a stern look. "Don't be so daft. *Sir*. The King is whipped. You know he is. Rolled up and dusted. He just won't admit it. It'll be a couple of weeks more in the spring and then we can all come home and that'll be it."

"Brat, if you had any *idea* -" Het's hand moved on his shoulder, gentling, as he stiffened. "Sat in a bloody cold ditch in Exeter with the Devil clawing your guts out, looking at your horses wondering which one you're going to eat next -"

"Think on your daughters, Hollie," Het said warningly, meaning this sort of talk was not seemly in front of little girls, and he rubbed his cheek against her skirts again.

"Aye. My girls. I wouldn't have been there if it wasn't for you three. I'll not have my girls live under that bloody bugger's yoke. Thinking of you three is about the only thing that kept me from putting a period to my bloody miserable existence, out there. And yes, Lucey, I *am* aware that's sinful talk, but till you've had six unrelieved weeks of the bloody flux, you have no idea what misery is. For which I thank God, and I pray you never do. I'd ha' bloody killed for some of your good bread and milk, lass. Rather than eating the Pig. I thought you wouldn't miss him, brat. So he went first."

Luce bit his lips and then laughed - a little weakly, but still, recognisably, a laugh. The Pig had been Gray's horse. And he had been a pig to ride, and *nobody* would miss The Pig. "I often wonder, you know - if the beast hadn't been so ungovernable with her, at the last - if she might have not -"

"I had not known your wife was killed in a riding accident, Lucifer," Het said, "I am so -" And then thought for a minute she could cheerfully have bitten off her own tongue at saying the wrong thing, as he ducked his head again, on a deep, shaky breath. Then he looked up, and his eyes were sparkling with tears, but he was smiling.

"His wife *was* a riding accident," Hollie said. "By God that lass was hard on her horses. D'you mind Rosa? That bloody witless mare -"

And then Luce was laughing, and half-crying at the same time, "As if I'm like to forget - d'you remember what she said to me, when Venning shot the mare? She called me some names, d'you remember?"

"Brat, I thought I was going to have to change my breeches. And then when she gave you such a slap -"

"My wife was - she was dressed as a trooper under Captain Venning's command," Luce said, looking at Het with shy pride. "She was a fierce lady. But gentle. She did truly care for me, God rest her, and -" he swallowed, but his gaze did not waver. "She was gentle. Only she and I knew how gentle she could be, I think."

"I reckon you probably hold the dubious honour of being the only living creature as that lass had ever loved," Hollie said, and Luce ducked his head as if receiving a gift.

"It was a privilege, sir."

There was a long, still silence, broken only by the crackle of the dying flames and the wind in the chimney. "My girls," he said again, dazed by his good fortune, and Het smiled, and put her hand out, and

Luce rolled over to her feet and lay all of a comfortable heap there.

"My boys," she said tenderly. "All together."

Thankful Russell had not moved. He was still lying in front of the fire, on his side, with his back to them, stiff and unmoving.

The lad wasn't asleep, though clearly he was trying to feign it. There was a distance of maybe six feet between Russell and Het, and to Hollie, it looked like the longest six feet in the world. It would be stupid of the lad if he was lay there waiting for someone to speak to him, be kind to him, to reassure him that he still belonged here. That just because Hollie was home, he was not to be turned out again from the place he'd made for himself.

Be bloody typical Russell, though.

"Hapless," he said gruffly, and his lieutenant sat up, rather too quickly for someone who was supposed to be asleep. Pushing his hair behind his ears and flinging his head up defiantly, trying to look like the old, chilly, unfeeling Russell, which was difficult when his eyes were wet and his mouth was trembling.

"I will go," Russell said. "I'm not - I will go - in the morning - as soon as I have said my goodbyes to Thomazine, you would not - I may have that, at least? She would be sad -"

"Thankful," Het said patiently, "if you were to leave so, *I* would be sad."

He looked up, hope and disbelief chasing each other across his face. Said nothing. Looked at Hollie.

"Don't look at me, Hapless. You know how it is in our house. What my lass says, goes."

"I am not your family, sir, you have no duty to- "

So bloody stubborn, and forlorn, and trembling like a stray dog and *still* trying to look fierce. Ah, Christ, it fairly tore at Hollie's heart. Like looking at himself twenty years ago, when Margriete had seen something worth the loving behind a seventeen year-old boy's frightened defences. And Hapless was twenty-one, and the lad had known no more of how to love, or be loved, than a barn cat - until he'd come here. "Russell," Hollie said, with a lump in his throat the size of a hen's egg, "Russell, get over here, where you belong."

Never seen the lad move so quick - so fast that he forgot to be graceful, and fell in an undignified heap at Het's feet. The three of them - "Piled," Hollie said aloud, "*piled* like your bloody mending, Henrietta. This is *your* doing, madam. I hold you *entirely* responsible for this."

"Mending-est lady in Essex," Luce said comfortably, rolling onto his back. "You always said so, Hollie."

And Het, who did not have quite enough hands to gather all three of them in, contented herself with a smile that was both smug and proud. "I know," she said. "Isn't it wonderful, dear?"

10403378R00154

Printed in Great Britain
by Amazon.co.uk, Ltd.,
Marston Gate.